m **McCulloch** is from the Highlands of
land. He currently lives in Oxford with his
ily. With his first novel *The Stillman* he became
Amazon Rising Star.

@tomamcculloch

THE
ACCIDENTAL
RECLUSE

Tom McCulloch

SANDSTONEPRESS
HIGHLAND | SCOTLAND

First published in Great Britain by
Sandstone Press Ltd
Dochcarty Road
Dingwall
Ross-shire
IV15 9UG
Scotland

www.sandstonepress.com

The publisher acknowledges subsidy from Creative Scotland
towards publication of this volume.

ISBN: 978-1-912240-18-0
ISBNe: 978-1-912240-19-7

Cover design by Mark Swan
Typeset by Iolaire Typography Ltd, Newtonmore
Printed and bound by Totem, Poland

For Ada and Orin – there are not enough words

Fade-in

A five-star hotel, a three-room suite. Laughing surgeons have dismantled me and put me back together very carefully, but in the wrong order. I want to be in my own bed. This will not be possible for a long time.

The maid has pulled the sheets so tight it almost seems malicious. She must have had someone in mind. A husband, most likely, her hands on his scrawny neck, tighter and tighter, and what blissful relief as he tenses, struggles and finally goes limp, a degenerate smirk on her plump face...

I tell my feet to move. All they can muster is a few desperate toe wiggles. I'm trapped, an outworn Pharaoh they got bored with, mummified alive in thousand thread-count Egyptian cotton.

At least one part of me is going to sleep. Despite the vague panic that comes with constriction this is not displeasing. It may be the only way I sleep at all tonight, the spreading numbness eventually reaching my buzzing brain. I should be grateful to the maid. I should insist on a new bedclothes protocol back home. Because jet lag is far from the only thing that stops me sleeping.

I shuffle up the bed, dragging my dead feet with me, and sit up against the headboard. A soft and giving material cradles my head. Velour or velvet, something expensive-feeling anyway.

The quick stab in the centre of my chest is a reminder

1

that luxury is always balanced by austerity in the end, usually of a physical kind. All aboard the Degradation Express! Heart failure, you say, what comparative *banality*, sir, step this way, back of the train, please, front carriages for the grim and imminently doomed only, the terminal must reach the terminal first, hoho!

Another sharp stabbing. I think of it as a warning jab. A finger in the chest, my father's looming face and something else I have done or not done. *Johnny! What the hell are you playing at?*

'Nothing, Dad.'

No response from the glowering dark. But he's out there, beyond the window that I know is beyond the dark rectangle of curtain across the room. I am no idiot, you understand. I did not rise to these bowel-loosening heights, able to insist on the finest of murderous bedding and the most luxurious of three-roomed hotel suites, without knowing that behind a curtain is a window.

More often than not, that is. For I am also a shrewd man, oh yes, a point emphasised across the years by media profiles, both fawning and abusive. A shrewd man is not dogmatic about curtains. He knows that occasionally there is something else behind them; a plaque, a naked dancer, night . . .

It was already dark when I got here, the curtains already closed. I am not yet ready to open them.

I sip water from the crystal tumbler on the bedside table. The thud as I put it down is startling in the silence. Like every five-star hotel room this one is soundproofed to ensure my privacy should the *bunga bunga* take my unlikely fancy. Yet the silence, as ever, is different. No two are the same, each permeated with the memory of what has just been extinguished. I have come from a silence full of buzzing neon and a million voices to one echoing to the scrawk of a lone seagull.

'I've never known silence like this,' Akira had said

earlier. We were standing in an extraordinary cold, a half moon rising huge and incandescent behind the bulk of an unknown mountain, as if the universe was a black curtain and the moon an aperture into a dazzling beyond.

The silence unsettles me more than opening the curtains. I wonder again why on earth I am here.

I pick up the device on the bedside table and press buttons until the room fills with Duke Ellington. *Money Jungle*. A sudden nostalgia makes me select *Solitude* but the desolate piano has me scrolling for *Switch Blade*. I follow the boomerang swells of Charles Mingus's double bass, step with Ellington's flowing keys into this return that I am too old for as I was once too young.

I slip lower into my sarcophagus.

I'm apprehensive about what's coming, Duke's making me uneasy. Not Ellington but my brother, named after the genius who is finally taking me closer to sleep. A sentimental choice by our parents, I always felt, as if to keep manifest in him what will inevitably be lost between them.

They're all out there in the dark, Anna too, lazy circling as Ellington now fades into that zany, plinky-plonky theme tune from the Japanese chat show, the director counting five-four-three-two ...

One

The famous old Irish playwright, Sam Beckett.

I do look like him. It is true.

I watch my face on the TV monitor as they attach my lapel mike. A later Sam Beckett. And *Sam* Beckett, note, not *Samuel* Beckett. As I have grown into that pinched, lined face and seen my hair become its white, flyaway fuzz, so too have I gained a friendliness with the man himself.

Tomorrow, I am seventy-five.

Sam too reached seventy-five, but not much further. The thought won't detain me too long for I have no intention of dying. Yes, brother Duke, I know. I hear you sniggering. Yet I will not. I will sit forever in a Parisian café, legs crossed and a glass of Burgundy, one of those small glasses in which the French specialise that somehow make drinking a profession rather than a pastime.

The sound engineer finishes attaching the mike. He gives an enthusiastic thumbs up, beams me a toothy grin.

Japan, that emphatic friendliness. I have lived here for over thirty years, yet it can still unnerve me. I fear its sudden collapse under the repressed rage of centuries, the engineer's smile become a sneer as he jabs his thumbs into my astonished eye-sockets and starts to twist, gouge ...

I notice Erin staring at me. My niece is sitting on a

canvas director's chair behind the camera. I used to have one of those! My initials stencilled on the back, of course. JJ. Sure, everyone knew JJ, no need for the full Johnny Jackson. I am too old now to have such a young name.

It's embarrassing.

Erin smiles, more lupine than reassuring. 'It'll be fine,' she says and goes back to staring at her phone. Her PA set up the TV show and in she flew this very morning, London to Tokyo, a bandy-legged Icarus in a Gucci suit. Poor child of the rickety genetics. If her legs were straight she'd be six feet six.

Takeshi Nakazawa has still not appeared. I admire the man. In the oppressive zaniness of Japanese showbiz TV he is a redoubt of solemn dignity. I have seen him interview presidents, PMs and popes.

Now me.

There is no audience in this tiny studio. When the interview begins it will just be me and Nakazawa, a cameraman and a sound engineer. My status is being emphasised. I am a man of such rarefied access that the plebs cannot look directly upon me. I have achieved the broom-cupboard . . .

Yet I will be watched. A monitor beside the one showing my face relays pictures from an auditorium elsewhere. I see people filing in to take their seats and watch the big-screen feed of my interview.

I like the sophistication of the staging, the emphasis on both the confessional and the voyeuristic. I can pretend that no-one is listening by focusing on Nakazawa, or I can play to the crowd by looking at the monitor. But I gave up the stage decades ago for a good reason. Spend any time with an audience and you start dialling it in. Start dialling it in and you start watching the watchers.

'Where is Mr Nakazawa?' I ask a floppy-haired

production assistant who has appeared with a tray of drinks.

'No English, Mr Jackson,' he says, absurdly, because I asked him the question in flawless Japanese.

'Find out.'

Off he goes. I shuffle in my chair and catch my face in the monitor. Heavy lines on the forehead. Arched eyebrows and a pursed mouth. Sour. I look sour. Sour as my breath. I regret the sashimi I ate an hour ago and the mint I forgot to eat afterwards. No much wonder the PA fled, my putrid breath fogging out at him. He may never come back. He may never eat fish again, the poor sod.

Erin gives me another smile, more strained now. She is urgently whispering into the physical appendage which is her mobile phone. If she removed her hand it would remain attached to her ear. I never hear the phone ring and presume it communicates directly with her brain.

Can you imagine any of this, Duke, what it has come to? I take a drink from my hip flask and feel a familiar anxiety at having to tip it higher to get a swig. Once more we are on the slide towards emptiness.

The crew is ready. They're staring but trying not to stare. Up on the monitor, the grinning audience is in place. The only absentee is the venerable Nakazawa-san. I await his grand entrance with sweaty palms.

I am nervous.

I regret asking Akira to wait in the car. This is my first public appearance in fifteen years. A rehearsal, a settler, before the more important ones back home. Home, do you hear that, Duke?

They think of me as some kind of eccentric, of course. I should have played up to it, sat here in a pair of Howard Hughes-esque white gloves, even a mouth-mask, but a

6

mouth-mask is not unusual in Japan. Hughes wouldn't have agreed to this. He would still be in his bunker, sat in the geometric centre of the room, surrounded by toadies and empty tins of tuna. Yes, indeed, HH would also have had fish breath, and fish breath is what this crew will call JJ. *Fish-breath has asked where Mr Nakazawa is*, that's what the PA is saying, somewhere beyond the curtain.

'Mr Jackson.'

I look away from Sam Beckett's face in the monitor into the anxious eyes of a goatee-bearded man. 'Yes.'

'You asked about Takeshi Nakazawa.'

'Yes.'

'I fear there has been a miscommunication. Mr Nakazawa does not present this particular programme.'

'I beg your pardon.'

'Shinohara Sugita.'

'What?'

'Our host. Shinohara Sugita.'

I look across at Erin, who is hurrying towards me, wide-armed in an exaggerated shrug with a sly grin. My mouth opens and closes a few times. Like a fish, a big cod, as would be expected of fish breath.

'Did you know about this?'

'I knew.'

'So when were you going to tell me?'

'Nothing to worry about. It'll be fine. Just stay general. Tell them the teaser trailer is coming but no details. Say they're going to be astounded, that in all your career this is a genuine landmark.'

There is flint in her gaze. Our inverted relationship is so strange, as if she is the elder and me the fifty-four-year-old. She controls via a studied arbitrariness in which I am forever wrong-footed.

I mime the drawing of a zip along my lips and make some muffled noises.

'What?'

I undo the zip. 'Mum's the word.'

Erin smiles but her eyes don't. I'm on a three-line whip. There were other plans for the fiftieth anniversary of Breda Pictures but the best-selling success of my autobiography changed them. Her Cosa Nostra-like ability to never forget dug out a memory of *The Bruce*, my never-made biopic of King Robert the Bruce. The ideal *anniversary vehicle*, she said, why not dust down the famous director at the same time, my first film in three decades in the year I turn seventy-five.

The perfect PR storm. I never liked the schmooze . . .

You know the game, Duke, the peddling of anecdotes to over-coiffed egomaniacs. My stomach lurches as I look at the monitor and the expectant audience. I stand up. In three minutes I could be back in the car with Akira. In an hour we would be back in the silence of Shuzenji.

I ask the PA for the bathroom, where I splash cold water on my face and take another hit from the flask.

'What am I doing?'

In the mirror, Sam Beckett shrugs. Never been much use that guy. And there's you, Duke, laughing at your brother who simply *must* make another movie, *darling*, if only to prove to himself that all that is long gone is not also lost. Did I really think Erin would let me direct? She tried not to laugh when I suggested it. Executive producer is as close as I'll get, which isn't close at all.

But to film in Inveran?

That was unexpected. You, Duke, have never let me be. It's all the others I'm not used to, like our mother; there she is, beside me in the mirror, a grumble of pots in the sink as the old man winks . . .

Back in the studio Erin looks at me suspiciously. I ignore her, closing my eyes as they dab make-up on my face.

When I open them, an improbably beautiful young woman has appeared. Long black hair and big moon eyes. She wears a tartan miniskirt, of course, and a tight white blouse. I stand up and shake her tiny hand. She very much enjoys my work, says she, which is very much over, says I.

Not at all and surely not, she says, so very coquettish that I even *blush*, all of which goes to prove that if flattery is the first instinct of the manipulative then delusion is the refuge of old men. I will indulge anyway, live on Japanese TV with this beauty whose legs angle away from the camera as she sits, yet are perfectly positioned to offer me and only me a glimpse of white panties.

She smiles! She knows! The floor director is counting down ten to one. I am ready for any and every question.

'Do you miss the monkey?'

Except that one.

I swallow. I make the mistake of glancing at the audience monitor behind the cameraman. They are howling with laughter. In front of me Shinohara Sugita stifles a little giggle.

'Because we have one.'

Oh dear God they surely do. The floppy-haired PA leads one into the studio. A monkey on a leash. Behind the camera Erin takes a picture on her phone and gives a gleeful thumbs up. This is the support for my re-emergence into the light which she flew six thousand miles to offer.

Along with the monkey, a massive cake is wheeled on, a six-tiered pink and white monstrosity, big enough to hold a person. I panic at the thought of another woman, bikini-clad, undoubtedly, bursting forth to give me a birthday kiss. The reality is infinitely worse. I struggle to control the shake in my hands as a wall of the tiny studio rolls open to reveal the audience I can still see

9

on the monitor, a floor director leading everyone in a rendition of happy birthday.

Even the monkey is clapping ...

What follows is not an interview, no Takeshi Nakazawa channelling William F. Buckley and deconstructing my career and comeback with the skill of a psychological surgeon, no references to the telling passages of the autobiography which has led to my being here in the first place.

What follows is instead a raucous celebration of the monkey films that made the Breda Boys famous.

A young man with acne and milk-bottle glasses is led on and presented as my greatest fan. He makes one deep bow after another, head almost at his feet. It is an extraordinary physical performance.

There follows a bizarrely complicated game involving old film clips, girls in monkey costumes waving little paddles with pictures of gorillas stuck on them and the young man being asked questions, each correct answer accompanied by a hooting monkey noise, an incorrect one by brown slurry pouring down on his head. This being Japan, I can't be sure the monkey shit is fake.

* * *

Erin is babbling. She's delighted. She sits in the limousine in the seat diagonally opposite, gesticulating wildly, saying things I'm not listening to. I look out the smoked-glass window and let Tokyo take me.

Cities by night, I've always loved them. I remain the wide-eyed bumpkin, greedy for neon. Give me favela Rio from a de Havilland Comet, ramble-tamble oranges in the shuddering night-black, a cigarette in one hand and a Martini in the other. Or Los Angeles from Mulholland, grids of light like the city's glowing bones.

Or give me tonight, this lurid Roppongi nightscape. I've not been in Tokyo for a long time. It does not change. It simply grows, metastasises.

Akira is a skilled driver. Fast enough to make trails in the neon but smooth enough to ensure my comfort. I look at the adverts in the sky, the mysterious flickering symbols of the multicoloured bar signs on every level of the fleeting tower blocks. Akira pulls suddenly left to avoid a taxi. I shift in my seat, the ice cubes clinking in the glass. I am never nervous when Akira drives.

He was standing beside the Mercedes when I appeared from the lift in the underground car park. I told him to drive. As I got inside I heard footsteps and looked up into Erin's face. Sensational, sensational, she was saying. I looked at her toothy smile and saw a grinning monkey.

I finish my whisky. We stop for a red light and a woman's impossibly sad face appears at my window.

Instantly, I think of Anna. It is the film clips they made me watch, that unexpected plunge into the past. Then the woman is gone, leaving a startlingly incongruous memory. I am standing with Anna outside the Sacre Coeur on a piercing winter night. Behind us, St. Matthew Passion is swelling to a crescendo. The lights of Paris, I'm certain, are a code about to be revealed.

'See? It wasn't all that bad.'

Erin is holding her phone out, a video playing on the screen. Orange light shifts on her grinning face.

'You came across really well. Relax. Don't worry, all publicity is good publicity.'

'You weren't the one sitting there.'

'Uncle Jay,' she says, ever so gently. 'That show goes out to millions. Some who've never heard of you, some who think you're a bit . . . odd. Now they're interested and that's what it's all about.'

She is, undoubtedly, a psychopath. I lie back in soft leather. I finish my drink with my eyes closed.

'You don't need to worry about anything like that when we get to the UK. Just your bog-standard interviews.'

'Recorded?'

'I promise. I know you hate it. Just think of the movie.'

The Great CEO tells me again about the interviewers, bright cultural lights who nevertheless remain dim to me. She emphasises the prestige nature of our anniversary project, making clear why she has decided to personally oversee it. Before the London interviews there will be a book tour, starting in my home town, where my life story will culminate in a civic gong which I already have. Perhaps they have forgotten, it was awarded so long ago.

'Inveran,' she says with a genuinely warm smile. 'Home.'

My stomach lurches. Automatically, I reach for the decanter. Going home, Duke, it feels like having you die all over again. Except this time you might have a few more things to say about it.

'Any music?'

My niece rolls her eyes and mutters something I will not ask her to repeat. Akira's voice is deep in the speaker.

'The library is synced to your own.'

'Ellington. *Far East Suite.*'

A few moments later music fills the limousine. I instantly tell Akira to switch it off. I am not ready for you tonight, Duke, neither you nor Anna. I press the button on the hand-rest and the cabin partition slides open. Akira's questioning eyes meet mine in the rear-view mirror. I hold this man twenty years my younger in an esteem that would make him blush if he knew.

'Where to?' he asks.

'Shuzenji.'

'Hey, hey, not yet!' Erin protests. 'We have a date. Don't you remember? You ready for one more surprise?'

I feel a little bit sick as Erin presses the partition button and Akira's head disappears from view.

'You want to know?'

An awful thought detonates as I watch her fiddle with her phone. On the screen that doubles as the partition, six smaller screens appear in a grid. Black-and-white images. Camera feeds.

One camera shows a forecourt full of the flash cars I have never taken an interest in. On another I read the words Minamo-Hirakawacho Tower. My niece's residence when she is on a rare visit.

Erin stares at me as she sips her drink. Her insistence on my delighted surprise is intimidating. The feed from the camera above the fiftieth-floor lift shows the apartment entrance hall. The lighting is low. The fake flames of the fire flicker across empty a leather sofa and a copper-topped coffee table. I have the voyeuristic certainty something bad is about to happen.

Other cameras relay the inside of the apartment. There are many people on the viewing terrace. They sit or stand and look out on circuit-board Tokyo, multicoloured neon become fuzzed white. Others cluster at the marble-topped bar. All are already boozed-up, ultra-HD making their features sharper than plastic surgeons have made their chins, cheekbones and noses. The faces only become indistinct where they stand too close to the searing glow of the cobalt and white LED lights. In my niece's feng shui masterpiece of interior design, with all the attendantly elegant evening wear, the banner above the bar is a jarring counterpoint.

Happy Birthday JJ.

There is a garish, pink and white cartoon character at each end of the banner. *Hello Kitty*, of course. But this is a light-hearted occasion; there is irony in the juxtaposition of opulence and tackiness.

'My birthday's tomorrow.'

Erin beams. 'Fashionably early is the new late. It'll extend the life of the hashtag.'

'What's that supposed to mean?'

'The social media campaign for your birthday, #notquitedeadyet.'

'You're joking?'

'Of course I am.' But she winks.

I wouldn't know how to check if she's having me on or not.

* * *

These people and their congratulations. They tell me it is wonderful to see me back in the public eye and tonight's interview was so funny. They tell me my autobiography is so poignant and they just love the title. *The Accidental Recluse*. And only volume one! They can't wait for the second.

I am supposed to know them, yes? This is surely the meaning of a birthday celebration. Yet if I do not recognise them then how can they know me? Their certainty in our non-existent acquaintance is unnerving, the way they cluster like medical specialists considering a rare and exciting disease.

Yet I chat, awhile.

And I admire, somewhat, their being masters all of the discreet retreat. Having circled the centre of tonight's attention until decency is achieved, they vanish like Botoxed wrinkles to indulge whatever sexual or professional machinations have truly brought them here tonight.

I find a table in the corner of the viewing terrace. Here, the shadows are deeper; dark oranges and yellows from hidden uplighters. A waiter deposits a bottle of Johnny Walker Blue. I sip and I sip, speaking now and then to a well-wisher, the lights of all Tokyo spread below me, so close I could reach out and pluck them one by one, pop them into my mouth like children's sweets.

A drunk girl appears.

Again, I think of Anna, who she doesn't look like at all. This attachment is a weakness, a failing in the land of Zen, where Dōgen waves an admonishing finger at all that cannot be let go.

She is American; Abby or Aimee. An actress or a model, the next big thing or perhaps the currently big thing. Not that she is big at all, more a willowy presence who may fly away on the breeze. I have no way of knowing who she is. My references are thirty years out of date although back then I would have screwed her without hesitation. Don't laugh, Duke, it would have happened, or it could have happened, or who am I kidding, it wouldn't have happened at all.

More of the delusion of age. I live vicariously through the ghost of someone who never existed in the first place. Even with five doubles of fantasy from my emptying bottle, it is clear Abby or Aimee has no sexual interest. She is just a fan, 'a massive fan'. She wants to talk about my films.

'Your *art*.'

Yet her only reference is to *A Man's a Man*. Not *Journey to the End of the Night*, say, Captain Bloom soaring over London, or *Fisherman's Blues*, the sequence as the *Makepeace* goes down in the storm, the cuts to Shelley staring at the sea as *White Rabbit* builds to a crescendo . . .

'It's a classic,' she says.

I offer a modest nod of my head. Don't give me that derisive snort, Duke. You know better than I that film was Oscar-bait. A saccharine-sweet biopic of Robert Burns. Redford was never sadder.

15

'Some say it's better than *Braveheart*,' I reply. 'I suppose people prefer a flyting to a defenestration.'

She doesn't understand. Her eyes flicker, let it pass. 'Your autobiography. It's so interesting, your *journey*.'

'Well, the time was right,' I say.

'How so?'

I watch myself talk, as if from a great and ever-growing distance. It is changing, I tell her, the land of my birth reconsidering what it is. I had such fixed ideas about what it was, my instinct always to look backwards. History meant then and never now. Change happened elsewhere and aspiration belonged to others, the grey skies an ever-lowered lid on dreams and schemes. In this renaissance there could perhaps be a rediscovery of Johnny Jackson, a forgotten son.

Forgotten son?

But the pomposity slips past her, as my entire monologue has. 'Yes. You're Scottish,' she manages to say.

'Exactly. You sound like my niece Erin. Have you met her? The one who looks like a giant stick insect? "Why not ride the zeitgeist," she said to me, something like that. "You're famous and you're Scottish, we've got a publishing division so why not write your life story." You know, before I die ...'

'Well, I'm glad she insisted,' she says, with such nobility in the face of my burblings that I could cry.

'*The Bruce*,' I say.

'The who?'

'My Robert the Bruce biopic,' I whisper, leaning in. '*The Bruce*. Keep it to yourself.'

'You're making another film!'

'One for the road. Talking of which, do you want another?'

As we drink, I give her a brief outline of the film. She's thrilled, in on a secret, a gleam in her deep blues and hands on her chin in a manner that hints she may, after all, be *carnally interested*.

Has she not seen the liver spots on the backs of my hands? Is she too drunk to notice my sashimi breath? Does she want to kiss me and find a tiny piece of ten thousand Yen black cod dislodged into her hot little mouth? I imagine her breasts and thighs as she bounces up and down on my spindly body and am suddenly thrilled that ancient art has made an old man desirable.

'Can you tell me any more?'

With half a bottle of Blue down his gullet the birthday boy thinks, why the bloody hell not. With reflection has come the gloop of sentiment and the return of Anna in the guise of this American girl who could not be more different. I take Abby or Aimee's hand. I have no more connections, I whisper to her, none at all. I feel like King Robert the Bruce in his dank cave, half-mad and talking to spiders, the exile trying to find a way back to the home he left so long ago . . .

'I can see why you have to make the film.'

'As I say, one for the road.'

'And what you've had to . . . endure. Your brother and your wife.'

'My brother was a troubled man and she wasn't my wife.'

'Sorry. I just mean I understand . . . A bit, anyway. My mother also had a heart attack.'

'Life goes on.'

She is quiet for a few long moments. I await a profound comment on the nature of fate and tragedy. Instead, she says, 'Tell me about the monkey.'

'The monkey?'

'It was just so funny, the way you talked about it in your book. The interview tonight, too.'

'You know Japanese?'

'I live here, don't I? Silly!'

17

I blink. I drink.

Has it been building up to this all along, the one thing that everyone wants to talk about?

I could sit here for days, pointing out every crucial detail excised from that most absolving of autobiographies, and back she would circle to the damn monkey. I lift her smooth chin, look into those beautiful cobalt eyes and say what is it you hide? Tell me all about that Nebraskan cornhusker life you left so far behind, what did you choose to bury in those endless fields?

Except I don't.

Two

Anyway, it wasn't a monkey.

It was a chimpanzee.

In time, it became the centrepiece of the act. But that was later, after the Day of the Menagerie and long after our mother and her disapproval had vanished. Then it was just me, Duke and our father, there in the old croft by the Sound of Skerray, peering over the edge of the world.

The act, our father's obsession. *I'm a man of Free and Easy heritage, greasepaint in ma lugs*, he'd say. Like his father before him, our old man was also a performer, once upon a lost time.

My brother and I. Slapstick at the shieling and pratfalls on the shore. It seemed so natural. Children of mountaineers will just shrug at the thought of dangling off the Eiger. A taxidermist's son will stuff the cat quicker than you can say here little kitty. We could sing *Arf a Pint of Ale*, bat our eyelids like Chaplin and slip into a Will Evans sketch, anything the old man remembered.

And he remembered so much, had an eidetic memory, it seemed, for every Music Hall and Variety bill from 1900 onwards, the Inveran Empire to the Ayr Gaiety, the Glasgow Alhambra to the Aberdeen Tivoli.

I say our father, but I mean Duke's. Of my paternity I was dubious. A blunt lack of affection combined with physical discrepancies that became ever more obvious as the years passed. From a young age I compared my stunted self with Shire Horse and Son, out again in the rowing boat.

'Give 'em to Bucket Boy.'

Then my brother's face, smugly looming as he handed me the bucket full of mackerel. 'Gut them, bucket boy. You heard.' Yet he would always seek me out later to apologise, Duke having a near-pathological desire to please. It made an inevitability, I suppose, of his future career.

Then again, with the old man you had to please. He was not a man to anger. A defiant melancholy defined his life and the stories he told. 'It was something else back then, boys. Listen to this, don't tell your mum,' his great belly wobbling with laughter as he reached the punchline.

I loved those tales.

The old man was so happy, freed in the telling, a foul-mouthed Peter Ustinov leaning on a spade, rambling on about the time Jimmy Nicol stood on the wrong mark and was knocked out by the sandbag dropped from the flies. Or *the not-so-alleged Scandal at the Alhambra*, this involving Betty Grable and two chorus girls. The stories tailed off as the present leached back into view. He would seem startled, as if he still hadn't come to terms with giving it up for the fields and the sea.

We would come to call these stories *Tales of the Fedora*. My father loved that hat. Worn at an angle he thought rakish but was actually ridiculous, a product of vanity, aspiration and too many Humphrey Bogart films. Women, as we found out, business or hats: always that tendency to push it too far. Although the fedora only appeared in my teens, when I think back to childhood it is ever-present, a later memory imposed on earlier ones. This is how I have chosen to remember him. In the same way, our small croft at the foot of Ben Chorain is not neat with lazy beds and geraniums, friendly smoke in the chimney, but squats cold and lonely, the flower tubs scrawny with the weeds of so many winters.

I recall so little about a deeper past that it might only exist as a series of dreams. Perhaps our mother was never alive at all to enforce, with military discipline, a tidy home and busy farm. Oddly, despite the ambiguities of my early memories, I have retained an absolute certainty about her voice: a lilt to mirror an ever-shifting temper, soft as summer surf or hard as a herring gull.

Already a distant presence, she achieved the ultimate remoteness by dying when I was thirteen.

Duke was five years older. He was different after our mother died, as if knowing his superior place in our father's affection conferred a responsibility to look out for me. I adored and hated him, naturally. I admired the easy way he climbed the Esha Cliffs and spoke to girls, who gravitated to him like pretty little planets. His affection for me was fierce. Dead arms and an ongoing series of playful humiliations. I accepted without rancour the apology that would always come.

'Sorry, Johnny.'

'It's ok.'

'No, it's not ok. It's just they kind of expect it from me and before you know it I've said something stupid.'

'Don't worry.'

'It won't happen again.'

Except it did. Duke needed the attention and I needed the apologies, as the old man needed his stories.

'You mother used to like those shows.'

We were deep into that frigid February of 1953. Our mother had been in the grave for two weeks. A viscous darkness had settled across the kitchen, only the fire holding it back. My father was midway down the bottle. Duke and I sat silently on the other side of the table.

21

With the firelight behind us we must have seemed mere shadows to him. Perhaps this made it easier.

'She loved them.'

That stillness, there was none like it in the universe. Only the music was moving. Ellington's *Mood Indigo* playing on the Garrard record player they had saved for three years to buy.

'She came to the Inveran show when I was working the coconut shies. Again and again and she was rubbish, boys, I tell you, couldn't hit a barn door from ten feet. I gave her a prize anyway. A teddy bear. And a wink. That's what she always said. *I was undone by a teddy bear and a wink.*'

Duke and I exchanged a quick glance. We had seen vanishingly little evidence of such fondness.

'My first show at The Empire she was there. Sneaked out and bought a front row ticket. I went down like a sack of summer sharn. A nineteen-year-old Harry Lauder in my head, Wailing Willy to the rest of the world. They booed me, bottom of the bill, but the buggers still booed me. MacDougall was frantic, waving from the wings, wanted me off pronto. Sod the lot of them, I thought. I started into *Mairi's Wedding* and it was bad, boys, really bad. But then they started to laugh. The worse I got, the more they laughed. Just roll with it, I thought. I decided to drop in a few heilan jigs as I belted it out, even tripped over my feet, legs in the air and arse revealed. Brought the house down so I did. Your mother was on her feet before anyone else. They clapped forever! It was called satire, apparently. My act was born, "Sorry Lauder".'

Then he chuckled. The old man never chuckled. 'Back she came. Once in Gourock, even, the Craigburn Pavilion. I near fell off the stage when I saw her. Three cousins with her, giggling away.'

It was extraordinary to think of my mother and father like this. That they could have been so happy.

'I proposed and she said yes. But they ground her down. Her mother. Jees-oh, a face that could melt yer wellies. There'd be no marriage so long as I worked the stage. It was unbecoming of a lady. Your mother didn't say a word. She forgot all those shows she'd sneaked out to. I got a job backstage at The Empire. Other folk got the laughs and I went home to your mother, three up in the tenement. Two wee rooms. Love, boys? What is love? Come on!'

We both jumped.

'Love is this song you're hearing on the record player right this very minute. *Mood Indigo.* Your mother loved Duke Ellington too. It's how you got your name, Dukey boy.' He sat back heavily in the chair and opened his arms wide. 'Dead easy, don't you reckon? Love. I'll drink to that.' He knocked his whisky back and poured another. 'But you know what else it is?' He looked from Duke to me and back. 'No idea? Well, I'll tell you. Love is taking over this farm in the middle of bloody nowhere when your granda died and your granny went doolally. There's love.'

He stood up. Glimmer of the pouring bottle.

'*Duke.* Up!'

Again, we both gave a start. The chair scraped as Duke stood up. A quick glance down at me, nervous.

'Away and get the coat stand.'

'The coat stand?'

'You *deaf?*'

Duke hurried out of the kitchen and the old man turned to me.

'You. Up.'

I too got up quickly. Duke lifted the coat stand into the kitchen from the hall and set it beside the old man. It was a solid, old-fashioned wooden one, seven feet high with three curving legs at the bottom. God knows where it came from, probably an aspirational purchase

23

by my mother, seen in the windows of Munro's department store, just right for hanging up the Sunday best.

The old man now threw his long raincoat at me. 'Put it on and get up on the stand.'

'Eh?'

'Don't *eh* me. Just do it.'

Still the short arse I would be until a growth spurt took me to my dizzying final height of five foot four, I pulled on the coat, which came down to my knees. Then I climbed onto the stand, pulling myself up by the hooks at the top and putting my feet on the circular wooden band that stuck out about a foot above the base, the place where you would keep umbrellas, if we had any.

There followed a few minutes of shoving and pulling, my father closing the neck over the top of my head with safety pins so it didn't pop out, until he was happy it looked like a bulky coat.

'Right. Here's how it works. Duke'll walk past and when I go "now", stick out a leg and kick him in the arse.'

The old man banked the fire and that is what we did. Over and over again in the dancing firelight.

'First rule of showbiz: everyone likes watching someone get kicked in the arse. Even your mother. We'll work up a routine. Get it down pat, practice makes perfect and aw that pish.'

That's how it began. Death can be a freeing, I suppose. The old man's passion was no longer an old story in The Clachan or a song belted out at shieling or shore, safely distant from his wife. Now it was shot through with new possibility. *JJ and The Duke*, he christened us, the surrogates of an ambition being rediscovered. Even though he wouldn't perform, it would always be 'we'.

'We'll get on the bill, boys.'

The cartoon light bulbs lit up in Duke's head and

mine at the same time. We'd been groomed for this our whole lives, all the turns the old man had drummed into us. The ambition felt like our own. I suppose the triumph in someone else's obsession is in convincing you it is actually yours.

And then it is.

Duke was a born performer. He was brilliant. I didn't enjoy it half as much, I was far too gauche, although that had its own comic appeal. My interest lay behind the scenes. The writing and the staging. The old man wouldn't have this. That was his job, to design and dictate. My best ideas he would first ignore then quietly reintroduce, changed slightly to prove they were his but thereby frustratingly less effective than my original concept.

'You got a problem with something, son?'

'No, Dad. It works well. I like it.'

My passivity. It made everything he did an affirmation of his unerring correctness. His violence.

* * *

'Whadaya think, Jack?'

'Well—'

'Needs work, I know. But there's talent there, eh.'

'Aye . . . there's something there.'

This last with a lingering look towards the exit at the top of the auditorium. It had gone midday. Everyone knew that Fat Jack McVeigh, erstwhile owner, proprietor and manager of The Inveran Empire sat down at twelve, Monday to Friday, in the snug of the Queen's hotel to a hauf and a hauf and whatever the lunch special might be, Fat Jack being a man who liked to live dangerously.

Though not as dangerously as to put JJ and the Duke on, even at the bottom of the bill. 'Coat Stand Surprise' had gone well, 'The Box' less so. The old man had come up with the latter a week or so previously.

Duke and I are two men in a pub, me the dopey one and Duke the wisecracker. There is a little wooden box on the table in front of us and I am telling Duke about my improbable world travels, how I went to Africa and bought a lion, which I keep in this box, and a giraffe as well. 'In the same box?' asks Duke. 'Of course,' says I. Duke now cranks up the ridicule, winking at the audience, more and more incredulous. Then I tell him I went on to India and was given an elephant.

'I suppose that's in the box too.'

'Don't be daft, you couldn't fit an elephant in this box.'

Except I kept forgetting the lines. No much wonder. This was my first time on an actual stage. This was the Empire, Variety's Outpost, a sandstone colossus on Stevenson Street. I nearly didn't make it past the sign jutting over the pavement like the prow of a ship. Empire – ten feet high, Art Deco letters on both sides of a V-shaped, neon sign. An unambiguous message.

My brother lit up the empty theatre. I noticed that *smile*. I heard the rapturous applause of five hundred ghost punters. Empty or not, I was still too terrified to look out at those seats.

Fat Jack lit a second Woodbine. The old man shifted in his chair. Something else everyone knew was that a second Woody during an audition was like Damocles being passed his sword . . .

He was in a forgiving mood. 'It needs . . . narrative.'

'*Narrtiv*,' said my father.

'Story.'

'I know what narrtiv is.'

'And it needs star quality.'

'Star quality?'

'Everyone's going to the pictures. The punters are

26

drying up. When they come here they want *Hollywood*. See who's top of the bill this week? Veronica the Voice. Songs from the big musicals. *Singing in the Rain. An American in Paris.* We're booked out. It's all about the silver screen.'

'The silver screen.'

'You got it, pops.' This being Jack's catchphrase. Because if you were going to be an eccentric impresario then you needed a catchphrase. 'Come back anytime. I'll always take a look.' Because Jack was also a fair man. In fact, he got his start alongside our father at the Inveran Show.

'Keep the coat stand though. I like that. You know the rule.'

'Everyone likes watching someone get kicked in the arse,' they parroted at the same time. This perhaps reassured my father, as he watched Jack hurry away through the stalls, that we still had a shot.

★ ★ ★

Duke and I were posted to The Ritz. Movies would become the core of the routine. *If that's what Jackie boy wants then that's what the bugger will get.* Hollywood was going to win us the bill.

Film after film. I lapped them all up. Loved Jack Palance in *Shane*, hated Richard Burton in *The Robe*, ogled at Marilyn Monroe in *Gentlemen Prefer Blondes* and had to cross my legs. The old man ordered an upping of the comedy intake: Abbott and Costello, Alastair Sim. He bought us season tickets for an Ealing Comedy retrospective. I must have seen the *Lavender Hill Mob* eight times. *Research, research* and never a word about school. I loved the near-empty matinees, the dust in the projector beam and the MGM lion, the lightning bolts around the RKO tower.

Duke loved westerns. He decided he bore a resemblance to Dean Martin and maybe he did. That light the room smile and slow lope – perhaps he'd always been like that and we just hadn't noticed.

There was no-one I wanted to be. It's hard to project when you look like Charles Hawtrey.

'I'll be the star,' my brother said. 'You can be the director.' That was just fine with me. I became fixated by the camera. I'd walk home with two hands in front of my face and my fingers in a square, filming Duke with my imaginary lens as he recreated scenes from the film we'd just seen.

It came together too slowly for the old man. I'd watch from the kitchen window as he stalked the yard, seeking the big idea with cigar in hand, cigars having now replaced cigarettes, a cheroot more in keeping with the persona of showbiz Svengali he had decided to cultivate. 'What about this, boys?'

I once suggested a song and dance routine that earned me a swift slap and a 'Don't be so bloody ridiculous.' Yet that routine would become the core of our revamped act.

I'd go over in my head, again and again, how I thought Howard Hawks would film it. In fact, that's how I now remember the second audition with Fat Jack; a series of shots, cuts and close-ups.

The Inveran Empire was softly lit, row after row of hundreds of empty seats. Beside the old man sat Fat Jack and those five hundred invisible but expectant punters. Jack looked bored, but at least he wasn't hungry, our father having been careful to set up a post-lunch audition this time.

Yet Fat Jack's jaw did drop.

He turned to my father. 'Well, Mr Jackson, I do believe this is the beginning of a beautiful friendship.' Because

Fat Jack was also a film buff. Some said he was thinking of buying The Ritz.

* * *

Saturday, 13th February 1954.

The opening night of Fat Jack's Empire latest: *Laughing Room Only*. Twice nightly performances, 6.30 and 8.30. A complete change of programme every two weeks. Lex McLean topped the bill, followed by Harry Gordon, Rita Cardle, the Moxon Girls . . . on down to JJ and the Duke.

This was serious company. If Duke became an instant star, if only in his own head, I became an instant basket case. We had to stop the Morris on the way to Inveran so I could be sick.

I was nearly sick again when I saw Lex McLean. The Variety legend shook our hands with true warmth as we waited in the wings. Then an arm round my shoulder. 'Breathe deep, son. An again, that's it . . . '

Then the orchestra was striking up, a few cheers from the audience as they recognised *Diamonds Are a Girl's Best Friend*. The MC winked before I walked onstage, Duke coming on from the opposite wing. A chorus of wolf whistles greeted us, hundreds of faces beyond the footlights I was so glad I couldn't actually make out. They laughed at the runt in Jane Russell drag, a ridiculous feathered head-dress, sparkly red mini-dress and runkled tights, the poor man's panto dame to a voluptuous Duke as Marilyn Monroe. He shook his hips and blew kisses while I smiled a horrible smile complete with three blacked-out teeth and pushed up my huge sagging chest.

The orchestra switched into *Two Little Girls from Little Rock* and we did our duet, working our way up and back down the flight of stairs set up at the back of the stage. Right on cue, one of my high heels flew into the stalls after a leg kick, forcing me into an over-exaggerated limp.

Coat Stand Surprise was next and then *The Big Sheep*. Duke was Humphrey Bogle, and me as Wee Betty – a dumpy farmer's wife – flirting with Duke and explaining that her prize ram had been rustled.

'Ah said, "take me instead, take me, leave Roger".'

'Roger?'

'The ram.'

'Of course.'

'You see, Mr Bogle, I need a good Roger in . . . '

'Don't look at me!'

' . . . the sheep field, to get them in the *family* way.'

'But now he's on the lamb, eh?'

The sketch ended with Duke holding his door shut as I tried to batter it down.

'Of all the joints in all the world she walks into mine. In the name of the wee man, why did she walk into mine!'

Backstage, Lex McLean dropped to his knees and kowtowed, bunnet in hand. Fat Jack twirled and beamed like the lighthouse at Mckeever's Point, stuffing a cigar down my fake cleavage, two cigars.

The old man grunted *well done* as three Moxon Girls, dressed as majorettes in white heels, made a bee-line for Duke. A Star had been born, oozing the charisma that washed across the auditorium and brought another standing ovation in the second show. I saw the glitter in Duke's eye, the deep need. Then later, at the aftershow party in The Empire bar, his anxiety.

I saw that look other times, across the years. A catch of my eye and a quick, uncertain smile, like *am I doing ok here?* As if he always feared, no matter how famous he became, that he might get found out.

Three

Very quietly, I leave my seventy-fifth birthday party. Like a ninja, Duke, the same way I slipped away from life itself.

'Take a right turn at every intersection.'

Through the open partition Akira's eyes glance up to the rear-view. He nods. The men in the security car will follow without reaction. They will not notice Tokyo, its stories spinning like autumn leaves.

We exit the garage and take our first right. I pour a drink. I have just begun to ponder where the geometric determinism of each right turn will eventually take us when my phone rings. Erin. Her frowning face was the last thing I saw before the doors closed on the express lift to the ground floor.

I let the call ring out then listen to the voicemail. Not without satisfaction I hear frustration in her voice.

'I don't know where you are ... '

Except she does, the limo being fitted with a tracking device in case of an abduction attempt. A lone wolf, the ex-partner with a grudge? Maybe Isis, dousing me in petrol in a desert cage, Zippo for the drop unless an unholy ransom is paid to absolve my contributions to western decadence.

'We need to talk, Jay. There's the arrangements for the flight, the PR schedule and all the other ... '

I stop listening to the message. What she really

wants to say is, how dare you not bow to my will.

I cut off the message. The sight of Akira through the partition is reassuring, even the back of his head. His eyes glance up to the rear-view. Gently questioning.

'Take a left at every intersection,' I say.

It is, I feel, very Japanese. If you intend to indulge a whim or follow a mode of behaviour then do it with utter integrity.

Japan is steeped in this way of being. It is the Zen way. If you are going to get drunk then get mystically drunk, like the stumbling, black-suited salary men I see from the limousine window; if you want sex then take it to the strangest extremes, sell used underwear in street-side vending machines.

And if you are going to take a left at every single inter-section then do it for hours and hours, until the action has exhausted itself of every possibility of meaning you may have initially intended and you are lost in a flood of people, sound and scenarios that would have been forever hidden had you not decided to indulge this whim and simply ordered your driver to take you . . .

'Akira.'

'Yes?'

'Let's go home.'

Tokyo. The Occasional City. I like it because I can leave. I settle into the high-speed drive back to Shuzenji. It begins to rain. We move from asphalt and neon to build-ings with progressively fewer storeys, here and there astonishing hints of the rural, patches of anonymous black which may be fields . . .

It takes two hours to get home when it should take three. The darkness is utter, the rain seething. As I get out of the limousine my legs give way. Akira stops me falling with a strong arm.

Gentle Akira.

32

I study his face when the security light clicks on. He helps me inside and tries to remove my shoes. I shove him away roughly and struggle to undress, eventually managing to strip to my boxer shorts. I hear your laughter, Duke, so come stumble with me, room to room, our dancing shadows on the *shōji* screens as Akira quietly follows. I know he follows, concern in his eyes.

He is so enduring he might already have been here when Anna and I moved in. Yet Akira came afterwards, one of the few things which did. I could call him my personal assistant but that's not quite right. I don't know why he stayed, given my once frequent exhortations to leave. I no longer say such things, grateful for a presence more permanent than Anna's ever was.

She found this place, an old wooden *ryokan* overlooking a long, tapering pond and surrounded by steep, cypress-covered hillsides. It's the funniest thing, she said. I don't feel like I've been here, I feel like I've never been away. A surge of affection brings a sudden wooze and I stagger into the *tokonoma* alcove in the living room. A vase is wobbling but it is me that falls, onto the sofa.

I look down. A testicle has popped out and lies trapped between my boxer shorts and left thigh.

It looks so forlorn.

In time, I make it to the bedroom. The bamboo blinds are raised but the light barely reaches the veranda outside. The windows are floor to ceiling and fifteen metres long, here and there a sliding panel door. I prowl along the glass, a slight and skinny creature, bone-white skin that has seen too little light. Beyond the glass is the night, behind the glass is me. Trapped between both is the disembodied reflection of someone I never thought to become. I slide open a panel.

Step into cold and near dark.

The rain is shocking. Instant goose bumps and

sobriety was I not sipping a tumbler of twenty-five-year-old-something as I walk carefully along the treacherous wooden decking. Below me, rain fusses the dark pond. I step down a short flight of wooden stairs onto a gravel path that snakes steeply down to the water through a beautifully arranged scatter of rocks and boulders.

Midway down is another path, leading along to an *onsen* that has been built into the bank. Tiled in black slate, the oval bath is half-enclosed by a mirrored wall inset with subdued stud lighting.

I know the view that I cannot see intimately, the pond, the trees on the hillside beyond. I wash myself before bathing in the habitual Japanese manner, savouring the alternating cold rain and hot water I pour over myself from a small jug filled from a tap in the bank. When I finish, I open a small wooden cabinet on the edge of the bath and make a selection on the iPod dock. Ellington kicks in. I crank the volume until the white-lit *onsen* is drowned in sound.

The American girl at the party was pretty, wasn't she, Duke? What would she think now, watching me clamber into the bath? Brittle bones and booze. My heart hammers. The specialist called it a cardiomyopathy, left ventricular swelling and reduced pumping capacity. 'Think of your heart as a deflating rugby ball,' he said, smiling brightly as if he looks forward to saying that.

Yet it makes sense; I have felt slightly deflated for years. Right now I am empty of air altogether, flopped on the rim of the bath, arse in the air and saggy old balls almost dragging on the tiles.

I turn and swing my right leg over. Now I have one leg in the water and one on the tiles. I wait for my heart to slow before swinging over my left leg. Both of them immediately slip, plunging me under the hot water. I struggle up, gasping and laughing. Then a quick *ta-daaaa*, arms out wide for the audience, befuddled

34

Tommy Cooper and another 'trick' gone disastrously wrong.

Ah, Tommy, a genius.

All we mustered, Duke, was a monkey. But take away the 'k' and at least we managed some of that.

Yes, I know. It was a chimp . . .

I am now facing the wrong way, towards the curving mirrors instead of open space. The man in the mirror disgusts me. I give him the V-sign and wish I'd got into the *onsen* the other way around. To turn now would involve complicated watery manoeuvres of which I am wholly incapable.

Hear that, Duke? *Reflections in D*.

A drift of lonely old piano, lost notes in the steaming darkness. Bicycle, limousine or *shinkansen*, we make those journeys and all our stories are eventually told. We start as soon as we speak and there's always some sucker willing to listen to the same old tales over and over. It's the auto in biography.

I'm coming home, Duke. Old Sam Beckett looking back from the mirror, he's coming to see you.

Who would you have become? I picture you Orson Welles huge, bald as the old man. It was happening as early as 1952. You inherited so much from him, you poor bastard. Read all about it in chapter six of my autobiography where the ghostwriter's words are particularly eloquent, I feel. His handling of your viciousness is as resonant as the lonely note Ellington is now holding.

The *Reflections* end. In the silent seconds before the next track, I feel your breath, Duke, on my neck.

I lie back in the water and close my eyes. Instantly, the world begins to spin, so I open them again. Alcoholism, of course, was a genetic trait that our father so generously bequeathed to both of us.

Yet I will rise to the occasion once more. I am, as you know, a professional. Tomorrow, before I get on the plane, I will do two things. First, a long shiatsu massage, soft fingers on my old bones. The background music will be meditative; sounds of the *koto*, clarinet and *shakuhachi*. Then I will eat *kaiseki* at that elegant little place in Shibuya, contemplating the art in each delicate dish as I sit in my *yukata* and look out on a tiny courtyard of dwarf cypress and tinkling water.

And I will remember how in this moment I saw my father's grinning face as his once-famous, seventy-five-year-old son leaned over the side of the bath and sent a jet of vomit into the darkness.

* * *

My first awakening is to laughter. Echoing belly laughs in an empty black cavern. There is a dream I won't recall except one image shining bright and oversized. That famous logo, the black-and-white outline of a monkey's head and the words *Breda Inc.* underneath, slowly fading back to black ...

My second awakening is to pale dawn grey in the window. Rain is silently angling, green foliage beyond.

My third is a slow rising from somewhere impossibly distant. My heart feels sluggish. Taste of sour dirt. I lift my hands, cover my face as the headache detonates. Exploding rainbows.

I feel sick.

Today is my birthday.

I can't remember much about the night before. The *onsen* in the rain, that's about it. My mother flashes. *You'll catch your death*. Like the time in Cuba when I sat naked in the deluge with a bottle of Havana Club and Anna said exactly the same words. Once more, I survived. I guess I must be lucky, although I did catch a horrible virus-cold that made me deaf in one ear.

36

Akira has left three pills and a glass of water on the bedside table. Lifting the glass, I study the back of my hand. It's hairy, mottled with liver spots. I think of dead flies with their legs sticking up.

'Happy birthday, hairy hands.'

They too are seventy-five years old today. That said, my first proper awareness of myself happened around the age of four or five. So I'm only really about seventy, which makes me feel a bit better.

I put down the glass and lift my hands in front of my face. Through the bars of my skinny fingers the window becomes brighter, the swelling sun making shadow-blocks of my palms and hiding their erratic, winding lines. Indeed, I have no desire to relive all those fortunes told.

I drop my hands and stare out the window. From my bed I can't see the decking and the pond separating the *ryokan* from a near-vertical, wooded hillside. The perspective is deceptive, my gaze immediately moving into the cypress, the trees seeming so much closer than they actually are.

Soon my niece will come and get me. I will go home for the final time. My ambivalence seems overdone. The greenery gives a shiver. First breath of the day. I notice that I have been holding my own.

Erin arrives at exactly seven. Six feet tall, immaculately dressed in a black trouser suit and open-necked white blouse.

Coming from a long line of short arses it amazes me how this giraffelike creature came about. Even as a newborn she was oddly elongated, tightly swaddled in her mother's arms like a length of guttering.

She stands awhile in the sliding doorway, a box in her hand, my birthday present. I look up from the *tatami* floor, where I sit at a low lacquered table.

37

Although she looms over me, it is actually me in the position of superiority. The white and fluffy guest slippers are chosen for that express purpose. As I look away to pour a cup of coffee she glances sourly down at them.

'Happy birthday,' she says.

'Thank you.'

Her knees fold almost to her chest as she sits down in the chair opposite me. Like an insect. She hands me the beautifully wrapped box which I place on the table. We both look at it for a while.

'We missed you last night. It was a great shame.'

'Who missed me?'

'The people at your party. Your friends.'

'My friends?'

'Why did you just leave like that?'

'My friends?'

'Yes.'

'But they weren't my friends.'

She shifts. She's getting annoyed. She has no idea who my friends are. I have no idea who my friends are.

'It was a great shame,' she repeats.

'Nothing to be done.'

'You did well with the monkey.'

'Chimpanzee.'

'What?'

'It was a chimpanzee.'

'Ok. Chimp.'

'A chimpanzee is different from a monkey. It's a Great Ape.'

She seems confused but quickly recovers. 'Are you ready?'

'Almost.'

'I'll wait for you. I have some calls to make.'

Her phone is already in her hand as she awkwardly unfolds herself from the low chair. She hates Japan. She was made for the biggest of canvases: LA. The City of Angels, although I never once saw one.

Akira has already packed for me. I don't bother to check the selection of underwear, suits and shirts he has expertly fitted into seven pieces of Louis Vuitton. Akira knows. This is something else my niece dislikes him for.

He has left one piece for me to pack, a thin, black artist's portfolio case. Yours, Duke. Stencilled 'DJ'.

I take the bag to the other side of my sparse, immaculately neat and tidy bedroom and slide open a door to a small office with one window, high up on the wall. Years ago, I could spend twelve hours a day in here. Seeking the lost magic of *A Man's a Man*. Or just seeking something to do.

This is where I wrote the script for *The Bruce* and designed the storyboards. When I gave the originals to Erin about a year ago I made copies and re-commenced my never-ending revisions.

On three sides of the room are long, angled drawing desks. Desks and floor are cluttered. Blank sheets, half-started sketches, dozens of balls of crumpled paper. There are empty glasses and at least five plates, a half-eaten sandwich, and is that cake? When did I eat cake? But there in a little circular clearing on the floor is indeed half a slice of what looks like fruit cake.

Yes, figures . . .

On three walls stretch neat rows of numbered black-and-white drawings. Dozens of them. I notice a section where some drawings have been removed. These nine drawings are arranged on the floor as the borders of the little clearing. I have made some corrections in red felt tip.

Script or storyboard, I veer from one to the other. At the moment, it is the images. I will present them, eventually and still unsatisfied, to the Great Director I can't stand, who won't even look at them.

I untack the drawings from the wall and put them into the thin portfolio bag, the nine loose ones on top to re-consider on the plane. Robert the Bruce smiles out from his portrait on the central desk, the famous one with the skullcap and the axe. He seems more bored than usual.

Rest assured, King Bobby, that closure is almost here. Beginnings, as you know, are so much easier than endings. I do feel a somewhat reluctant relief in having a stranger finish what I haven't managed in decades. Maybe that's who your gormless face has been pining for all these years.

Erin is in the living room. She talks loudly on her phone, legs folded underneath her on the semi-circular white leather sofa, every inch the tycoon I have created. She holds up a hand and rolls her eyes, mouthing a name I am supposed to recognise that will explain her exasperation. I don't have a clue who she is talking about, and cross over to the sliding windows and outside.

It's not that I doubt my affection for her. Yet its depth has always troubled me. She is a child of privilege, and compulsions that yell Asperger's. Take the pre-teen mania with short-wave radio. I had a small cabin built at the bottom of the Wendlebury Manor garden, which she insisted, for some reason, had to look like a Yukon trading post. She'd sit there for hours, turning the dial a Hertz at a time, noting the stations in a leather logbook. I'd see the yellow glow from the top windows. I still remember the names: *World Harvest Radio, HCJB Quito, Super Power KUSW* . . .

Football came soon after. An obsession that only a girl could bring to such a masculine game. Not that she ever played. She simply recorded. It wasn't enough to

40

read the statistics in the newspapers; she had to copy them into another logbook, as if she didn't quite trust them. Then animals. Pets of all kinds.

'Finally.' Her appearance startles me. She peers into the rain, chin in the air, moving her face left then right, as if checking herself in a mirror only she can see. She is still holding her phone. I feel a slight annoyance that her footprints have messed up the pristine shininess of the wet decking.

'That man can go on.'

'Who?'

'Peterson?'

'I don't know him.'

'The lawyer. Peterson? You met him last night.'

'Peterson?'

'Yes. *Peterson.*'

She is looking at me with impatience. It is my age she despises. She always has.

'I suppose we should go then.'

'I suppose we should.'

I look around the room, as if suspecting I won't be back and want to retain as many details as I can. None of them will stick, crowded out by all the others to which I now must return.

Four

Fat Jack booked us at The Empire several more times in 1954. At the same time the old man tried to get JJ and the Duke signed. He eventually came back from another trip to Glasgow with a contract from the Galts Agency. This meant regular work, two weeks in one theatre then on to the next, if only the 'number threes' circuit, outposts like Motherwell, Hamilton and Paisley.

A Galts contract also brought the summer seaside gigs. Fourteen-odd weeks guaranteed money.

You worked for it.

Twice nightly shows and a change of programme twice a week. Fourteen acts per programme and a small cast meant you'd done half a dozen turns before taking the stage in your own right.

We started in July 1954 at the Beach Pavilion, Leven. Fourth on the bill. We finished in the same place.

Back home, Fat Jack had a 'wee proposition for us'. We were crammed into his tiny backstage office.

'That being . . . ?' the old man asked.

'Headline tour.'

Duke and I exchanged glances.

'Sounds intriguing,' said our father. 'Doesn't it sound intriguing, boys?'

'Indeed it is.' When Jack spun back around in his chair he had three cigars in his pudgy hand. He raised the other, rubbing his fingers together and frowning, the MC searching for the right words.

'*To Barra and Beyond.*'

'Come again?'

'Eh?'

'The islands boys. The western lands. Gonna take some culture to those *teuchters.*'

'The islands?'

'A December tour. You'll hop from place to place on the mail steamers.'

'Mail steamers?'

'There's no competition. They don't do panto. Too pagan for them.'

'I was thinking about the sea,' said Duke. 'The Minch.'

'Well, boy, those island lassies are surely lonely. One thing you can guarantee is plenty of Minch.'

* * *

'Pay the dues,' the old man said. We paid them all winter, Castlebay to Portree, Stornoway to Ullapool. 'Play every stage like it's the Palladium.' When we finally did play the Palladium it wasn't filled with whisky-pissed fishers and crofters. Fat Jack had tapped an unknown market. There was decent money here. So we paid more dues the following winter, headliners in *The Stornoway Way.*

It was quite the ramshackle bill.

A Harry Lauder wannabe, a magician and a couple of catastrophic comedians, on up to number two, an ageing husband and wife dance team, Brigitte and Paulo (actually Mary and Watty McPhail). They didn't make it back in 1955, Brigitte rupturing groin and career when she attempted the splits in Benbecula village hall. A ventriloquist replaced them, Swanney and Magoo, a

43

naughty schoolboy dummy with a tendency to explode into foul-mouthed tirades depending on how drunk Swanney was. Magoo never made it home, hurled into the Minch on the run home, Swanney laughing as he bobbed off into the blue yonder. He really did hate that dummy.

'These are the lands of the sheep shagger,' Duke told me, mock-serious. 'Be careful.' But he was the pretty boy who needed to keep a wary eye, not for lonely farmers but enraged boyfriends. I watched this with a studied perplexity, barely able to look at a girl. Every encounter was gruesome, the treacherous way my mouth went AWOL, my words randomly re-arranging.

'How do you manage it?'

We were in our room at the Marine Hotel, Kyle. It was 10am, Duke already with a drink to hand.

'How do you get so many?'

'Dunno,' said Duke. 'It just kind of happens. Few drinks and . . .'

'Easy as that, eh?'

'I don't want to let anyone down. The girls, it's what they expect. Same as they expect your greeting face.'

'My heart bleeds.'

'Piss off. You just hang about in the background, pretending to be invisible. It's me picking up the slack. No bugger wants to talk to you so where's old Duke? Duke'll smile. Duke'll give us a laugh.'

'I'm not having a go at you.'

'I feel like I'm being crushed, sometimes. Tight, in the chest. All these people and sometimes I could cry.'

It was almost shocking. I'd glimpsed this anxiety, now and then, but he'd never talked about it.

Almost immediately, it vanished.

He jumped up. The Duke was back. Lopsided smile and lazy blue eyes like he'd just fallen out of bed. He stared at me, took a slow drag of his cigarette and winked. 'I go through the same patter every evening, darling, so trust me, I'm not gonna give you any. You're gorgeous. That's all that needs to be said.' Then he slumped back down on the bed, the smile disappearing. 'Give it a go, some such shite. Telling you, it works wonders for old Jekyll and Hyde here.'

I preferred Jekyll. The good doctor had the smile which sold the tat.

My merchandising ideas had been well received. Signed photographs and photo opportunities. Postcards of stills from our most popular sketches. I even arranged a special performance at Portree hospital with a journalist in tow. I wondered if I might have a flair for this kind of thing.

'An entreprenoor, eh, you must've got that from your mum.'

Money was the one responsibility the old man gave to me. He knew if he wanted to make any poppy then an attitude almost conscientious in its recklessness just wasn't going to cut it.

* * *

Fat Jack broke a promise. He didn't put us top of the bill for the spring show after *To Barra and Beyond*. Nor in January 1956 when we got back from *The Stornoway Way*. Lex MacLean's bow on the night of our debut seemed a lifetime ago. 'Nothing wrong with being journeymen, boys.'

I watched my father's fists clench and unclench.

'Work the act,' said Jack.

I didn't want to. I was on the verge of quitting. I was tired of seasick winter tours and endless summer seasons, the grind of a week to week existence. My life was slipping past in a depressing show reel of flea-bitten boarding houses. The problem was what else to

45

do. I wondered about some kind of business. Or maybe making films. I had bought my first camera, a Kodak Brownie.

Back home we went to work the act. The old man's momentary faltering of optimism was lost in a blizzard of stale ideas, re-treads with a tired twist, waiting for something to click. Again and again my ideas were shot down when I could have done it so much better and he knew it.

I was going to take a stand. Sure I was. And then I did, on the night of the storm that changed everything. A somehow liquid night. The carry of sound as if we were underwater. We huddled by the fire as an extraordinary wind surged and the walls groaned, the roof about to rip and spin into the darkness any moment, then the cottage itself, the three of us Wizard of Oz-ing up, up and away. If only.

'Just what is it that you don't like about it?'

'It's too fancy.'

'Too fancy? What's that supposed to mean?' I had an idea for a comedy chase sequence, Duke and I on a static motorbike with a projection of changing scenery behind us, a daft montage that would make it seem as if we were driving over mountains, the sea, along railway tracks. 'You still think Buster Keaton rip-offs are going to cut it? It's not the nineteen bloody twenties!'

'Shut it, Johnny!'

'Let me run with it.'

'It won't *work*.'

'Why are you so jealous? I've never got that. Just what—'

He slapped me. Hard on the face.

I blinked away the tears but held his stare. 'What is it that *threatens* you so much?'

When he made to strike me again I grabbed his hand.

46

'Stop it!' Duke stepped between us and pushed us apart. He looked as if he was on the verge of tears.

'Away and get some coal in.'

'Me?' said Duke.

'Not you. Him.'

'C'mon, Dad, it's a hurricane out there!'

My father and I stared at each other. 'No worries, Duke.' When I reached the door I said, 'I quit.'

'What?'

In the noise of the wind he hadn't heard me. When I said it again it didn't sound right any more.

'That so?'

The wind wrenched the door from me. I struggled across to the byre and filled the coal bucket, hurrying back to the cottage in a howling black that suddenly swelled into bright white.

A flare was slowly falling, illuminating the remains of the outhouse, the long grass in the fields a wildly undulating sea. I ran to the end of the cottage and looked towards the Sound, a blackness pricked by a line of blinking red dots. The night swelled white again under another flare, revealing a violent confusion of waves, the red dots the running lights of a large cargo vessel.

It was no more than a hundred metres offshore and listing heavily to port, fuzzy behind explosions of spray. Men were braced at the rails, staring at the sea rising to meet them, uncertain about jumping. A lifeboat dangled from a line, battering against the hull. Another flare went up.

Then I saw people in the water. Three of them, closer to the shore, maybe twenty metres from the asphalt slipway. They struggled, gone then reappearing, fading into black as I waited for the next flare that never came. My vision closed on an expanse of smooth metal as the ship finally rolled onto its side and, on the darkening edge, figures tossed here and there by the waves.

I swam out. I swam back. I brought three men to the shore.

I knelt beside them on the shingle. I saw the catch of light in their bulging eyeballs as they focused on mine, a confusion lost in a spluttering of salt water. No sound but the wind. No words from Duke and my father, who stared at me, soaking wet in the doorway, with the same incredulous look as the sailors I had left on the shore.

We helped them back up to the cottage and Duke and the old man drove them to hospital in Inveran. I watched the car all along the shore road and up the hill, until the tail lights disappeared as it dropped over the brow, just as, on the Sound, the ship's running lights had also vanished.

⋆ ⋆ ⋆

The next day I remember as a series of highly stylised set-pieces. Everything I looked at or said was infused with a crystal clarity. Yet I was conscious of not trusting it, neither the broken fences which had turned four fields into one big one, nor the line of detritus that followed the salamander shores of the Sound of Skerray west towards McKeever's Point and east towards Inveran.

Nor the big ship, lying on its side a hundred metres offshore, gentle waves lapping the near-submerged hull. The newspaper told us it was the SS *Breda*, built in 1921, a single-screw cargo steamer out of Rotterdam. A hundred metres long and 7,000 tonnes, all hands lost but the three Chinese sailors I had pulled from the sea, now babbling in Mandarin at Inveran Memorial.

Duke, my father and I stood in the yard, each with our hands on our hips. As we stared out at the Sound the *Breda* finally slipped under the waves. I accepted this fact with alacrity, the situation so far beyond normal that this vanishing seemed confirmation it had never happened at all.

Then a sound behind us, a movement at the byre.

Afterwards, we would each claim to have seen it first. But, as I say, I didn't trust any of it.

'Unreal.'

'Unreal.'

'Can't whack it,' said my father.

Up on a beam of the ramshackle byre, which had miraculously survived the storm, sat a bedraggled monkey.

'What are we gonna do with it?'

'Chuck it a tattie.'

'A tattie?'

'Why?'

'I'm not throwing it a tattie. What if he doesn't eat tatties? I mean—'

'Everyone eats tatties.'

'How do you know it's a he?'

'*Everyone eats tatties!* Away and get some.'

When I returned, my father opened his arms wide as he looked at the monkey, as if apologising for his idiot son.

'The hell's that?'

'A tattie.'

'I can see that, ya cheeky wee shite. Why'd you not peel it?'

'I dunno.'

'If you were a monkey. If you were eating your very first tattie, would you not want it peeled?'

He had a point.

My father removed his fedora. A sure sign of uncertainty. He began to scratch his bald head.

'Old Donny's got a phone. I'll call the zoo and get them to come and take it away.'

49

He hefted the potato in his hand and lobbed it into the byre. A short second later the potato re-appeared, rolling to a standstill at his feet. I looked to Duke, looked to our father, looked to Duke.

After a few moments, at exactly the same time, we each took three slow steps into the byre and peered up. There was the monkey, sitting up on its beam. Grinning, I'm sure it was grinning.

'Bring me some more tatties.'

He threw another one. A high-arc towards the monkey, who caught it smartly and lobbed it back. Three more with the same results. The fifth time the old man put his hat back on and pointed at it. And lo and behold the monkey tossed it back and knocked it off. The next time my father threw the potato over his shoulder. Back it came, once more knocking off his hat.

'Boys, I have a wonderful idea for our act.'

'Dad!'

The old man and I turned and followed Duke's outstretched arm. In the field opposite the byre a horse was prancing, shaking its mane and snorting. Not just any horse, a truly magnificent one.

'Christ almighty,' my father said. 'It's the day of the animals.'

I am sure that was when the second idea detonated in his head. He had finally worked out the angle he had been pondering since the drive to Inveran with three half-drowned Chinese sailors. The horse should have reared up, whinnying, a lurid emphasis for the long-awaited eureka.

There followed another set-piece of that over-exposed day. Our father is on one side of the table, the two of us on the other, the inevitable bottle between us. We watch him drink and gesticulate, stand up in excitement and sit down in contemplation, shirt open to his waist and big belly straining, listening as he expands upon his strategy and *the possibilities, think of the possibilities.*

'Are you sure about this, JJ?' my brother asked me later. 'I mean if you're not then just say.'

'It's what he wants.'

'Do you want it though? If you don't we can fix it.'

Duke didn't want to fix it. I saw it in his eyes. This would make him the big star I had no desire to be.

'It's ok, Duke.'

* * *

The next day was bitter. A slicing wind off the sea. The old man had called *The Inveran Courier* and we were waiting for the promised journalist. Providence and the old man had cracked their knuckles.

It was 1pm and he still hadn't appeared, so we took turns going into the yard to look down the shore road.

I saw a figure in the distance, walking along the road and up the slope to the cottage. It took me far too long to realise it was a woman. The trouser suit confused me. She was blonde and pretty, a bit older than Duke, I would have said.

She waved and I waved back, not with the desired nonchalance but with a weird, Nazi-like salute. My casual lean against the gate also failed, it was just too far away and I nearly fell over. I blushed as only a seventeen-year-old can blush.

She looked at me closely and bit her lip. Tried not to laugh. 'I'm here to interview you. I'm from the *Courier*?'

'Sure. Right. Eh—'

'Duke Jackson. A pleasure.'

Her gaze moved past me, eyes opening wider to admit The Duke, who had appeared out of nowhere.

51

'Anna Chambers,' she said. 'Delighted to meet you.' Her smile had become something altogether different.

She apologised for being so late. Her rubbishy old jalopy had broken down, a fact illustrated with a thumb over her shoulder, which all three of us dumbly followed, our gazes stopped by the whitewashed kitchen wall. She very much appreciated Duke's offer to run her back into town afterwards and then, all business-like with a clap of hands, asked if we were ready to begin.

My father spoke of the Day of the Animals, a phrase he'd become quite attached to. 'That should be the title of the article, hen.'

She offered the most carefully non-committal of smiles. 'Perhaps we should hear from Duke,' she said.

'A pleasure,' said Duke.

He needed no deep breath. No tense, *here I go then*. The all-new Hero of the Breda showed no first-night nerves. He told Anna how he saw the men in the sea and didn't think twice, just swam out and brought them in. It was truly impressive, my brother clearly a genius or a psychopath.

'Brought them home,' was what Duke actually said. Turned out the hero had a gifted turn of phrase. He didn't settle the angst on his face as he would in later performances, although he did flash me a wary look. Testing my contempt, maybe, or making sure I didn't give it away.

Anna looked at him very closely. She had stopped writing in her notebook. Her lips were slightly open. That was when I noticed the day's bitter cold which I still feel now, colder than the waters of the Sound as I swam back to the shore with the Chinese sailors and out of my own story.

At first, I looked back with anger.

Then incredulity.

In time, I avoided thought of it altogether. Later still, I was completely reconciled. It would even come to make me laugh. Because it could only have been this way. We are all children of myth. Every story has its creation legend: the Cherokee and their water beetle, the Vikings with their ancient giant. Some might say The Breda Boys foundation myth was of less cosmic significance. But all these myths, they're just tall tales round the fire. They're showbiz.

★ ★ ★

You had to hand it to Anna Chambers. She only escaped the *Woman and Home* pages for the Breda article because the feature writer had ruptured a hernia trying to reach the second of the Inveran links in one.

She never looked back. Her story was a sensation. The Day of the Animals became the *Day of the Menagerie*, a quick-smart syndication for our heroic, Boys Own tale. I imagined it flashing around the country like in a film montage: a dramatic, read-all-about-it spinning of a dozen front pages.

She took the famous photo too.

The three of us stand outside the old byre, left arms outstretched as we lean towards the camera. It was extraordinary how long we spent discussing whether it should be our left arm or right, the old man eventually holding sway with the unassailable argument that if in doubt, veer left.

You might have seen that photo. I have a confused look on my face, as if I don't quite get the punchline to the joke. There was this shipwreck, right, the only survivors a monkey, a horse and three Chinamen . . .

Anna was also there a week later at Inveran Town Hall. One of the hundreds pouring inside, who occasionally shook my hand but much more often my brother's. The people intimidated me less than the building, with its Jacobethan pilasters and flagstoned staircase leading up to the arcade. Heavy double doors then opened into the hall, the wooden floor polished to a glassy sheen, and ornate, white painted balconies on three sides, chandeliers like sparkling wasps' nests . . .

I looked down from the table on the stage where we had been seated with the other dignitaries. There was Anna with her notebook in the front row. A green dress, hair the colour of summer barley.

Again, she acknowledged me and again she did not see me, those big blue eyes only for Duke. As his were only for her. He fixed her with that lopsided smile and she quickly smiled back, another blush. His problem was the others he saw. The others he smiled at who she had not yet noticed.

Ah, Duke, the machine greased by need. There was genius in his aw shucks, it was nothing. He was just the Everyman who happened to be in the right place at the right time. He was just like you. In fact, it might even *be you*, next time. Anna fell for it, we all did, including the tubby man with Himmler spectacles sitting at the other end of the table. He was the main reason we were in the Town Hall, the culmination of the events triggered by Anna's story going national.

Fat Jack was the bearer of the news, driving out from Inveran in his new Austin 30 to tell us. It turned out that the horse we rescued was *Sunflower Star*, the Aga Khan's favourite, being taken to stud. None of us knew what an Aga Khan was. Not until he turned up with his entourage two days later.

We traipsed into Inveran Memorial and another photo: the Khan, the three of us and the bewildered Chinese sailors. The Khan wanted to reward us for Duke's heroism, although I suspected he was more relieved about the return of his prize horse. 'You are very welcome to the monkey,' he added.

Not to be outdone by the acclamation of an exotic aristocrat, the council leapt into action, informing us we had been awarded the Freedom of Inveran for our act of civic responsibility. The news was conferred by the chairman in his office overlooking the town green with growing alarm, as if he had just seen a troubling vision of the old man grazing his cows.

Hence the reception in the Town Hall and the chairman's toe-curling speech about how we embodied the best of this hard-working community. The London hacks grinned as they scribbled, the Aga Khan a bewildered presence at one end of the table while at the other the old man beamed, Duke smouldered in his blue blazer and I wondered if he might stand up and croon.

'This is just unreal, isn't it?' he had said to me a few hours ago when we were getting ready.

'Just a bit.'

'You look like you're going to court.'

'You look like you've already been convicted.'

He grabbed my hand, suddenly and genuinely anxious. 'There's still time to change this, you know.'

'Your tie's squint.'

'Bloody hell, JJ. I can't do this. It's not right.'

'Careful, you don't want the old man dropping dead, not now. He's reached the gates of paradise.'

After a long and bumptious speech, the chairman presented us with a grudgingly small silver quaich. The Khan followed with nothing so gaudy. Just a simple handshake, having already handed over a cheque for £5,000, an almost unbelievable amount of money. All of which continued to explain my father's beaming face as the Fleet Street flashbulbs popped and the audience broke into applause. Then the old man waved his hands up and down, asking for quiet.

He scanned the faces, very grave now. 'For those who say you can't do something. For those who say something is beyond your ability ... I say,' and he tipped back the fedora. 'You Aga bloody CAN!'

* * *

A few days later we sat in the kitchen pondering the quaich, which my father had placed in the centre of the table.

The absurdity was palpable. Any moment I expected to hear the laughter explode, the great cosmic joke revealed and everything instantly vanishing: money, monkey ... even the ridiculous clothes worn by Duke and the old man. The Khan's money had been put to swift use at Archibald and Son's, the stop-off of choice for the huntin-shootin-fishin set on their way to the grouse moors and salmon rivers, a toff's paradise they had once mocked.

A secret envy was now manifest in Duke's yachtsman attire, complete with stripy cravat and canvas deck shoes. My father had gone for the classic tweeds and walking stick, a sterling silver handle shaped like a whippet's head. Yet he still wore his greasy fedora, making the somewhat redundant points that country gentlemen are born, not made, and you can't polish a turd.

They both knew it, of course.

The old man folded his arms and looked at me. 'So, Master Johnny. You decided yet? You still retiring?'

'What do you need me for anyway? Duke's the big star. That's why you changed the story, eh?'

'Don't be jealous, son.'

'I'm not.'

'It's just the *act*. What does it matter who dragged three half-deid chinks out aw the sea? You know the truth. We know the truth. So what if no-one else does? Would you be happy trotting out the tale every time some journalist wants to hear it? Never mind telling stories, you clam up when someone asks you the *time*. We're on the move here. Need to make some hay while the sun shines, and trust me, it's dazzlin. Everyone wants a piece of The Breda Boys.'

'The Breda Boys?'

'Trips off the tongue, eh?'

Then Duke. 'It's just an act, JJ, you said so yourself.'

'Ok, so you get to be the hero. What do I get?'

'You get the monkey,' said the old man.

'The monkey?'

'Sure. Everyone loves the monkey.'

Everyone loves the monkey. It would be the final line in *The Breda Boys go to Monte Carlo*.

Five

The lawyer, Peterson, is one of our entourage, a nervy, whey-faced man of indeterminate age and personality.

There is also Erin, Akira and myself and three security guards, two of whom followed me around Tokyo and out to the Shuzenji compound last night. Yet there is no irritation to be found in their faces. Perhaps it's in the eyes hidden behind the Ray-Bans, although I suspect a more Android-like disinterest.

We sweep into Narita Airport like a flock of black-suited vampires, black-shaded against the day that has transformed during our high-speed drive from cemetery grey to vivid autumn blue. I glance up, a last look at those delicate watercolours and then we're inside the terminal.

As VIPs, we elicit gawps and unclipped security barriers, a *time is money* arrogance undermined by my slowing, old man shuffle. Each time Erin glances back impatiently, Akira's grip tightens on my arm.

In my dotage the contrary has come to please me. The absurd too. I doff an imaginary hat at a wedge-faced boy sitting on his father's lap. His smile will help me through the weirdness. For although the VIP brings a private gate, it offers no shade from the white masks and gloves of the Customs People, who patiently wait for us to remove our shoes and shades and jackets.

Still, departing is easier. I shudder at the thought of the return flight, remembering the last one I made, years ago.

Eleven hours from LAX into Tokyo dawn, a customs officer thrusting a sheet of paper with cartoons of people blowing their noses. 'Bird flu, you have fever?' I decided not to waggle my arms like a chicken, and shook my head, stepping to another officer asking about *pork*. Did he say pork? I Indeed he had, for importation of pork products to Japan is illegal. I patted my pockets and reeled deeper into strangeness, the retinal scan and closed-circuit mugshot that instantly transformed me into a terror suspect, the drug dog with an alarming interest in my crotch. The craze of Tokyo was still to come, yet I had already been disassembled into a million, neon-lacquered pieces . . .

I am being beckoned impatiently forward by a security officer.

'I have no salami in my pants,' I tell him as he efficiently pats me down. 'I have not eaten spam in years.'

Beside me, Erin frowns.

Slow-burning dementia. It's what they think now and probably then, back in the late-eighties when I was removed as CEO. I can understand it. I was in a manic phase. Who knows how long it might have lasted.

Ironically enough, the film that is now the prestige, fiftieth anniversary production of Breda Pictures was the straw that sent the camel sprawling. I had jettisoned a board agenda to present the latest script for *The Bruce*. I had even hired actors to read through the pivotal scenes.

The manicured hands that fidgeted with such exquisite awkwardness wasted no time in swiftly propelling me down the back stairs. I had long since lost all interest in the company by then anyway. It was a small miracle that they hadn't bumped me years before. The board was magnanimous, however, making me president. And, like most presidents, I have no power at all.

Erin glances again at the portfolio bag containing my storyboard and script re-works. For the next twelve hours she will fear the demented daftie babbling on about a movie that isn't his to make. Not that she'll care, guilt being an emotion somewhat alien to Erin. She was too young to be part of the coup that replaced me but it felt like its final act when she became CEO years later.

'It's quite the plane,' Peterson says as we strap for take-off. He's sitting beside me, the man who drew the short straw and feels he must now engage.

'It is that.'

'Global Express 600.'

'What?'

'The name of the plane.'

Peterson, Akira, Erin and I sit in a square of seats with a table between us. We each have an octagonal, port-hole window and an angular, light and dark grey seat like something out of *Star Trek*. The internal fuselage has the same two tones, the bulkhead separating our compartment from the next, decorated with an abstract design of marbled greys. Like mountains, or stylised breasts.

'Cruising speed 500 knots. 6,000 nautical mile range,' says Peterson.

'Do they look like tits to you?'

He blinks a few times then turns, following my gaze. On my left Erin too looks up. Another frown.

There will be a board meeting on the plane. As president, I periodically drop into these meetings, just as a reminder that if it wasn't for me there would be none of them. Today, the spectre will again squat at the feast, with the regional directors patched in via some high-faluting tech link.

My *wisdom*, Duke.

They may imbibe if they so wish. I am a giving man. Yet even wisdom must prepare, for the wise man is also humble, yes? I ask Akira to get me a drink, throw it back and ask for another. Opposite me, Peterson pulls a screen down from the cabin roof and connects a projector to Erin's iPad. I finish the second whisky and Akira re-fills the glass. This time he leaves the bottle.

This is why I love him.

That's right, Duke, you heard. Raise those cartoon eyebrows high and higher, high as they reached at the punchline, turning to the laughing audience as I stood hands on hip all mock-offended, the butt of another joke as the curtain closed and the band crescendoed, the two of us exiting stage left, the old man's arm around your shoulder, a grin in the fog of a cheap cigar ...

'Hadn't you better slow down?'

Erin has assumed a look of concern.

'There's no rules in the sky, pet.' I raise my glass. 'Up here in the blue we is ... free.'

'What about your DVT socks?'

'What?'

'Deep Vein Thrombosis.' She leans down and pulls up her trousers, revealing a pair of long red socks that come up her skinny knees. 'They stop blood clots forming. Stop them reaching the brain.'

'Blood clots.'

'It's an issue.'

'That so?'

'On long-haul flights.'

Now I am looking down at my legs. Peterson too. And Akira. All of us peering down and wondering about the time bombs about to detonate in our heads. Erin proceeds to hand out packets of socks.

Ah, people, the life of the Global Executive. That sleek private jet you see parked up as you queue forever to cram into a budget airline that charges you a pound to piss, you wonder and dream, do you not, about the champagne and the caviar, the undoubted mile-high kicks? Perhaps this will finally be you, one day, puce-faced and embarrassed as you roll up your tailored trews to reveal your bunioned tootsies, struggling into a savagely tight pair of red safety socks.

Erin seems pleased.

She fiddles on her iPad and some graphs appear on the projector screen. 'Look at the numbers.' The numbers, the numbers, once upon a time I too was greedy for those Kabbalistic shiftings. Erin says, 'Twenty points up and rising.'

I imagine one point for each thousand feet we climb to the cruising altitude of thirty-eight thousand and whoa Trigger, let's plateau awhile, no need to overheat. I see my father. The unimpressed Scotsman. One of the biggest companies in the world, ye say?

S'no bad.

And a puff on the foul-smelling cheroot. Even with all that poppy in his pocket he wouldn't splash out on a decent Cuban. Ever the stretch for a respectability to which he was genetically indisposed.

What a sprawl I created. First Breda Pictures then Breda Investments. Both became subsidiaries of Breda Inc. when we branched out in the seventies, more affiliates following, an all-consuming media and leisure monster. Few of these later ventures and acquisitions had anything to do with me. Yet the original sin was mine, the decision to 'aggressively diversify our portfolio'.

Can you remember, Duke, how I actually used to say things like that? Early on, say, when we turned the idiosyncratic Sirocco hotel in Mustique into soulless clones, one on each continent, boutique hideaways for the super-rich. Or later, when we turned Jefferson Publishing into Breda Books.

That desire to get ever bigger . . .

It was almost physical, an anxious churning in the gut, like the swelling logo on the projector screen, a tiny black dot becoming recognisable as the familiar monkey in silhouette, side profiled, the tail curling up to the right of the head and Breda Inc. in small, black block capitals underneath, becoming bigger until it fills the whole screen before reappearing as the tiny, swelling dot.

It is wise, I feel, to get drunk, even if it means breaking my promise to hold back until we reached China. Sentimentality demands it too. Look there, a little Chinese boy hurrying home from school, stopping to look up at the contrails, as we used to stop and look up, Duke, whenever a plane passed, hands cupped over our eyes and who was it, up there, would we travel like that one day, the possibility so unimaginably distant that it didn't even cross our minds to be envious . . .

I have no choice but to raise a glass, at exactly the moment, I hope, that the little boy looks up.

'Erin?'

'Viggo?'

I look up at the projector screen, now showing five smaller screens in the pattern of a domino. Each has a clock in the top left-hand corner and a location underneath, as you might see behind the reception of an old-fashioned hotel. New York, 10.32; London, 06.32; Johannesburg, 08.32 . . .

'Peterson?'

'Erin?'

'Viggo?'

Peterson frantically taps on the laptop. A sudden meld of multicolour rectilinear shapes appears on the centre screen, greens and reds shifting as the image behind the digital shatter tries to assume form. I have met Viggo a few times. Chief Financial Officer. I can hear but not yet see him.

'Ah, *Viggo.*'

'Erin!' Viggo's face beams. His skin is a shiny pink, like ham. He looks as if he has been chemically peeled.

63

'Mr Jackson,' he adds, the forehead creasing as the video feed reveals my unexpected presence. 'A pleasure.'

'Liar,' I say.

He explodes into laughter that sounds like Bluto from *Popeye*. 'Nothing changes, nothing changes.'

'Gentlemen,' says Erin.

The screens are filled. Five faces and five locations. London. New York. Johannesburg. Los Angeles. Mexico City. Personality-type or location, all are interchangeable.

Like any other corporation, ours is Old Testament in its will to create a world in its own image. The faces are introduced to me, nebulous interchanging entities. I imagine Anna Bernstein in the top left of the domino falling asleep in her LA penthouse and waking in London, but only the vaguest sense of dissonance as she limos down to Canary Wharf, something about the sad pasty faces, the absent sun . . .

Did I really enjoy this? Did I talk like this, back then?

Abbreviations. Not a wasted syllable. It is how a spreadsheet would talk. Such a pressing need to cheat time. Except there isn't. When this meeting is over we will have nowhere to go. To speed with hyper-efficiency through each agenda item is all too quickly to bring the realisation that up here in the sky there is only time. And nothing to kill it, each one of us with a sociopathic inability to engage in small talk, never mind the sharing of confidences.

Erin sits very straight. The five screens become one as she taps the iPad, the face of each director filling the screen in turn. Between each report she clicks back to the five-screen view, as if to check the reaction from the rest.

Her movements are precise. I realise that she has never stopped turning the dial of the short-wave radio set that used to obsess her. She remains on that perpetual quest to tune in and I am struck again by the absolute contrast to her carefree and hopelessly innocent mother.

She should crack her face and make her arse jealous . . .

Quite right, Duke.

The sketch lacks a punchline. The drone-faces are confusing me. I crave complete sentences. Yet something is happening in Mexico City. I know this. We're back to the five-screen view. Viggo is talking and Erin makes no move to click to the one-screen view, perhaps unnerved by the thought of Viggo's hammy face in movie size. The deal is on the table. The price right.

'JJ?'

'Hmm.'

'Well?'

The faces are peering. A patient expectation. To my right, Peterson has leaned away, as if making room in the space between us for my wise and erudite response to a question I have not heard.

'The acquisition of Cinematica,' says Erin, gently.

'What about it?'

'What do you think?'

It is touching for them to seek an opinion they don't care about. 'Do what thou wilt shall be the whole of the law.'

The drone-faces blink.

Viggo lets out a savage laugh, Bluto with Olive Oil, Popeye tied to a barrel of dynamite and the fuse lit.

Cinematica, I come to learn, is an independent Mexican film production company. A workers' cooperative, in fact, two words relayed by Viggo with the most perplexed of emphases, like a naturalist looking in wonder at a species long thought extinct. Several films in the bag. Neo-realist and edgy. A route here. The 25–35 demographic. Huge emerging market. We benefit from their credibility . . .

And here they come again, the ghost-words that

65

have accompanied every one of my successes, whether earned or vicarious.

Well done, son.

The old man's sentiment is as grudging as ever. Once more it is me and not you, Duke, who has succeeded, whose company has acquired Cinematica, the latest in a forty-year stretch of accumulation.

'Twenty million plus,' says Viggo. 'The re-make projections of their Mexican hits. Porfirio closes tomorrow.'

'Still a risk,' says Erin. 'But what's life without a few of those?'

On-screen, the five faces become Porfirio's alone. The man delegated to drown Cinematica's independent spirit in a waterfall of dollars nods his acceptance of the role. 'She has cojones, your niece,' Porfirio says, then a dirty laugh like Eli Wallach in *The Good, the Bad and the Ugly*. Except he doesn't, being the cliché not of the sleazy Mexican but the Harvard Business School graduate.

The plane suddenly lurches, dropping into turbulence. Peterson gives an odd little squeal and grabs my hand. He seems reluctant to let it go, as if waiting for the next pitch of the plane. When it doesn't come, he looks up sheepishly. His touch was clammy. I want to wash my hands.

'Sorry.'

I refill my drink. Peterson's eyes follow the glass from table to mouth to table. He licks his lips and I shake the glass. He refuses the offer by clearing his throat and turning back to the screen.

I close my eyes and settle back. It is an incredibly comfortable seat, a perfect ergonomic fit for my skinny frame. I raise my whisky and the ice rings against expensive crystal, a tiny, lingering sound like a distant temple bell. I am filled with a vertiginous longing for our cottage by the Sound, Duke.

Some wonder about the next stage of human evolution, but surely the ability to delude ourselves with the most forgiving of nostalgia is already the pinnacle.

Our father would have been astonished by all this. If his brain hadn't exploded in Soho, all the gaudy baubles of wealth would have done for him soon enough: the starlets, the mansions and the swagger. I can see him, Fat Croesus in the Jacuzzi with Brigitte Bardot, washing his socks. Bring on the money. Money meant acceptance and he sought both with epic singularity.

Erin too has the family ruthlessness.

She clicks unhurriedly from face to face, the goddess of her flying Olympus, dispensing condescension and encouragement but, more than anything, uncertainty. None of the domino faces have any clue where her whim might take them tomorrow, a week, or a month from now, an unease in their eyes like the bands of colour swelling off the starboard wing, aquamarine stacking upwards through mauve, deep purple and black, as if outer space is falling down on us.

The plane banks to port and downwards, trying to outmanoeuvre the storm, but when we straighten up, the same troubled colours are on now both sides, the storm coming in from all directions, no escape from the deepening gloom. Soft uplighters flick on beside each seat.

The plane begins to shudder.

I am smiling like a child.

Beside me, Peterson grips the armrests. I reach out and pat his hand, his eyes turning to me in bemusement and not a little alarm. He is likely wondering about my smile, my grinning death's-head silhouetted by sudden lightning flash as the plane drops violently into an air pocket.

'You have to admire it,' I say.

'What's that?'

'The drama of it all.'

'If you say.'

'I do say, I *do* say.' I raise my glass to the roof. 'To the great director in the sky.' I drain my drink.

Somehow, the internet connection survives the turbulence, now and then a pixilation on one of the screens but the face always re-emerging. My grand-daughter's only reaction to the violent rollercoaster is a slight frown, her body elegantly shifting into each lurch of the jet. She *is* a goddess, I am convinced of it, Duke! She will bring us safely through by sheer force of will to *get to the end of the agenda*, which finally arrives at the blessed relief of Any Other Business.

'Bravo, bravo,' I shout, Peterson now looking at me with panic as I start to applaud and rise in my seat, feeling a hand on my shoulder. Gentle Akira. I pat his hand too, in acknowledgement.

Erin's gaze is blank. She has spent so long on the full range of reactions to me that she cannot be bothered offer any. She turns away. One by one the domino faces say they have nothing to say.

★ ★ ★

Music fills the stateroom. Ellington's *Such Sweet Thunder* was inspired by Othello, Duke. Did you know this? Did our father? It seems unlikely, sat there in the midnight kitchen with the bottle half gone.

Ahl shake a spear. Right up yer erse!

Never a funny or a maudlin drunk. Just dangerous, moods like a roulette wheel. I see him as me, shirt unbuttoned, sitting on the edge of the double bed that fills most of the width of the plane. He's as perplexed as I am too, scratching an armpit and wondering how it ever came to this.

The door to the main cabin slides open. Erin steps inside. I have a brief view of Peterson's bald head above the headrest, improbably red and shiny, like an over-polished cricket ball.

'Can I turn the music down?'

Before I answer she has picked up the remote control and sat down at the small mahogany table on the port side. She is holding a hardback book which she places face-down on her lap.

'We need to run through the itinerary.'

I look at her blankly.

'For the award thingy and the interviews. The council is presenting you with the Freedom of Inveran.'

'I already have it.'

'What?'

'The Freedom of Inveran.'

'You do?'

'Surely do.'

'Looks like you're getting it again. Maybe it lapses after a few years. Freedom. It's always conditional.'

'Isn't that the truth.'

'You've got a book signing in the town as well. Once we're done it's on to Edinburgh and London.'

'BBC interview?'

'BBC interview.'

'Monkey?'

'No monkey.' She offers a thin, papery smile and looks at the scatter of storyboard illustrations on the bed.

'You're working hard.'

I look at the picture in my lap. 'Can't seem to get this one right.' Robert the Bruce is sitting in a crowded tavern. An imbalance in the frame that I can't pinpoint. Too many people? I just don't know.

'Quite the labour of love. All this.'

'You mean, why am I bothering with this when someone else is making the film?'

'I didn't say that.'

I pour another drink as she watches me. She has the

patience of the desert but I have no idea what she's waiting for. I remember a sombre little girl, handing me her latest drawing of ponies, waiting for my reaction that will only disappoint her. I feel a familiar sense of failure which I bat straight back in the forlorn hope of trading my guilt for hers. 'Maybe there's something he might like.'

'Stone?'

'He's still the director, isn't he? Unless you've changed your mind.' I smile. 'Happy to step in, you know.' In truth, the thought of making another film fills me with something close to panic.

She nods, almost imperceptibly, her gaze moving back to the pictures. 'What about Inveran?' she says.

'What about it?'

'Are you not looking forward to going back? Going home. It's been so long.' Her voice is gentle, nostalgic for somewhere she knows so little about. 'I got this for you.' She hands me the book.

A Hundred Years of Inveran.

I flick through old black-and-whites. The railway station, Shore Street and the spire of the United Free Church, the promenade and children on bikes, George Street with dark-clothed men and women in hats, frozen in their stroll past signs saying druggist, bootmaker, Kodak supplies.

I drain my drink, the hum of the jet like the persistence of memory. Look there, Duke, it could be me and you on Bowen Street, stopped outside The Ritz and looking up at the big block letters of the films.

'Check this out,' says Erin, reaching across and flicking to the back of the book. 'Do you recognise it?'

It is a cottage in medium-shot beside a single track. *Machair* falls away from the road, down to a pebbly shore and the sea. On the gable end is a blue plaque, a smaller image of it in close-up.

70

The Breda Boys. Entertainers and film-makers, lived here from 1935–1957.

'Did you know about that?'

'No. I didn't.' I search for an emotion that won't come, as if my presence in this deeply personal place has become conditional on something I am again not quite ready to admit or to face up to.

I flick through the photos some more. Town shots, mainly: pipe bands in the square; HMS Cumberland lit up in July 1919 to celebrate the end of the war; the sweeping horseshoe bay from the air.

Then a waterfall.

My flinch is automatic. A coldness rushes over me like the water pouring into those black pools. The Craigie Falls, that day with Anna we know so well, Duke. The cold is now becoming a rising heat in my cheeks. I remember what I said and the reply I didn't catch, the thundering waterfall turning her words into the first of the dozens of versions I told myself across the years.

'Keep it. The book. It's for you.'

I run my finger across the photo. It the first time I have thought of the falls in a very long time. I see the falling water and feel the wet spray. Now the slow turn of Anna's head, my own filling with sound, a disorientating fizz that slowly rises to a deafening peak then suddenly stops.

I look up from the book and realise I am grimacing. Erin looks at me carefully then opens the stateroom door.

'Oh. One other thing. Do you know what a *Shinigami* is?'

'A *Shinigami*?'

'I think that's how you say it, yes.'

'Can't say I do.'

'It's a Japanese god. Shinto, to be precise. A god of death. We had to look it up. That's what he's been calling you.'

71

'Who?'

'No idea. We've been getting some emails, off and on for a few weeks. No name, of course.'

'The god of death? Decent gig, I suppose. Never likely I would get wisdom, or love.'

'I'm surprised he isn't typing in purple font. You've never seemed so interesting.'

'Can I have a look?'

'Believe me, that is not time well spent.'

'What about you?'

She frowns slightly. 'Did I never tell you about the onion?'

'The onion?'

'I was once sent an onion with pins it. There was a note saying it was a voodoo spell to make me go blind. A punishment for all the evil that Breda Inc. has done. Ever since then I get a weekly review from the cyber-bods. There's some strange people out there, Jay. It's completely fascinating.'

'Sure you don't fancy another hobby. Stamp collecting?'

'There's rumours about protests too. The security context is ever-evolving. We keep an eye out.'

Her own eyes have narrowed like a lizard's. A monitor lizard.

I look back down at the Falls as she slides the door shut. I am left with a startling quiet, just the hum of the jet engines and the erratic thumping of my heart. *Shinigami*, I say. The word hangs oddly in space. I turn Ellington louder and louder until I can't hear it. Or you, Duke, you and Anna.

Shinigami? Don't make me laugh. If I truly am a God of Death then why can't I instruct my memories to kill themselves? I should email this lunatic straight back. Tell him to have a re-think on his mania.

Six

Ivor Cutler, in a dry, mock-offended aside once said, 'If you think I'm a liar, I'm not.' Neither, I assure you, am I.

So here it is.

Duke, my father and I sit on a train. First class, Inveran to Edinburgh Waverley, changing at Glasgow.

At our feet sits a monkey. Inevitably, we have decided to call him Charlie. Charlie the Chimp. He's being held on a leash by a sad-eyed Russian called Leonid Baltacha, whose fearsome baldness lends him an uncanny resemblance to Yul Brynner. Both stare out at the magnificent landscapes, while now and then curious faces appear at the carriage door to gawk at the chimp.

Leo appeared the day after our call to Edinburgh Zoo requesting assistance with a shipwrecked primate. He once trained monkeys for the Moscow State Circus but defected during their first UK tour. In thanks for this propaganda coup the Home Office found him furry new comrades at the zoo.

The Russian went immediately to the byre and closed the door behind him. When he emerged an hour later he was holding the monkey by the hand. We were told three things – by Leo, not Charlie. First, Charlie was a male chimpanzee. '*Genus pan troglodytes*. Like Cheeta, Tarzan's chimp,' he added, in response to our blank stares. Second, the chimp likely came from West Africa, probably the Congo. Third, Charlie was tame, very biddable and had 'professional ambitions'.

As we looked at each other, Leo's sad face exploded in laughter. 'A joke, gentlemen, a joke.'

From Waverley, we took two Hackneys to the Victoria Hotel. Here was where the old man decided the Breda Boys now belonged. Charlie, Leo and I waited in the lobby while the old man and Duke went over to the reception. The cane swung 180 and the silver whippet rapped the desk. For my father, the manager offered a one-look assessment. For the monkey, a double take.

Yet having money, in some places, does not mean instant recognition of it. Such was the case at the Victoria Hotel, ground zero for the Scottish-holidaying Mayfair and Klosters set. It took my father's raucous, ten-minute insistence on the equal value of his poppy to get us rooms.

Charlie, undoubtedly, would have preferred the hotel to the zoo. Yet that was his home for the night. Half a dozen chimps squatted in the rain like forlorn convicts on Death Row. They stared at Charlie sadly, one of them manically chittering what must have been a warning to flee.

There in the rain, watching a bald Russian stroke the head of shipwrecked chimp, a dozen other simian eyes peering at me, I realised how insane the idea of adopting a monkey actually was.

'We used to have dogs, Leo. Half-daft collies with black eyes. I never trusted them. I don't much like animals.'

'Ah, but a monkey is more like a person.'

'I've never been too good with people either.'

'Yes, I hear you, my friend. Most of the time it is indeed easier to like a monkey.'

'And Charlie likes you.'

'Yes.'

'So do you understand what I'm saying?'

Across one long moment, Leo looked confused, then dubious and finally hopeful. A smile slowly creaked into place. He was happy. He couldn't have been happier if I'd tossed him a banana.

A Pathé newsreel team arrived the next morning. Leo brought a grateful Charlie back from the death cell and they filmed us wandering around Edinburgh. In the Royal Mile, the old man slipped into his best Oliver Hardy, turning to waggle his tie at the camera as Charlie lobbed an apple and knocked off his fedora. The crowd swelled, the sun shone and Duke doffed his brand-new trilby: autographs for all the pretty girls and a peck on the cheek for the old women.

'The hero of the Breda proving a big hit with the ladies too,' the overly cheery voiceover would say.

The media blitz didn't end there. The old man was relentless. *The Daily Mail* eventually offered the interview deal he'd been looking for. They offered to send a journalist but the old man said we'd head south, paid for by the *Mail*, of course. There were TV possibilities in the offing he needed to follow up. Andy Stewart's manager had given him a contact for *The Good Old Days*.

Duke and the old man headed south while Charlie and I returned to Inveran. Leo came too, a week's holiday where he would look after Charlie on a trial basis before deciding if he wanted to join us.

Then as later, making films, Leo and I just clicked. He was sombre yet sharp, an old man in waiting whom I instantly liked.

I had an old magazine I'd been holding on to. A feature on Houdini with a diagram of one of his contraptions. For Charlie the Chimp's debut we simply ripped it off.

That's showbiz.

Duke and the old man got back a week later, purring about London. 'You hear that,' my father said, pulling the door back and fore. 'That is the sound of doors opening.' Leo and I took them out to the byre for the gala performance of *Monkey No See*. We had an instant hit and the old man knew it. All he managed was a nod of the head. I think this was the first time I'd been able to follow through on an idea without it being instantly dismissed or represented as his. He didn't like it.

So began the Breda Boys era. Leo signed on and Johnny Walker led the celebrations. When I couldn't take any more of the endless toasts, an increasingly morose Leo was proposing I headed into Inveran, to the Ritz and some western double bill. There was no escape there either.

As I walked in I saw myself on-screen in the pre-movie, Pathé newsreel. My guts twisted as I listened to the jaunty voiceover, my sour face in huge size. No wonder the old man changed the *Breda* story. Who'd have listened to Hercules if he had a face like a burst settee?

Yet the camera loved Duke. I was watching a film star being born. At one point I looked at him with such furious disgust that I almost expected myself to attack him. I had to leave the cinema.

I felt even worse when I passed the door of Miller's Café and Anna Chambers suddenly appeared.

'JJ. Where's the monkey?'

'Chimp. It's a chimpanzee.'

'Called Charlie?'

'How did you know that?'

'Well, it's a chimp, JJ. What else were you going to call it?'

'Well, I—'

'I'm only teasing.' She squeezed my arm. 'That was quite the event at the Town Hall.'

'It's quite the story.'

'Certainly is. You boys are heroes. What is it they say, *you'll never buy a drink in this town again.*'

'It's what my father wanted all along.'

She smiled. Then looked at me a bit more closely. 'Can I ask you a favour?'

Standing there on the edge of the streetlamp light, her eyes gleaming and her hand again squeezing my arm, I'd have done anything she asked. Instead, I said, 'Depends.' I didn't sound casual, my mouth so dry that my voice made a strange squeak – it sounded more like *deep-end.*

'Duke. Can you ask him to call me?'

'Call you?' No squeak this time, instead my words sounded more like air being let out of a tyre.

'At the newspaper. I want to do a follow-up interview with him. I want to call it *The Man Behind the Smile.*'

I smiled weakly. 'Sure you don't want to do a piece on me instead? *The Man Behind the Frown.*'

'Can you talk to him?' She was looking at me very earnestly. And now holding my hand.

The next time I'd touch that hand was when I shook it on her wedding day, a few minutes after I'd handed Duke the ring.

Three weeks later *The Man Behind the Smile* was syndicated. 'A poignant look at a vulnerable man,' a TV host would say to me gravely, years later. 'You must miss him so much.'

'You have no idea,' I replied.

* * *

28th June 1956. *I'm Laffin, You're Laffin* at The Glasgow Empire. Rita Cardle and the Gibson Sisters, on up to Harry Gordon. Then The Breda Boys, second on the bill with Jimmy Logan at the top.

Backstage, we were terrified.

Two thousand seats. Two thousand Glaswegians whose default setting was unimpressed.

Never mind the English Comics Graveyard, this was ground zero of all Variety. We'd never played Glasgow, never mind The Empire. It was the *Breda* fame which landed us a contract with Moss Empires theatres. They were keen to cash in and this was the first night of a UK tour. We were just wannabes. I could feel it backstage, everyone waiting for us to die on our arse.

'Sure boys,' said Jimmy. 'Nothing to worry about.' He mimed a noose around his neck, pulling it upwards.

Then we were on. We went through *The Big Sheep* and *Diamonds Are a Girl's Best Friend*.

Afterwards, Duke and I met stage front.

'So that's it then, JJ.'

'Sure is, Duke, sure is.'

'Sad, innit.

'Innit just.'

'Shame we don't have a big finale.'

'Everyone loves the big finale.'

'They surely do.'

'You know what, Duke.'

'What's that?'

'I've got this ... thing.'

'Have you been to the doctor about it?'

'No, I mean—'

'They've got ointment for things like that.'

'I mean a monkey.'

'JJ, I've told you this before. *People* go to the doctor, animals go to the *vet*. Did you get mixed up again?'

'I can make it disappear.'

'Using the ointment?'

During this patter, the contraption Leo and I had built in Inveran was lowered from the back of the stage, a ten-foot-high, red-painted wooden frame with stanchions allowing it to stand freely. A sign hung at an angle from the top, stencilled with the words *Breda Boys Magic Inc.*

At the same time, Charlie joined us, led by the obligatory bombshell in a swimsuit. I led him behind the framework and went back to Duke. We stared at the girl as she sashayed off stage.

'That's what you call misdirection.' I said.

'I thought she was Ms McGurk?'

'Boom, *boom*,' I said and a noise like a gunshot went off at the same time to gasps from the audience.

'Well, would you look at that,' said Duke, looking to the back of the stage.

'All hail the Great Magnifico,' I said, with my arms in the air. Through the wooden frame all that could be seen was the blue curtain at the back of the stage. Charlie the Chimp had simply vanished.

'How'd ya do it, JJ? How? *How?*'

'Well, Duke, you know how it goes, all it takes is a bit of monkeying around.'

Down came the curtain. If Harry Houdini could do it with an elephant, why couldn't we with a chimp?

* * *

If the Breda rescue made us heroes, Charlie the Chimp made us stars. As the Moss Empires tour went on, I worked him into other sketches, the old man accepting my ideas with a strained demur that was more about his fear of fucking up a good thing than any new-found faith in me. He needn't have worried. The public gets what the public wants and the public wanted a chimp.

And Duke.

You could see the superstar emerging. Every town we played, I filmed little scenes with my Brownie camera: Duke silently clowning in a hotel room; Duke cartwheeling along a street; his crushing hangover in the back of a car . . . I had this vague idea about making a

79

documentary. I was an *entreprenoor*, see, as the old man said, savvy enough to overlook any envy in the quest for cash.

Dine with the Duke was another of my ideas, wheezing a PR trail through the pheromone fug. We would hold a raffle before a show, the lucky winner getting a signed photo and a lunch date with Duke, a photographer on hand, of course, a write-up for the local paper. I must have really hated myself to come up with that idea. Anna must have thought I hated her too.

In Leeds, we recorded *The Good Old Days* Christmas special at the City Varieties Theatre. The Music Hall sentimentalist that was the old man listened with dewy-eyed delight to Leonard Sachs sonorous introduction. *Inimitable. Incomparable. Lifesavers . . . and escapees . . . of The Glasgow Empire. Your very own Breda BOYS*. Then the famous gavel came down to introduce our first television appearance, *Diamonds Are a Girl's Best Friend* followed by a rendition of *Walking in a Winter Wonderland*, where Charlie, dressed as Santa, comes on to join us.

Another performance on *The Good Old Days* helped get us onto the bill for the famous *Five Past Eight* revue show at the Glasgow Alhambra in 1957. Then *Sunday Night at the London Palladium* came calling, which opened another door in November, the Royal Variety Performance.

Pinch yourself time.

Judy Garland and Tommy Cooper. Harry Secombe and Tommy Steele. Never mind the Queen, it was all about the Count. The old man was almost in tears watching Basie and his orchestra. I filmed him in the wings with the Brownie, the fedora held respectfully in his hands, eyes closed. Anna, there to cover the Breda Boys' big night, was beside him, head on his shoulder.

That night was also the first time we went to Soho, tagging along with some of Basie's band to an 'All-Niter' at The Flamingo Club on Wardour Street, a subterranean concrete bunker flooded with a sea of dancing people. The jazz I recognised, the blues less so. The soul was something else.

Elated by his arrival in the promised land, the old man vanished into the crowd, an arm around one of Basie's trombonists. Sharply dressed black men stared at me, one opening his jacket to offer me over-priced miniatures of whisky from the dozens held to the inside lining by little pieces of elastic. 'Big Time,' he said, 'why so serious?' Then he burst out laughing. Intimidated, I bought one, sipping as I glanced at the shadier types, heavy-built and hyper-kinetic, as if barely controlling some internal energy. 'Gangsters,' Duke whispered. 'Maybe the bloody Krays.'

I found out later that this night of firsts was also the first time the Duke had taken Drinamyl – Purple Hearts. It explained the bear hug when we met in the toilets, the hands gripping my shoulders.

'Can you believe it? I mean, it's unbelievable. We just played the *Palladium*. We met Count *Basie*.'

'I know, it's unreal.'

'What if we get found out?'

Then we were laughing hysterically. No Purple Hearts for me but I must have seemed just as high, the two of us waltzing around the toilet to the indescribable luck that had landed us here. Then another amphetamine jump cut. Duke suddenly serious. 'Anna. She's wonderful, isn't she?'

My brother's wide-eyed question didn't want a response. No validation was required, not yet.

'I think she gets me. I really think she gets me.'

I filmed them on the dance floor. Watching through the camera made it easier, somehow. I watched the scene again, hours later, projected onto the wall of my hotel room. No soundtrack except the *ratatatat* of the feeding film, Duke and Anna laughing and dancing, there and gone in the seethe of people, their movements spastic and peculiar in the absence of music.

* * *

Providence once more gave a simian smile. We made the leap from stage to movie screen, moving to London in 1958. The deal with Rank demanded it. Five films, comic capers starring The Breda Boys and Charlie the Chimp. We'd tackle thieves in Tangier, gangsters in New York, crooked casino owners in Monte Carlo, just like those Bing Crosby and Bob Hope *Road To* . . . movies.

Duke and I had said barely a word at the contract meeting with Earl St John, aka the Earl of Pinewood.

'Yer gonna want to sign us, I tell ye that,' my father told him.

The Earl smiled. 'Now why in the world would I want to do that?'

'Because you're clearly a man of wisdom.'

'Wisdom?'

'Aye, Norman. He musta done wonders for your bottom line.'

The Earl leaned back in his chair and laughed, slamming a hand on the table. A cigar sealed the deal.

We moved to Notting Hill, St. Stephen's Garden, a whitewashed Victorian terrace on three floors. Charlie became a celebrity resident at London Zoo, chauffeured to Pinewood by Leo when needed on set.

Our lives had changed so quickly. Maybe that explained the ease with which I took to London. I just didn't spend all that much time thinking about it. It would be a long time before I did.

Late-fifties London had a distinct, gloomy appeal. Still so many bombed-out streets. Piles of rubble. Men and women as grim as the buildings. Yet all so exciting for the country boy in the big smoke. I walked with the Brownie, gravitating to the little parks that dotted west London, and the canal, the windings of the Grand Central, east to Northolt and west to Paddington.

Meanwhile, Duke soaked up the attention. That was the deal, what the re-engineering of the *Breda* story demanded. The Rank contract catapulted us into showbiz society. The Breda Boys were a sought-after presence at parties. Bumpkin Jocks, that's what the metropolitans wanted, a stereotyping slightly less lurid than that of their ancestors, who craned to see Buffalo Bill's 'Red Indians' or poor John Merrick, Saartjie Baartman paraded half-naked at Piccadilly.

Coached by the old man, Duke tried to throw the 'r' away. He learned how to wear a Savile Row suit instead of seeming like he'd just fallen into it. He worked on That Smile and the optimum moment of deployment. He believed enough of his own hype to be credible but disbelieved even more, a headshaking Dorian Gray pouring another double in his Notting Hill bunker.

'I feel like I'm breaking up. He's got these expectations and I can't keep up. Who's the performing monkey again?'

'It's all a performance, mind?'

'I know that, for Christ's sake.'

'Remember the first time we did coat stand surprise? In the kitchen. I thought the old man had gone mental.'

'He is mental!'

Both of us must have had the same memory flash. A smack on the face, *just get it bloody right.*

Then we were laughing, affection for a memory that deserved none. Shared moments like this became increasingly rare. They seemed to bring complications Duke didn't want to deal with.

He would head north every couple of weeks, trying

to persuade Anna to move to London. Every other week she came down, testing the waters while Duke hedged his bets with an ever-revolving cast of party girls and the inevitable morning-after guilt I hated myself for indulging.

'I was squeezing breasts right and left, Johnny. They were being *offered* to me.'

'What are you gonna do, eh?'

Anna herself turned a blind eye. She was a journalist, she must have seen the rumours in the papers about Duke and Linette Rogers, his co-lead in *Moscow Monkey*. Yet nothing was ever said, as if this new world was so bizarre and dreamlike that nothing in it could actually be happening.

The old man was living his own dream.

He established a near-permanent presence at the Mingo. This brought new friends and connections, and epic, late-night parties back at Notting Hill. One Saturday night, just weeks before the race riots, we had our windows smashed by a gang of Teddy Boys, incensed by all the black faces. We joined *The Stars Campaign for Interracial Friendship*, set up to fight against racism. Duke and I were photographed putting copies of *What the Stars Say* through letterboxes. He'd even claim, with full amphetamine delusion, to have prevented a second race riot.

Yet if we'd somehow landed on the crest of the counter-cultural wave about to break across London, the *zeitgeist* captured by our films was of a 1940s vintage. *Moscow Monkey* was terrible. As were *That Touch of Chimp* and *Peking Chimp*. Yet I loved them, Pinewood Studios more so.

French streets become Alpine vistas become narrow Chinese streets become a medieval castle ... I wandered the sets. I hung out in the editing suite with bespectacled men who took serious and generous delight in explaining the process. I bored the trousers off Doug Fotheringham, erstwhile director of the monkey films, who would say, 'We're not making Kane, dear boy . . . '

Leonid hated the premieres as much as I did. Invariably, we walked up the red carpet together, one on each side of Charlie, holding a hand, Charlie's sidekick and 'the man behind the monkey'. Charlie stopped now and then, a grin for the cameras and a clap for the crowd. A few steps ahead, Duke and the starlet *de jour* sashayed. Inevitably, she would crouch down and blow a kiss at Charlie, who would put a hand over his eyes and fall over in love-struck delight.

'I grew up watching Sergei Eisenstein,' Leonid whispered to me during the first screening of *Peking Chimp*. 'This is such *shit*. If he angled the camera by 30 degrees . . . much more interesting.'

He would say much the same about my efforts.

I was still walking the city, making my stream of consciousness epics, moving further afield, Epping Forest and Hampstead Heath, a bus to Southend, filming in the rain at the end of the pier. I spent the night in a decaying boarding house and filmed three hours of the darkening sea.

London Bucolia, I called these films, boring and amusing people by telling them narrative was over-rated. What can I say? I was twenty years old. I would screen them at our parties, a second-floor living room that me and only me called *The Inter Zone*: low light and joss sticks, Mingus or Monk on the turntable. It was mostly the tokers who watched, smoking and staring.

Leo appeared one night, finally worn down by my nagging him to come and tell me what he thought. He watched silently for half an hour then said, 'Why do you think only potheads are watching?'

I didn't know.

'Because they're potheads!'

After I stopped moping, I asked Leo if he wanted to work together. He turned out to be a wonderful cinematographer, his feel for composition and lighting uncanny. Our first film was a short called *Rooftop*, shot in a snowstorm, about a man who may or may not be about to jump.

My brother's response was sarcasm. He didn't get *Rooftop* and because he didn't, he somehow thought I was taking the mickey out of him. I remember another party, Duke surrounded by the entourage he had acquired. When Anna was around she must have counted every skirt.

'What's it all about? You're too clever for old Duke here. I mean, have you *seen Rooftop*?'

Laughter rippled among the acolytes.

'You know what I call this cat? Brother Grimm. Lighten up, little bro!'

I just shrugged.

'Duke, you're such a tease.' This from the willowy blonde on his arm.

'You've *nooo* idea, sugar!'

This was another recent shift, Duke's odd appropriation of black slang. 'That white brother sure wants to be black,' I heard someone say. He dropped it whenever Anna was around.

'Be easy, little bro. Be *easy*.'

Then he was gone, his devotees trailing. Increasingly, even though we were still living under the same roof, this is how we communicated: through awkward set-pieces at parties and PR events.

There is drift in every relationship. You watch it happen, you know it is happening and sometimes you just let it go. I cared less and less, even as I watched Duke untethering. The UK's most popular actor in 1959 according to the *Mirror*. A constant presence in the gossip pages. It was sometime around then my brother went 'full Duke', when he decided, I *am* the Star they're calling me, a teeth-grinding Benzedrine epiphany, setting mine permanently on edge.

I was sick of it, disgusted with him, the shake in his hand when the bennies and booze washed out, the glittery-eyed insistence that I'm going to get my head together, I'm serious, bro, and there's only one person who can help me do that, only one, I'm bringing her south, telling you, a one-way ticket this time and watch, just watch, our feet won't touch the bloody ground . . .

Seven

Tiny angels drift out of velvet black. You never expect them to be so small. You imagine soft beating wings and a silent hovering, a porcelain-faced boy or girl with the eyes of your first love. Yet angels are tiny, Duke, and legion, flurrying like the snow dancing round my head. This is why I have always loved winter, its holiness, the profound silences. Great distances. Great space.

Others are watching. I feel their eyes. They peer from the three Mercedes stopped and purring in the lay-by. The cars were waiting at the bottom of the plane steps when we landed at Glasgow.

Petersen was delighted. I watched the strange, caterpillar moving of his lips, like a silent prayer. Oh God above, I give thanks to my outrageous fortune, to the opulence that awaits my big arse and clammy hands. It is touching, how he appears not to take providence for granted.

Everyone but Akira, Erin and have remained in the cars. I am trying to ignore my niece, standing behind me in the boneyard cold. She's loiters like some kind of spooky Jungian archetype. I sense her even when she's thousands of miles away, when I hear again the static rush and theremin-like undulations of the short wave as she moves hertz by hertz along the bands of her Vega 206, never settling on one station too long. Passing through, an addict of empty space.

'I have never known silence like this,' says Akira. 'I

can almost touch it.' He is standing very still and looking up, a sentry who might have been here forever. The snow is starting to lessen, allowing a milky swelling in the sky gradually to reveal itself as a huge and looming half-moon. I feel unexpectedly relieved. A full moon would have been far too much.

'Not far now, Johnny,' he says, the only man who calls me Johnny, the 'y' stretched out like an 'ee'.

'No. Not far.'

Above Akira's shoulder the outline of a mountain becomes more visible as the snow clouds further fade.

Another sentry, guarding the west.

For a giddy and fleeting moment, I am convinced that I have become the mountain and it has become me. I feel an enormous pressing of geological time and memory, and an awareness, at the same time, of the mountain's quietly respectful acknowledgement of my own hinterland.

'A true place of Zen,' says Akira, a man of perspicacity. He can see the temple in the wilderness.

'It sure is beautiful,' says Erin. Her voice is almost in my ear. I did not hear her creeping closer. The *sure* grates on me, the mid-Atlantic drawl cheapening the moment. I am no more the mountain.

'Why on earth did you move away?' she adds.

'Sometimes I ask myself the same question.'

'It's stunning.' She raises her phone. Takes a picture with the flash on that makes Akira turn and look at her for a moment before getting back into the car. 'This would make quite a scene.' She takes another, flash-less picture and is suddenly business-like. 'We need to go now.'

I watch her hurry to the Mercedes behind mine. The picture now taken, the moment can be re-run as required. This one might merit a longer pause on the slideshow: it sure is beautiful ...

89

Her car moves forward then stops. Likely a word from Erin, the driver told to wait for us to move off first. She suspects, not unreasonably, that unless the headlights are on me at all times, I may flee into the darkness. It is deepening, the moon fading as the snow blows in again, harder now, the angels now dancing furiously, my hair a flyaway Christopher Lee in *The Wicker Man*.

I'm smiling.

I open my mouth wide. The cold makes me cough as I breathe deeply, emptying my lungs of the last of the recycled plane air. The flight seems improbably distant. I'd slept, finally, waking to the orange lights of Glasgow strung below me. Immediately, I was catapulted into this high-speed drive west to Argyll, a rollercoaster eventually bringing nausea. Hence the stop in this lay-by.

I get back in and slump in the seat.

In and out of sleep.

My father's ghost voice as Akira leans us in and around the bends. *Helluva road. If yer goin' to be sick I'll stop the car . . .*

I wake to the blue and red LEDs of the car's interior displays, the buttons to press to open the drinks cabinet and the white-outlined numbers on the phone, unknown switches with strange hieroglyphs that make me think of *kanji* characters on Tokyo buildings. I feel a pang of nostalgia that I put down to alcohol. Tokyo seems impossibly distant and Akira has been driving for days, across land and sea, thousands of miles, hands always at ten to two on the steering wheel . . .

It is just after seven am.

I tell myself there is a faint lightening in the east, where the darker patches of unseen mountains meet open sky. In truth, it is as dark as when we landed at Glasgow. I stave off the hangover with another drink. Cotton-mouthed, I tell Akira not to stop until we reach the top of the pass above Inveran. I want the last of a more distant perspective before I plunge down, down, down . . .

This time no-one gets out from the two other cars which stop behind us. This place used to be called Diarmid's Leap. It has become Diarmid's Rest, with picnic tables and information boards, a 20p telescope. Inveran is below me, orange lights following the long, horseshoe sweep of the bay like the runaway of a goofy airstrip, ending in the darkness of a headland I cannot see.

They will ask me questions. They will ask me questions and I must smile, I must remember to smile.

★ ★ ★

'Mr Jackson! A profound pleasure.'

The name badge tells me this is John Houston, Manager.

'How was your flight?'

'Well, they caught me in the end.'

A flicker of uncertainty before he realises he can laugh. But no idea what to say. 'Yes, yes. Excellent!'

My spirits had sunk a few moments after we swung in the high iron gates of Inveran Castle Hotel. Through the windscreen, the headlights illuminated the snow-covered gravel of the long drive. Then the castle itself was looming, and, horror of horrors, two lines of hotel staff, an upside-down V extending from the doorway and down the entrance steps, twenty pairs of eyes following the three Mercedes as they swung around the fountain and came to a halt parallel to the steps. They were all smiling, rictus grins in the bitter chill, despite the alarming uniforms that must have been designed by a deranged toddler with colour blindness, all green waistcoats and odd reddish trousers, skirts. How long had the poor buggers been waiting?

Houston walks alongside me, up the stairs. At the top stand two well-built men in dark suits. The two other security men from the plane follow behind. I glimpse Erin. Already she is talking urgently into the mobile phone clamped to her ear. I wonder if she has even noticed the line of staff.

'Nice to meet you,' I say to young 'Alison', who blushes.

'Helluva cold,' I say to 'Lewis', a prematurely balding thirty-something with a big ginger beard who, in his Christmas-coloured uniform, looks like a grown-up version of one of Santa's little helpers. 'I found a wee ice-cube in my bed this morning. When I threw it on the fire it went *fart*.'

Lewis looks as if he is on the verge of panic.

'One of Billy Connolly's. I'm not that funny. Good to meet you. See that?' I hold out my left hand. 'Steady as a rock, eh?' Lewis nods, a flicker of a frown. 'But this is the one I shake hands with.' I take his hand with my right, start juddering it up and down: fake DTs, not far from the truth.

There is a ripple of laughter up and down the V. Gotta give the crowd what they want, Duke. But as I reach the top of the steps and enter the reception hall I am glad of its vast emptiness.

'This snow,' Houston suddenly says. 'It's completely unseasonal.' As if he feels he must apologise.

I have never liked this place. Inveran Castle was a tumbledown waiting to happen when I was growing up. Rarely remarked, just there, a place of black windows and geriatric aristocrats, drowning in a rising sea of empty bottles, unpaid bills. The Big House, it was called, of course, with that complex mix of Highland deference and scorn. You'd see them, occasionally, clambering out of a battered Jaguar, creatures from a lost geological era, into Archibald and Son's to buy tweeds and waders for cauliflower-nosed relatives who would fish, drunk among the midges, and catch sod all.

'I hope you like what we've done with the place,' says Houston, as if this is my home and he the steward, anxiously watching me poke around, re-familiarising myself in a swell of sentiment. It is indeed a Breda Inc. accumulation, but the nostalgia is Erin's. She bought the castle ten years ago. One for us, she said, *the family*, the rags to riches so captivating she spent twenty million on a refit and so disaffecting that she's never visited until now.

A championship golf course lurks in the darkness, beyond the crenellated Victorian ridiculousness that brings rich, daft Americans to pay thousands for romantic dreams of emigrant roots.

It was the final nail for the Royal Inveran in the town centre, apparently, whose five- star clientele immediately bolted. I mean, who can compete with a castle? The bankruptcy was swift, I hear . . .

A shuffling makes me turn.

I hide my unease in comic surprise, an Inspector Clouseau-like jump and Karate-chop but Cato not there, just the grinning staff arranging themselves into another line. Houston re-appears with a remarkably ugly Monarch of the Glen sculpture, the stag looking more constipated than regal. There follows a rousing rendition of 'Happy Birthday' that will have the suite-dwellers unhappily roused from dreams of Rob Roy. I lift the stag and offer a smile fit for an Oscar.

'It is good to have you home for your birthday, Mr Jackson,' whispers Houston. Erin appears to kiss me on the cheek and gently turn me to the right. A photographer seals the moment in eternity.

So doth complete another circle in this crescent life. I

am led to the tight, tombstone sheets of the three-room Discovery Suite. As I close the door, Houston tells me that Vladimir Putin stayed in this very room during a summit a few years ago. The information is unlikely to help me sleep.

* * *

A silhouette against the window, a figure opening the curtains. Silver light pours in. The arrhythmia that rocked me to a jittery sleep remains. I feel it as a lightness in my chest, a waiting for sudden pain which has long emptied of anxiety and is now more expectation of an inevitability.

'You've got the best view in the house,' says Erin.

There is a wetness on the sheets. My heart gives a massive thud, a tolling for the arrival of incontinence. I am horrified by the thought of avoiding the coronary to instead moulder in an overheated nursing home where the staff tick off your days with the disinterest of deleting email spam.

'Better to burn out than to fade away.'

'You can see right . . . ' Erin shimmers as she turns. 'What did you say?'

'Nothing.'

Sitting up, I see a glass on the floor, the wet sheets actually caused by some troubled night-flailing.

'The islands in the distance, I can't remember what they're called. You can see the weather coming in.' She comes closer and looms above me, her face blocking the window. 'You look bloody awful.'

'Believe me, I feel worse.'

'You should cut down on the booze. Doesn't go well with travelling. Not at your age. Quite a welcoming committee, wasn't it? Just needed an anthem playing. What's with that Houston guy?'

'What time is it?'

'Eleven thirty.'

'For Christ's sake, Erin.' I have been asleep for less than three hours.

'Bad idea to sleep. Ride out that jetlag!' There is an unusual levity in her tone. 'Try and stay awake.'

'Not much choice now.'

She sits on the edge of the bed.

'You know, I have the strangest feeling. I've been here what, twice? But it's like everything I look at I've seen before. I can't work out if it's things I've actually seen or I'm just telling myself I did.'

I was here with her only once, an overly attentive, eleven-year-old Erin. She probably does remember everything she thinks she does, the islands and the white wake of the ferries, the scrawl of gulls on washed-out grey. I have a vivid image of her on a beach, arms wide and her face raised, as if urging the universe to give her all it has. Maybe that's been her problem all along.

'But I can't picture Mum. I know we were here with her but I can't even imagine her. It makes me miss her even more.'

I can't do this. I am not ready to think about Anna. 'Give it a rest, you've been here five bloody minutes.'

My harshness surprises me and I immediately regret it. Her body tenses, the head dropping a little.

'Thanks. Thanks for that.'

'I'm sorry, Erin. I'm just—'

'Maybe I deserve it,' she adds. '*The Bruce*. Having Frank Stone direct.'

'You buy the ticket—'

'You take the ride ... Sure. I still don't understand what you've got against him.'

'He hasn't made a decent film in years.'

'What about *Time Passages*?'

'What about it?'

'It got him Best Director.'

'James Cameron won Best Director. Ron Howard, for crying out loud. You shouldn't use the Oscars to measure quality.'

'Didn't you win an Oscar?'

I ignore the smirk. '*Time Passages* is schmaltz.'

'That's harsh, he's—'

'He's a hack.' My ego just can't get past Frank, the poster boy for cosmetic dentistry and hair plugs.

'He'll be here later this morning.'

'Wonderful. What about Renner?'

'Still not sure. He's being an awkward git.'

Brad Renner will play Robert the Bruce. A-list gold but the Dick Van Dyke of Scottish accents. I remember the video of his read-through and have a near-physical yearning for my *ryokan* at Shuzenji.

'We'll stick with the press conference tomorrow morning. You and Stone. If Brad's here, he's here.'

'Be still my beating heart.'

'Look, it's *your* film. Your script. That's why we're building a set in your home town. You don't need to direct the damn movie for it to be yours. It's all about you! People love you. Look at your biography...' And so on. She justifies herself via emoting, plain old wheedling and a peculiar grammar of arm and hand movements that leave after-trails in my jittery, jet-lagged eyes. She's what I would see if I peered inside a Punch and Judy booth and watched the puppet master.

'Two o'clock lunch with Frank. Is that ok?'

I remember Frank's last visit to Shuzenji. An exhausting, six-hour gush of California enthusiasm.

'How could I refuse?'

She takes my hand, presses it to her cheek. 'I'm sorry. I am. But you're home now and we're making your masterpiece.'

It is humiliating, to lie in bed while she patronises me.

My feet are also demeaning me, poking out all bony and pale from the sheets. But I won't get up, I can't bear the thought of her watching me struggle out of bed. Therein lies more humiliation, a condescending *here, let me help*.

'Be nice to Frank. He's a good man.'

She always speaks so highly of him, which is surprising considering he is even shorter than me.

I watch her leave.

There is, ultimately, nothing to be done.

I sit for a while longer then push back the sheets. My pyjamas have rolled up to my knees. I wonder again why my legs have become bald as I have aged, yet my ears sprout like the cress we used to grow at primary school. Perhaps it is the cress rather than the sound-proofing which creates the silence that envelopes me as I walk across to the window and look out at the sea.

Japan knows a different space. That world resides in the infinitesimal. Waterfalls in miniaturised gardens. The bonsai approximations of trees. I reel against vertigo as I look out the panoramic window, down from my tower to the marina and its cruisers. My gaze moves past the pincers of the breakwater, across the open sea to the dapple of the inner islands, the mountains of far peninsulas in the hazy distance.

The Castle sits on a low hill, a couple of miles outside Inveran. To my left is the whole sweep of the bay, the town spread along it. Behind the townhouses and hotels of the seafront, terraces of trees and bushes step up a steeply rising hill, bisected by a line of elegant Victorian houses. Post-war pre-fabs cluster on the southern end of the ridge, a cemetery dominating the north.

I look back to the seafront. Flags line the long promenade that becomes Shore Road and continues over the headland, down to the Sound of Skerray. A few more miles and you come to an old croft . . .

'You're home now,' Erin said.

So let's get out there, see what's what. It's the reason I'm here, Duke, is it not? I'm here to see you all, one more time. Not to make a damn movie, although without *The Bruce* I doubt I'd ever have come back. There's the crux, good brother. I'm here so I won't ever have to come back.

* * *

Standard protocol dictates that I should be accompanied by a minder wherever I go. This, I can easily slip.

More difficult is escaping the hotel itself. It is almost impossible to leave a five-star hotel without being seen. The need to please means near-universal surveillance. Fart in an empty corridor and someone will instantly materialise with a can of air freshener. Put on your jacket in the lobby and the concierge is there. Isn't it a fine day, sir? Going anywhere in particular?

'We need a ruse, Akira. I'll put on a dressing gown so it seems I'm going to the spa but I'll have my tracksuit on underneath, see, Nikes in my bathing bag. I'll whip off the gown and we run for it.'

He is momentarily unsure if I'm serious. Then we're both laughing. In the end, we make it to the back entrance and the staff car park without being seen by anyone. No opportunity to dive into a linen trolley. It's almost disappointing. I get in the passenger seat of the black Mercedes.

'Your choice, Johnny,' says Akira, and points at the sound system.

'Charles Mingus.'

The soundtrack to an escape.

Stretched double bass, the tenor sax kicking in and the music settling to a driving beat. I turn and look out the back window and here's another black Mercedes swinging around the corner, coming up fast, tyres kicking up slushy snow like a chase sequence in a James Bond movie. Akira steps on it and we've lost them, but no, the Merc suddenly fishtails back into view . . .

Instead, we ease through the back gates and head down the access road, walled on both sides by Sitka or maybe Norway spruce. No-one is following and I am smiling. As is Akira. We drop down and round a steep hairpin left and leave the dark trees behind, taking a left onto a single track.

The Albannach Road.

We used to cycle out this way, I think. My memory is unsure but these days I don't spend much time questioning. In imagination there is also truth. So there we are, Duke! In the wan distance of another winter day, miles from our cottage, cycling along a potholed road that can't have changed much between then and now. The sea is a ten-metre drop from the verge on the right-hand side, small islands across the water and larger ones beyond, sombre greens and browns.

'Is it always so cold here?' asks Akira.

Leonid once asked me something similar. He was always moaning about the cold and the rain. I used to joke that only a Russian would defect to a country where the weather was almost as bad.

I offer Akira my hipflask. 'A little warm-you-up?'

He declines.

I drink for both of us, the road becoming a cindery winding through memories that whip past too swiftly to keep up with, like the dead leaves blustering across the car as the wind rises. A rough sea comes closer, a dark band on the horizon promising sleet, which reaches us as the road becomes the promenade. Soon we're in Inveran proper, the hurrying umbrellas of Abraham Street. One by one people look up the car. I seem to recognise every face.

Don't worry, folks, I'm only passing through . . .

A sign says *Esha Bay, 6*. On Stevenson Street I see that the Inveran Empire has fallen to an Odeon. If I look out the window and up I might be able to see the cemetery on the heights. Not today. I am not ready for tears that I will explain away as the coldness of the ever-slashing wind.

The Clachan, though. That is another matter altogether. I might not even have noticed it on the opposite side of the road if we hadn't been stopped by a red light. My flask is empty, after all.

The décor, of course, has changed. No longer the 1950s austerity of smoke-stained walls and punishing wooden chairs, as if any pandering to comfort was disrespectful to The Clachan's alcoholic function. The stained-glass windows on each side of the main door have been restored. In one, two coopers make a whisky barrel, in another, several musicians sit at a table.

Yet the basic structure is unchanged. The Clachan still has two bars, separated by the same door with the murderously low lintel. We stand and wait at the counter in the first, the only customers and no sign of any staff. After a while, we head through to the second bar, a smaller, darker room: faux-mahogany, dimpled, copper-topped tables and cosy booths, red leather seats.

He looks as old as I, the barman. A similar thinning of white. He stands behind the polished brass taps. Squints as he holds a glass up to the light. 'What'll it be, son?' A smile makes another line in a magnificently creased face as he notices his doppelgänger, who eases slowly onto a bar stool.

'Double Highland Park.'

'And why not.'

100

'Fancy one yourself?'

He does.

He moves away to find the whisky, revealing a mirror behind him. It is framed on the left and right by gantry shelves filled with bottles of spirits, while a third runs along the top, lined with a collection of old water jugs advertising Johnny Walker, Teachers ... There is nothing in front of the mirror except two ice buckets, making clear the mirror is the main feature of the bar.

It is rectangular, about two feet by three, a frame covered in fake, peeling gilt. The surface is stencilled in curling gold letters. *Nostalgia*. I stare at my reflection until the barman hands me a glass.

We drink. It is 11.15am. Whine of the wind outside. It could be any day, from now back to 1950.

'Just passing through?'

'Coming back.' I nod to the mirror behind him. 'Not much choice with that looking back at you.'

He chuckles. 'Not exactly needed in a pub, eh? Nostalgia. The drink'll get you there soon enough.'

'Isn't that the truth? *Freedom and whisky gang thegither!*' I raise my glass and the barman does the same.

'Tell you though, I've seen a fair few who've spent a bit too long staring at that.' He jabs a finger at *Nostalgia*. 'It'll make a *cowran, tim'rous beastie* of anyone. No much freedom in that.'

I smile in delight. I feel oddly grateful to the barman but have no idea why. 'You like Robert Burns then?'

'I just know a few.'

'You want another?'

'I wouldn't say no.'

He doesn't. He pours us two more doubles. Fixes me with a gimlet eye. 'Why'd you stop making films?'

'Ah, you've recognised me.'

'C'mon. The whole town knows you're coming. No

101

many folk turn up here with a limo and a bodyguard.'

He points with his chin. I turn and smile at Akira, sitting quietly at a table. 'No. I suppose not.'

'What happened to the films?'

'That's why I'm back. I'm making another one.'

'Really? An old man like you?'

I laugh loudly and point at the mirror. 'Nostalgia, my friend. Who can resist?'

And soon a fraying.

The little voice saying we must go now, go now nags for a while longer but is eventually silenced.

Fraying, Duke, it sounds just like freeing.

I tell the barman about *The Bruce*. He's intrigued, clearly a man who also likes his myths to be muddied.

I even offer him a part. The old retainer, who brings Bruce some wine as he stands alone, looking down from the ramparts the night he took Edinburgh Castle. Frank Stone can only agree, what does it matter to that hack anyway? What matters is that it matters to me. It's so rare to meet someone I can talk to, about Bruce, about Burns, who can reel off lines. We're laughing like a couple of old pals and maybe we were pals, Duke, at primary school, why the hell not?

'There was a group of us that used to go about together.'

'Proper wee toerags, so we were!'

'Down the Esha cliffs, remember?'

'That circle of big boulders down on the shore. Like a den. Or a castle. Didn't we used to call it Esha Castle?'

Maybe the barman was also with us that autumn day, Duke, when we cycled out the Albannach Road and went fishing from the rocks, the mackerel coming in on the tide and we were in them, in them, five, ten, a dozen . . . heading here afterwards, the three of us, did we really come in here, The Clachan, showing off our catch to our fathers, who toasted our skills, as The Breda Boys were toasted a few years later, remember, the barman also here the night of that farewell party, listening to the old man's speech, watching you serenade poor embarrassed Anna . . .

'Some night, some night.'

'Half the town was here.'

'Sinky fell in the harbour on his way back home. Poke of chips and he didn't see the mooring rope.'

'Sinky by name.'

Soon we are telling others these stories, who appear as if from nowhere, filling up The Clachan, office and shop workers on their lunch break, delight in their eyes as they meet and greet old Johnny Jackson, Goretex-clad tourists clutching *Lonely Planet*s like bibles, sipping their first malt.

And over there, the old man, that tatty fedora, shouting in old Donny's ear, you in the corner with Anna and *yes, we're going to be making films*, in London, and *no, I can't believe it either*.

Yet I am outside it all, watching myself, completely present yet a thousand miles distant from everyone, who ask occasional, shy questions when the barman and I are momentarily silent, scrabbling for the next detail in memory's murk. Even Akira is persuaded to have a drink.

'Just one, Johnny.'

Again he makes me think of Leonid, something in the tone or something I am forcing, a way back to another occasion in The Clachan, Leo's sombre words of condolence at the old man's wake.

'Your brother, eh?' the barman is saying.

'Still gets me,' I say. 'Right here.' I'm thumping my hand on my chest, my heart. 'Right *here*.'

'A lot of shocked people. You don't expect that kind of thing. But he was loved, you should know that.'

'I do, I do.' And do you, Duke? Do you see the light in this stranger's eyes as he raves on and on and on . . . ?

I come across myself again.

It is silent.

I am sitting on the same bar tool and staring in the mirror. *Nostalgia* scrolls across my forehead.

I realise the barman and everyone else has gone. I feel a strange kind of slackening. I dread these moments of lucidity and turn uncertainly to Akira, who is sitting beside me. There is nothing in his eyes to suggest I might have caused a scene, or said or done something to empty the pub.

'What time is it?' I ask him. My voice begins some distance away and slowly works its way back to me.

'Two thirty.'

'There's an old joke in there . . . the Chinese dentist?'

Akira just stares.

I point at the mirror. 'I think I want that.'

Akira shrugs.

'Serious, I like it.'

My gaze moves to a new barman, who places a tray of glasses on the bar and gives me a double take.

'You're that famous film director,' he states.

'I am.'

He's wearing a black T-shirt that says *I Eat Lions* in bold white letters. Even drunk I don't believe him.

For I am, as you know, Duke, *perceptive.*

It is written in the frown lines like the skeleton of a bird's wing that I see reflected back at me.

'How much?' I ask the barman.

He looks back at me. Frowns. He seems barely eighteen. 'For what?'

'The mirror.'

'Eh? Well, I don't think it's for sale.' He smiles nervously, the flush swift-rising from neck to cheeks.

'Five hundred quid and a hundred for you.'

Akira gets off the stool and takes out his wallet. He counts out five hundred pounds and puts the money on the tray. Then he walks behind the bar and hands the barman two fifty-pound notes.

'You can't ... It's not mine. What'll I say?' He definitely doesn't look like someone who eats lions.

Akira has already lifted the mirror off its hooks. Then he pauses and laughs. In the empty space where the mirror used to be is a faded poster of a naked redhead. *Patty Mullen*, the poster tells us in block letters. *Penthouse Pet of the Month, August 1986*. She has an immense eighties perm and high-hipped white panties. One hand is demurely covering a large breast.

'I apologise for my behaviour, son,' I say, sliding carefully off the bar stool. 'Sometimes I feel a right tit.'

Eight

When Anna moved into St. Stephen's Garden, I moved to Kilburn. A room in Leo's flat on Albert Road, where old Irish matrons stood in their doorways like frosted sentries. A two-ring hob and barely a ray of natural light, the overground train rattling on the other side of the scrubby back gardens.

The old man headed to Soho.

He spent most of his time there anyway. Not among the Bohemian wannabes but the Poles and Jews, French and Italians, exiles who crafted a new place while holding firmly to the old culture brought with them. Soho was somewhere to play up that identity, almost to professionalise it.

Thus entered the Gregarious Gael, propped at the bar of The Coach and Horses or the French pub on Dean Street, telling the old Clachan stories and those of more recent vintage, lurid tales of showbiz London and *no names but can ye no guess*, a rap of the cane and a doff of the fedora, hugs for the Greek proprietors of his favourite cafes. An effortless maker of his own myth, he might have lived in that tiny flat across from the Prince Edward Theatre his whole life.

Yet as the Rank films rolled he became antsy, nothing to do but set up a few marquee Breda Boys bookings now and then. Soho's delusions rubbed off; he wanted to be a player and The Aga Khan's money meant he could buy a way in. I called him the Angle Grinder, always chasing the connections. As the financial boy wonder, most negotiations deferred to me. I made some savvy property deals in Pimlico in the early sixties, all off the back of the old man's contacts.

More than anything, he saw it as somehow preordained that he become the proprietor of an exclusive nightclub. I bought us into *Delilah's*, a second-division hostess club off Berwick Street haunted by chancy politicians and fading call girls. He became its public face, his ego placated until it could be fully indulged with a something that would be his alone, The Cannonball Club.

I saw him less and less, Duke and Anna more often.

She came south at a good time. Journalism was opening up for women, no longer the lone voice of Marjory Proops. Yet the horizons remained limited: fashion, society gossip.

It didn't irritate her, to begin with, how her talent as a writer was so much less attractive to *The Mirror* than what she offered as the fiancée of Duke Jackson, Film Star. They wanted the razzle-dazzled country girl in the big city. *Through the Looking Glass*, her weekly column, was styled accordingly, full of uncontroversial showbiz tittle-tattle, playful hints of scandal.

I watched her at the parties they threw in Notting Hill. A natural hostess, effortlessly friendly, drawing confidences like blood: an arm around a tear-streaked Diana Dors, fending off Peter Sellers, still burbling his drunken, little boy confidences as she helped him into the back of a cab.

'These people are children,' she told me. 'It's like being in a kindergarten.'

Duke was the child she couldn't control.

This was the era of amphetamines and barbiturates. Bennies to start the day, whisky and downers to end it.

Before Anna moved south, Duke could hide it for the few days they spent together.

'I'm worried about him, JJ,' she said to me. 'He's drinking an awful lot. He's not usually like this.'

'No,' I lied. 'I don't know what's up with him.'

'Can you speak to him?'

A squeeze of my arm that went through me like an electric shock. A kiss on the cheek that finished me.

I didn't talk to Duke. I stopped going to their parties, and then I stopped visiting altogether.

It was a Sunday morning several months later when I went back to Notting Hill. Anna's smile was genuine, if fleeting. There were new lines on her face, and wariness too, like an expectation of disappointment.

For a moment, I had the strangest feeling, as if time had concertinaed and instead of five months having passed, it had been four years. I saw again Anna's happiness when she showed off her engagement ring. I felt so sorry for her, for her certainty so quickly vanishing.

There was no sign of Duke. When I asked where he was, she started to cry. Then the outpouring, sitting on the couch with her knees drawn to her chest. I listened with a hot, growing guilt that I had let her endure this alone, convinced, absurdly, that I was responsible for her loneliness.

Duke appeared hours later, dishevelled, still in his Saturday night clothes. 'Good to see you, little bro.' He shot me a sheepish grin, fixed himself a Bloody Mary and slumped on the sofa, head bowed like a little boy as Anna viciously castigated him. I should have left, but there was such insistence in their frequent glances. They needed me there. And if each of them were looking for an ally then they were also seeking normality, a respite from their spiralling dysfunction.

I played the role. I visited every couple of weeks, all

the while hating Duke's self-absorption and Anna's weakness for it.

Yet the emotional abuse they inflicted on each other was so stylised, a psychological equivalent of the objects they surrounded themselves with: the Florence Knoll furniture and the Weegee prints, the zebra skin rug à la *Breakfast at Tiffany's*. They needed forgiveness and I let them have it, just enough to briefly convince them that all was the sweetness and light suggested by their public image.

Although that, too, was becoming tarnished. The old man with a hand on Duke's throat one morning at Pinewood, the other thrusting a newspaper in his face. *Don't you fuck this up!* Something had happened in a West End restaurant, a photo in the *Express* captioned *Cracks in the Fairy tale*.

It was the latest in a series of incidents which culminated at Ronnie Scott's, the night I wanted to whisk her away, back to the little croft by the Sound, the two of us at the end of the world.

The Monkey and the Showgirl had wrapped. Another undoubted hit. The champagne and the old man were in full flow.

'Tenshun. Tenshun,' my father was rapping his silver-headed cane. 'The award season is upon us again.'

A great cheer went up, one or two drum rolls on the tables. It was time for The Oxters, the old man's customary, post-movie prize-giving to cast and crew who had brought *honour upon the chimp*. Their prize was a twelve-inch plastic replica of Charlie instead of the famous Oscar figure.

'For artistic licence, for putting the Grouch in Groucho, The Oxter goes to our dear Director, the venerable Mr Douglas Fotheringham.' The old man rummaged in a plastic bag for a statuette and tossed it across to Fotheringham, who stood up with great dignity and played exaggerated tribute. 'To all those friends and enemies who have brought me to this career pinnacle . . . and to those I hope never find out!'

This was acknowledgement that the plot of *The Monkey and the Showgirl* turned on a scene that ripped off the Marx Brothers' fake mirror scene from *Duck Soup*, where two Grouchos mimic each other. In our film it was Charlie the Chimp copying everything the drunken villain did while Duke sneaked in the window to rescue the girl.

'Once again, and his *third in a row*, The Oxter for simian relations, commonly known as the Doolittle, goes to . . . Leonid Baltacha.' Leonid raised his glass and, with a loud *Na Zdorovie*, knocked it back.

'And now. Best newcomer. It could only be, it will only be, Ms. Lana Roberts.' The old man reached into his bag as Lana, sitting beside him, squealed and stood up, her epic, Mansfield-esque bust lifting and falling like a cruise ship on a swell (great numbers would also sail in Lana). Then the old man had a sudden fit of coughing. He held up a hand and slowly calmed down, finally able to take a drink of water. After setting the glass down he put a hand on Lana's shoulder to steady himself. 'Sorry about that, Lana,' he said. 'I'm just feeling a bit chesty.'

The tables exploded. More drum rolls. Fake-affronted, Lana waved her Oxter in the air and blew kisses.

Then Duke, sitting on the other side of Lana, stood up and grabbed her, kissing her hard on the lips. The cheers became louder, and a few wolf whistles, which soon faded into uneasy silence. Duke wouldn't let her go, Lana struggling and Duke holding on for a few more excruciating moments, the old man now pulling at his arm, before letting her slump down, mouth open in shock. Duke remained standing, wild-eyed and grinning, staring across the table at Anna.

'That's how you do it. That's how you do it in the *movies*.'

The viciousness was the most disconcerting thing, some unknown slight become a fixation, bursting out.

Very calmly, Anna stood up and walked out. Two days later they announced their wedding date. Only five weeks away and in the middle of November 1962, as if there was a deadline they suddenly had to make.

★ ★ ★

'You're my best man, little bro.'

Duke shouted this in my ear as we stood at the bar of The Coach and Horses in Soho. A thump on my shoulder and he was gone, back into the noise, the throng and the congratulations. It was the first of several celebratory parties that would mark the run-up to the wedding.

'Bloody *ask* first,' I shouted.

That was the first night I drank, properly drank. Three pints, two whiskies and the pub soon a wurlitzing spin with me in the middle. *My brother . . . my best man . . .* Flushed faces peering and laughing. Claps on my shoulder and conversations I cannot recall. Then Anna suddenly appeared, somehow resisting the party, a curious look my way and then my nausea quick-rising.

Leo helped me to the toilet. A hand on my back as I bent to the toilet bowl. 'Let it go, Johnny,' he said. But when he added, 'Many loved before,' I realised he wasn't referring to my spasming guts.

I haven't been back to that pub since. It's probably the haunt of vegans now, polenta eaters.

I didn't go to The Clachan either. This, the stag party the night before the wedding, would have felt like a wake. Yet I walked past a few times, drawn by something like grief to those shifting shapes on the smoked-glass windows, the relentless *bodhrain* like my heartbeat made audible.

When the pub door opened, I hurried into the

darkness, light and laughter spilling out behind me. Then Duke's voice. 'Is zat you, little bro, zat you?' An echo from tenement to tenement and now quick footsteps behind me. I ducked into a close and when I peered out he was standing under a lamp post at the far end of George Street like the loneliest man in the world.

Many loved before. Yet, Duke, in the slanting rain and soft orange light, looked as if he never had.

'Find him.'
   'What?'
   'Your brother. Find him.'
   'What time is it?'
   'Seven thirty. He needs to be at the church by eleven. Where the hell were you? You're his best man, you're supposed to keep an eye on him. He just disappeared. Christ knows where he is.'

I dressed quickly. Mackintosh and boots. The fizz of rain as I hurried down to the road. I walked parallel to the sea, the choppy waters a corpselike grey and the wind a coldness inside me. Where the road began to angle steeply upwards, I took a muddy path back down to the shore.

The tide was out. I rounded the headland on the flat, no need to scramble over the seaweed rocks. Esha Bay stretched before me, a mile-wide scallop of flat sand. At its western edge the cliffs rose two hundred metres. Among tufts of grass, rock streaked white with their shit, I could just make out nesting fulmars; black, scrutinising shapes, the hardier riding the up-draughts.

We played there as children. In the familiar cluster of sandstone rocks at the foot of the cliffs I saw a round black shape. It took five minutes to reach it. An umbrella. Duke was sheltering behind it, knees pulled to his chest. Despite the noise of the buffeting wind, he knew I was there.

   'Can you remember the time I left you stuck up there, on the cliffs?'

'It kinda stays with you.'

'Sorry. Did I ever say sorry about that?'

'About a hundred times.'

'I'm sorry anyway. I don't think I've ever properly looked out for you.'

I sat down beside him on a flat step of rock. He was pale. He disgusted me. 'Not really the time for this.'

'Time for what, little bro?'

I stared at my feet. Pushed it back, *back*. 'Stop calling me that. Little bro. I hate it. I fuckin' hate it.'

He looked round. 'What's up with you?'

'You. You're what's up with me.'

'Whatever.'

He reached down between his legs and picked up a near-empty half-bottle of whisky. I tried to grab it from him and he wrenched it back, the two of us now standing, struggling for the bottle. I finally managed to rip it free and hurled it as far as I could, the bottle spinning and spilling.

'Thanks a lot, *little bro*.'

'What's your problem, Duke? Why the self-pity? You're getting married today. You forgotten that?'

He raised his face to the sky and rain and stood like that for a long time, his eyes tightly shut. 'I don't know.'

'Don't know what?'

'I don't know what I'm doing. I feel like if I let her go I'll just float away.'

'Give it a break.'

'It's true. I look at her sometimes and think what's a—'

'Girl like you doing with a guy like me?'

'Don't take the piss. But well . . . yeah.'

'Christ's sake, who's writing your dialogue, Duke? You know what?'

'What?'

113

'Don't be the wee boy. You let this go you'll always be the one who couldn't hack it.'

'It's not that I can't hack it.'

'What then?'

'It's not that I worry I'm going to fuck it up. I *know* I'm gonna fuck it up! That's what I *do*. Isn't it? Hey, she might be better off with you. Think she'd let you take my place?' A little laugh but a careful look.

'What's that supposed to mean?'

'A joke. Just a joke. Why so defensive?'

'I'm not being defensive, I'm pissed off. The old man sent me out here to find you. Bring you in.'

'I'm not a spy.'

'Eh?'

'That's what you do with spies. You bring them in. From the cold.' He thrust out his wrists towards me. 'Here you go then. I give up. Slap on the cuffs on and bring me in. It's a fair cop, gov.'

I walked away, into the wild rain, passing the bottle lying in the sand. I only turned when I reached the headland. Duke was following, about a hundred yards away, lifting the bottle now and then, still seeking the final drop. He was dawdling, but the tide still too far out to catch him.

Weddings are all the same unless you are the one getting married: a marathon of over-exposed idiocy.

I smiled for the reptilian cynics of the Fleet Street press pack, still drunk after a sleepless night in the buffet car of the Glasgow sleeper and the bone-rattler that finally deposited them at the end of the world. I waved to the locals crowding outside the church, who stared with greedy, forensic attention at the stars and the frocks with a shifting mixture of mockery and desperate hope that some of the starlight of the famous guests would briefly shine on them.

I was told that my speech in the function room of the

Queen's Hotel was hilarious. I sang along as loud as anyone else as Duke led a rendition of *Mairi's Wedding* (name changed accordingly ...). I smiled as I watched their first dance. Yet I was not there, not really. I barely spoke to Duke and only once to Anna, a quick *good luck* as I had handed over the ring. She mouthed a *thank you* and squeezed my hand. I searched for certainty in her gaze and tried not to find it.

* * *

1963 fell on me with a great weight. A time of isolation and deep cold. In my memory it snowed for weeks.

By day, I sat in the Kilburn flat, reading cheap paperbacks in the sickly scent of the lilies that Leo bought to *cheer up winter*. I even heard, occasionally, a petal falling on the sideboard, like an underscore to my isolation. I would anxiously wait for the next passing train to shatter the silence.

By night, I sat with Leo in front of the fire, dissecting the films we had recently seen at the Curzon in Mayfair, these the only times I ventured further than the shop at the top of Albert Road.

I didn't see anyone else, the old man lost in Soho, Duke and Anna on extended honeymoon.

Then, in three frenzied days, I wrote *Wrecking Ball*, a story for my hemmed-in mood, set mostly in the cab of a crane operator as he knocks down bombed-out buildings, haunted by flashbacks to the Bethnal Green tube disaster when an air-raid panic killed 173 people, including his wife.

The day I finished the script I received another.

Charlie Goes to Tangier. This was the crap I would be forced to make instead of *Wrecking Ball*.

I phoned my father. That was it, I was done. He said give me three days but called back in two, telling me Earl St. John had agreed that I could direct *Charlie Goes* ... My mood veered an instant 180. The old man feared only for the franchise, I know. But I was going to be a proper director.

He left it to me, naturally, to tell Duke.

I went round to Notting Hill after they returned from their Italian honeymoon. My brother opened the door.

He was smoking a cigarette in a ridiculous, white ivory holder and wearing a yellow polo neck and suede cardigan. Something about his appearance was instantly suspicious and I remembered why as I followed him inside. He was dressed almost exactly like Richard Burton in a photograph I had recently seen in a magazine. I was so infuriated I almost punched him in the face.

Then Anna was there, a whirl of movement and a bright smile at the end of the hall. Arms around me.

'JJ! It's wonderful to see you.'

During their honeymoon I avoided the papers and the inevitable paparazzi shots of the yacht in the bay of Capri. Duke filled me in, monologues so polished they had to be rehearsed, all 'turquoise waters and limestone cliffs, like marble . . . meandering walks and the air like silk.'

'Come on, Duke, you're boring your brother.'

'He wants to hear. Don't you? Not every day old Dukey boy gets married, eh?'

'Sounds wonderful.'

'You know Capri was popular with homos? Before the First World War.'

'No, I didn't know that.'

He poked another cigarette into his ridiculous holder. 'How's Leo anyway?'

This, I decided, was the ideal moment to tell him I would be directing him in his next film.

'You're having a laugh, right?'

★ ★ ★

116

Filming took place in March. I made the welcome discovery that my remote personality, far from being a hindrance, was ideal for a director. I became notorious for my disdain for actors. 'Essentially, he's a psychopath,' someone said, years later. Yet they invariably gave me what I wanted. Perhaps that deep need for validation found my contempt more gratifying than luvvie drooling.

Not that there was much angst on *Charlie goes to Tangier*. As Fotheringham had said, 'We're not making Kane.'

Still, I knew that a garrulous assistant director helped to ensure peace among the peacocks. This was Leo. Only a particular kind of misanthrope could take issue with a man who spent half his life babysitting a monkey. Even that notorious curmudgeon, Bernie Butler, director of photography, loved him, even if he suspected Leo would have taken his job in a heartbeat.

There were only a couple of occasions Duke took issue with me. Generally, he was placated by the script re-write that took me off-screen almost completely. Kidnapped by Berber bandits early on, I didn't re-appear until near the end, leaving the film to Duke and the born-to-be-a-Bond Girl Thea de Kok, his Dutch co-star, a pill-popping diva who put the high in high-maintenance.

Charlie goes to Tangier was the biggest hit of the franchise, Earl St John so delighted that he agreed to back *Wrecking Ball*. This was the first production for Breda Pictures, which Leo and I had recently set up.

'Let's do it,' he said. 'My life's achievement should not be the ability to make a monkey smile on cue.'

'Chimp,' I reminded him.

We found a demolition site on the Isle of Dogs. A five-day location shoot and then four weeks in the studio.

It was mostly the same crew from *Charlie Goes to*

Tangier but with Leo as DP. He crafted some beautiful visuals; empty, deep-focus street-scenes and over-lit POV shots in the cab of the crane. We developed what would become a trademark, the tracking shot that started just after the action began and ended just after it finished. There was something provoking, almost stalkerlike, about that slight movement, the way it led you that bit further into the scene.

The Earl of Pinewood did not approve.

He stalked out of the screening room without a word and summoned us to his office the next day. He was furious. He thought he'd been hoodwinked by a couple of god-damn beatniks. The ending, in particular, appalled him, the police turning up en masse to arrest Dan Smith, who laughs maniacally as he swings the steel ball and smashes their squad cars one by one. I had only seen a man having a nervous breakdown, not a countercultural attack on the social order.

I thought we would have to re-shoot the ending. Then I thought it would be canned altogether. In the end, it was strangled it at birth. Rank had five hundred plus cinemas and we made it into thirty. We premiered not at the Leicester Square Theatre, but the Curzon, Mayfair.

The old man put in an appearance. *Wrecking Ball* perplexed him. For once, he had little to say, just an indecisive 'S'interestin', I'll gie ye that.' Press interest fell away when Duke declined to attend, Leo and I taking the applause of an auditorium full of people we knew from all the evenings we too spent there. Sight and Sound liked it as well, offering praise to a 'sombre study in Polanski-like paranoia.'

I heard from my brother a few weeks after the premiere, through Anna, a phone call inviting me for dinner.

Duke let me in.

'Aha. Orson McWelly is here!'

A supercilious grin and again a cigarette in that ridiculous holder. Anna appeared and hugged me. As beautiful as ever in a white and yellow checkerboard shift dress, but weary, it seemed, overly made-up. She sat me next to her on a garish, purple velour sofa I hadn't seen before.

'We saw your film,' Duke said, leaning forward in the red pod chair that clashed horribly with the sofa.

'And?'

'And what?'

'What did you think of it?'

He took a drag on the cigarette. Considered the ceiling. 'A bit . . . niche, don't you think?'

'I liked it,' Anna said.

'That's not what you said,' Duke shot back. 'You said it was interesting.'

'Yes, and interesting means I liked it.

'Something can be interesting and shite.'

'Don't listen to him, Johnny.'

I felt the familiar tension. They were looking at me intently, expecting the conciliator to step in. I refused, for once. I wanted to ratchet that tension, ratchet and not release it. Screw them both.

'So you thought it was shite?'

Duke smirked. 'I didn't say that.'

I considered him for a moment then said the one thing guaranteed to provoke. 'So you didn't understand it?'

He leaned forward. 'I understood it. I'm not an idiot. I mean, it's not exactly going to make a lot of money.'

'Like *Charlie Goes to Tangier*?'

'Yes. See, you *can* make something entertaining!'

'Well, why don't you give it a go?'

He smiled. A bit coy. 'I've got ideas. Maybe I'll surprise you one day.'

'Why not start with the next Breda film?'

'Maybe I will. It's not going to be you.'

119

'What's that supposed to mean?'

'Stop it. Just stop it!' Anna burst into tears and rushed out of the room.

I looked at Duke, whose face was impassive. He shrugged and sat back in the chair, took another drag.

'She gets like that,' he said, vaguely.

I found her in the kitchen. At the sink, staring at her disembodied reflection in the window, a G&T in her hand. When she saw me she quickly wiped her eyes, turning to me with the saddest of smiles.

'I missed you,' she said.

'I missed you too.'

'I don't know what to do, Johnny.'

She held my gaze, waiting for me to say the right thing, the definitive something I could never find.

I said nothing.

Her look of helplessness was utter, then gone, becoming a swift defiance. *I will do this myself*, it said.

'You're still writing,' I said, absurdly, an eternity later.

She sounded tired. 'Yes, Jay. I'm still writing.' She swirled her drink. 'Tales of excess and debauchery.'

'Are you ok, Anna?'

And though her face immediately fell, there would be no more tears. I had missed my cue, once more.

'Happy as anyone else,' she said. She even managed to sound bright.

It was then I noticed, high on her cheekbone where the make-up had smudged, a red mark; a bruise.

Nine

Dusk is falling.

I sit up front with Akira. We return from The Clachan to the Castle. In the backseat is my new mirror.

Nostalgia.

I fight my nausea. I watch seagulls cartwheel above a morose sea, the lights of the promenade elegant curve from brightness to uncertainty. I decide not to ask Akira to put on some jazz.

'There's a time and a place for frantic sax.'

He glances across.

'This isn't it,' I add.

'Do you feel ok, Johnny? I can stop the car.'

I feel a slight acceleration. He wants to get me back to the hotel quickly, before I cover the windscreen in a watery omelette of vomit, no visibility, the car veering, smashing through the seawall.

'They'll be waiting,' I say.

They are. Top-lit by the light outside the staff entrance as we drive into the back courtyard of the Castle Hotel.

Erin is wearing a long coat and has her hands on her hips. On each side of her, their hands clasped at the stomach, stands a black-suited minder. They look like the start of a dance routine.

My niece is cold fury. An assault about to happen. People keep out of our way. This is how God might pass.

'Why are you laughing?'

'Because I'm a daft old man.'

'Knowing it doesn't mean you should indulge it.'

'You couldn't be more wrong, pet.'

'Where's your cell phone anyway? It keeps going to voicemail.'

'Japan.'

'Japan. Right. Of *course* . . . '

Akira opens the door to the suite and she quickly pushes past him. I catch up with her in the lounge, slumped on the sofa. 'I missed lunch then.'

'Don't worry. So did Frank. Some problem with his chopper. Who calls it a *chopper*, for Christ's sake?'

My mood plummets. I haven't avoided Frank Stone after all.

'You can't disappear like that.' She's insistent, genuinely concerned. I form my fingers into a gun and point it at my head.

'Look at you. You're a mess. Did you really think we'd let you direct a hundred-million-dollar movie?'

I chuckle. Yes, I *chuckle*. A chuckle that says I don't care when I clearly do. I go through to the bathroom. Splash cold water. Do my best to avoid the mirror. When I lift the towel she's there.

'Read this.' She thrusts a piece of paper at me.

I have no choice.

Mr Shinigami. I saw you in town today. This is a time of nostalgic return, I suppose. Therefore, I can understand the mirror. I hope you mount it in a very prominent place. Somewhere unavoidable. All those faces. It's coming, you know, that reckoning, don't overindulge the . . .

'He's following you. Can you understand now why you need to be accompanied?'

By now I'm laughing.

I'm thinking of Frank Stone. One of his OTT studies in big-budget melodrama. We need music, the spook of skeleton strings as I peer into the mirror with a concerned frown, wondering who the maniac might be. Cut to a dark apartment, a three-bar electric fire, someone with his back to us. We see fingers slowly typing, another email taking shape on the blue screen.

I look up at Erin. This time I circle a forefinger and point it at my temple. A moment later she's gone. I saw a look like that once on a chef hammering a schnitzel flat in a Munich restaurant.

I sit down on the toilet and read the rest of the email. I am advised to fend off my inevitable hangover with a painkiller, maybe codeine. I am told to *go easy, don't mix it with alcohol . . .*

Now my heart is hammering. I scrunch the paper up and throw it in the toilet, flush it away.

* * *

It's impossible to believe now, but Frank Stone was a 1970s heart-throb. The winsome teenage lead in *Babes in Brooklyn*, a comedy about a gang of street kids in 1920s New York, *The Waltons* meets *Happy Days*.

Fading from view in the eighties, he re-emerged in the late nineties as a sentimental visionary with a mystical ability to milk the multiplex masses. The man with the wizard's touch transformed himself, All-American Jock into wannabe auteur favouring black suits à la Warhol.

'JJ!' he exclaims and gives me a bear hug.

'Look,' he adds, stepping back and holding out his arms, offering me up to the consideration of his entourage. 'The legend himself. Johnny Jackson. I can't tell you how this man has *guided* all I've done.'

He is indeed a man who can fill a room, not with the gravitas he craves but through simple insistence. I smile indulgently. I let him take me aside, where he whispers loud enough for everyone to hear that he is humbled and indeed honoured to contribute to my final work.

'Final?'

He seems surprised. 'Final. Yes, final. Every day is our final day, every film our last, don't you think?'

Scientology.

Surely that is the explanation flickering in those piggy little eyes. 'You're a man of . . . perspicacity,' I say.

His eyes narrow, looking for a mockery he decides not to find. 'Let's tell them about our masterpiece,' he shout-whispers, taking me by the arm and leading me across to the door to the media suite.

Stone arrived out of my semi-conscious hangover fug at 7am. A heavy but directionless beating that confused me. For a disorientating moment I thought it was something inside the room. When I realised it was a helicopter I knew that the Great Director was here. I immediately fell into a deep and near-perfect sleep, like some kind of biological threat-response.

And now another chittering.

Voices and occasional laughter on the other side of the door. I am reminded of every terrifying Breda Boys intro. *Ladies and gentlemen . . .*

Gallant Stone insists I go first, flashing a magnanimous tombstone smile, right hand on my shoulder while the left checks his hairpiece is still in place.

I step into applause.

My raised hand is no greeting but a fending off. The world lurches. The last time this happened I fell off the stage at the BFI Southbank, a Q&A session after the screening of the thirtieth anniversary print of *A Man's a Man*. Quite the finale to the retrospective of my films, fifteen years ago now, almost as bizarre a public appearance as my next, the TV show in Japan a few days ago.

I walk very carefully up a short flight of stairs and sit on one of two leather chairs. Stone sits at the other. I am faced by a bristling of microphones on the small table between us, beyond that the crowded auditorium. Alcohol would make it easier, but that's why I fell off the BFI stage.

In Shuzenji, I am sliding open the bamboo screen. The air is cool and I do not mind the rainy smirr . . .

'The story is always there. But destiny calls at a given time. When that time comes the story needs to be re-told.'

Stone has been asked why he is making *The Bruce*.

'This nation is flowering,' he adds. To demonstrate, he raises a fist in front and slowly opens his fingers.

I resist the urge to close my eyes or shake my head. Buddha is right, all existence is indeed suffering.

'The myths are rising again . . . Like salmon in your great rivers.'

I think, *salmon*?

'What is the salmon but the symbol of wisdom. Strength. That's what Robert the Bruce is. Wisdom and strength. The one who had not only the *perspicacity*,' he glances my way, 'but also the will to follow through on the story he knew he had to tell. Destiny might call but it can also suggest.'

Oh, dear God.

Yet the titters don't come. The hacks are smitten. They ask and they scribble as Stone expands on his theme, how our myths are entertainments and while the most enduring are the most straightforward, that does not mean sacrificing truth or complexity, for we are thinking beings . . .

'There is room in this film for contemplation, for the wind in the barley . . . we all know that famous scene in *A Man's a Man*.' He reaches an arm across my shoulder. 'It is truly an honour to have such a legendary figure as Mr Johnny Jackson producing this film.' He gets to his feet and starts clapping. Soon the entire auditorium has followed suit and again it goes on uncomfortably long.

'I want to remind you,' Stone says when the applause dies out, 'that *The Bruce* is Johnny's script. His film, not mine. I mean, I've read his autobiography. Would you get on the wrong side of this man?'

Laughter now. Stone flashes me another dazzler and sits down. My turn for the questions.

The trick, as ever, is displacement.

There is an empty seat beside a pretty blonde in the centre of the auditorium. I will settle there, looking back at the table and watching myself respond to the inevitabilities about why I have chosen to make another film and the enduring influence of *A Man's a Man* . . . I am surprised and impressed with the gregariousness of my responses, the leavening of Sam Beckett's usual scowl.

When the questions end we are ushered stage front. Stone puts his arm round me. Photographers cluster. A young girl in a wheelchair with a bald head and a tube in her nose appears through the side door, pushed by Erin. She is wearing a *Kid Whizz* T-shirt, one of Stone's better recent efforts. She hands him an autograph book. He signs and smiles, bends for the cameras.

'Mr Jackson?'

I turn to an earnest-looking young man with a Dictaphone. 'The dispute, do you have a comment?'

'What's that?'

'The union recognition dispute with your hotels? We're in one of them right now. The underpaying of—'

He is jostled in the sudden movement around me. There are hands on my shoulders and a calm voice saying, 'This way, Mr Jackson.' The journalist shouts after me as I am hurried through the side door.

As it closes, I glance back and see the little girl in the wheelchair. She is crying, shrunk down and clasping her autograph book while the journalist still shouts his questions, Dictaphone in the air.

'I love it!' Stone says.

We are in The Ghillie's Bar, the VVIP annex of the main lounge, hustled in like politicians to a safe area following an assassination attempt. Erin strides to a far corner, fury on a phone.

'I most *surely* do,' he adds.

He scurries back and fore in front of a buffet set out on either side of a vast fireplace, stopping now and then to pop another grape in his mouth. After a few circuits he stops, suddenly reflective, and wanders to the window. There, he becomes a silhouette, looking out on a flat expanse of patchy snow that ends like an infinity-edge pool and becomes the gauzy grey of Inveran Bay.

'Incident,' he suddenly bellows and throws his arms wide, turning around. 'What is life without incident?'

He's delighted. LA life is as regulated as a call-sheet. The most innocuous of departures becomes an Event.

'It reminds me of this one time,' he says as he comes back over, then tells me something about Aspen, Colorado, and an environmental protest. A sudden claustrophobia sends me to the bar. I feel Erin's eyes drilling into the back of my head as I ask for a bottle of beer, yes, just a beer, Duke, a little settler, to deal with the grape-munching burbler that is Frank Stone.

Lewis with the big ginger beard, who I met when we arrived at the hotel, places the bottle in front of me. There is a momentary pause in Stone's monologue, filled with rehab judgement and envy (he knows old Betty fairly well). Lewis takes the opportunity to say something but Frank's off again before he can. I roll my eyes at the barman and watch him turn away. Soon, a sense of great ease flows through me. I watch how Stone's mouth makes a little pout when he talks, the voice somehow emerging from just behind the teeth rather than the throat.

And his *hands*. He has the most extraordinary hands, oddly small and rounded palms but long Nosferatu fingers. I wonder briefly about what the journalist had said. Then I gesture to Lewis.

'I'm making a film, a documentary,' he blurts out as he places down the beer, his face colouring to an alarming red.

'Good for you,' I say. 'I hope it's better than ours.'

Stone starts laughing. A cartoon *yuk-yuk-yuk* that grows into a full-throated guffaw. He's worked on that laugh, I know he has. Lewis too seems alarmed, smiling nervously and backing away.

* * *

As Akira and I had the day before, we leave from the back entrance. I sit in the back of the Mercedes, Erin beside me. On my insistence, Akira is driving. On Erin's, a minder sits up front with him. Another car pulls out behind us. The incident at the press conference and the latest email have spooked them.

The schedule dictates a visit to MacIntyre's Cave, where the famous scene with Robert the Bruce and the spider will be recreated. Then on to my old primary school and a performance in my honour. The possibility of subversion – as at the press briefing – seems remote, although an attack by eight-year-old anarchists with cream pies cannot be completely ruled out.

'You'll listen now? You see?' She clicks her fingers. 'How it happens?' She looks out the window and I follow her gaze into the rush of passing spruce. I have a flash of childhood, the windblown conifer in Dulston Wood; the bird's skull, white pebble and toy soldier I placed in the roots, a strange altar I felt somehow compelled to build. Imagine coming across that on a stroll in the forest.

'Nebulous intelligence. It sometimes coagulates. You know, like blood?' She turns back to me. 'Could have been blood. Why not? That journalist. Maybe he had a knife. A gun. He was in the strike zone.'

Strike zone?

I am convinced, again, of my niece's basic madness. The staccato sentences remind me of the way she described the share prices on the plane. She lives in a Manichean world. Profit is up or down. People are friend or foe. Abbreviation is the psychotic tell. There is only danger in nuance.

'Did you notice his hands,' I ask.

'The journalist?'

'Stone.'

'Stone?' Her momentary confusion becomes weary resignation. 'No, Jay. I didn't notice his hands.'

'Quite extraordinary. Look at mine.' I hold them up, the backs of the palms facing her. 'I've got liver spots like Rorschach blots. Do you think he's had plastic surgery? He's not much younger than me.'

'You know what, Jay? You're right. You're absolutely right. It *is* all a big joke, the cave we're turning into a bloody film set, Frank's hands, I mean, how can we take *any* of it seriously?'

Sarcasm has always made her ugly. A narrowing of the eyes, teeth bared to the gums. Like a baboon.

The car comes to a sudden stop.

Erin turns and peers through the windscreen. A lorry stacked with logs is emerging from a track leading into the spruce woods. A skinny man in a yellow bib is standing directly in front of us, one palm face-out towards us, the other beckoning the lorry forward onto the main road.

Two minders from the following car have materialised. They stand one on each side of ours.

129

The lorry eases into a slip road just ahead. The driver's door has opened. I look up as we pass. He's smoking, leaning down to talk to the man in the bib, who starts to laugh, then doffs an imaginary hat.

As we drive away, Erin continues looks out the back window.

'Maybe you're right. Did you see the way they looked at us?' She turns back to me. 'You wonder how people see us, really see us. All our self-importance. It must seem completely bizarre.'

As if on cue, I glance outside and see the sign for the cemetery, which Akira and I passed yesterday. Erin too has noticed it but says nothing. She will not speak of that place, not yet. As I will not tell her that McIntyre's Cave is somewhere else she has been. If she is meant to remember, she will.

I see it all again, of course.

Don't laugh, Duke, at these incessant thoughts of time and how nothing truly passes. In McIntyre's Cave, King Robert the Bruce is still watching the spider try and try and eventually succeed in spinning his web, while as my car reaches the brow of the hill and McIntyre's Bay spreads beneath me a day from long, long ago continues to spool, gloweringly grey, a young girl with a red kite scampering across the sand towards the incoming tide and I'm shouting, shouting, my voice catching on the wind and Erin finally hearing my warning, rushing back towards me and into my arms, her smile fading as she looks at her mother, beside us but a universe away, a woman who would walk, if we let her, into the implacable surf, water to knees, waist . . .

The caves now have a clifftop car park, commandeered for the production. A man with a clipboard waves us through the security barrier. Two marquees have been set up. People with beards and wellies rush around.

130

Straightaway, Erin walks to the fence and looks down on the arc of white-yellow beach. Joining her, I notice that she is breathing deeply, in and out to the rhythm of the surf. For a startling moment, I am sure it is her breath drawing and releasing the waves.

'Just a beautiful place,' she says, opening her eyes. I know now that she does not remember being here before. She turns to me and smiles. She seems to be offering both reconciliation and invitation. All I have to do is follow. I feel the same claustrophobia as in The Ghillie's Bar.

* * *

I stand at the cave entrance and watch him. Frank Stone. The colossal echo of his laughter, the waving of his strange hands. He walks slowly from one side of the cave to another, stopping to touch the floor. I remember an interview. Jay Leno, I think, Stone gushing about his 'obsessive need to inhabit the worlds I create'. Dear Lord, what I would give for a falling stalactite . . .

Then he sees me. A hurrying, an arm round the shoulders. He guides me out of earshot of anyone else.

'What do you think of the set?'

From the entrance, the cave funnels into a bulbous chamber some thirty feet wide and high. Lighting rigs have been positioned in front of the entrance, bathing the set in a dim mustardy light, an ethereal strangeness enhanced by the uplighting of various stalagmites. The crane camera has a platform, complete with heated seat. Up there will loom the Stone God with his toasty bum.

'It's coming together,' I say.

'Coming together?'

It isn't enough for Frank. There's a fretfulness in his eyes. He needs validation I cannot give. My storyboard perfected these scenes years ago. Their essence is sparseness, the only prop a rough blanket on which Bruce lies and looks up at the spider, the only lighting a mean little fire. He's on the run. He would not have had that chair and table, or half a dozen candles. Nor a wooden *bed* . . .

A spotlight snaps on from a lighting rig. A technician directs it to an overhang of rock. I understand straightaway. This is daylight, pouring through an opening in the cave's roof, picking out the spider at its web. It will be a cudgel-like depiction of Bruce's epiphany. Brad Renner will sit up on his bed and look suitably illumined, a swell of strings as Frank intercuts a montage of victorious battles to come with the spider's painstaking but ultimately successful efforts.

'It's going to be a dream sequence,' he says.

'I love it.'

This seems to reassure him. He takes me on a directionless meander round the set, arms flailing and those fingers, those *fingers*, like a wizard's, casting spells. Maybe that explains his two Oscars.

'We've had trouble though.'

'It's a complicated staging.'

'No. The set. It's been vandalised. Generator lines cut. Some lights smashed. It's why we beefed security up top. Incident follows you about, like at the presser? I thought the locals were friendly?'

'Make a friend, you make one for life. Make an enemy . . . '

'Rabbie Burns. Right?' He pronounces it like *rabies*.

'No. Johnny Jackson.'

He looks confused then slaps me on the back and laughs. 'Tell you, Mister Jay, you've still got it, still got it.'

As I wonder what I still have, a young brunette in an oversized, fur-collared parka and clipboard appears with a deferential flush, the thrust of a wilting hand and the declaration of 'Susie, a pleasure.'

Again, I am compelled to follow. Susie points with proud uncertainty to two canvas seats, printed, in neat gothic script, Frank Stone, Director, and JJ Jackson, Executive Producer.

'Do you like it?'

She takes my arm and walks me towards my chair, still holding on, gently helping the old man down.

'I'm counting on you, Jay.' Frank Stone plonks down beside me. He's pointing at my face with a serious look. 'That *eye* of yours. Standing on the shoulder of giants. That's all I'm doing. Tune me in.'

I get up and walk the set. I make a pretence of studying it. I see Akira by the entrance tunnel and offer a little gesture. He turns and disappears. A few minutes later I meet him outside. We walk across the watery sand into a razor-edged wind and flurries of snow. He hands me the hipflask. By the time we turn back the snow is heavy. The pouring light from McIntyre's Cave has become a gauzy yellow, making an uncertainty of the figure waving and shouting to me as I once called to her.

Though only mid-morning the day already seems to be calling time. The cold deepens. I hike up the steps and across the car park. A fleeting smell of coal smoke makes me close my eyes, breathe deeply.

Erin is already inside the car. 'We're running late.'

I nod, trying to catch my breath. 'The kids won't mind.'

'You need to take it easy.'

'Tragedy might improve the PR.'

A massive heart attack in the assembly hall of my old primary school, say, at the very culmination of the special event being held in my honour, the children's singing becoming horrified screams.

'True.' This seems to cheer her up.

She spends the journey back along the coast to Inveran staring out the window and humming a little tune I can't place, eagerly following each winding of the road, the revelation of every spectacular seascape. 'Look at that,' she says, and 'isn't that something.' She wants me to join in. To agree. As with everything she says or does, her cheerfulness is relentless, exhausting.

A lassie of pairts, my mother would have said. Knows what she wants and how to get it. But my mother wouldn't have liked her. It's ok to be that *go getter* but gonna go get it somewhere else?

In some ways my approach to Erin's upbringing was much like my mother's. A dour *just get on with it*. That first day of primary, Duke, it was likely the same for you as for me, Mum unclasping your gripping hand at the top of Campbell Street and shooing you away towards the school, where the other mums were crowding the gates, hugging goodbye to their children. I remember that walk so vividly. The dreadful uncertainty mixed with anticipation.

I take a drink from the flask. Dark outskirts become the shiny orange of wet streets. Still the snow is falling. We take several turns and my bearings falter. Then, with a surge of recognition, I realise we're in Campbell Street. There, there she is, Duke, tough love in a long black coat . . .

Just get on with it.

I will have another drink.

Only one more, I am not a vulgar man. It's not as if the car door has suddenly opened, spilling me onto the ground, the smile on the face of the head teacher become a horrified gawk and a hurried shooing of the children, who peer like amused little animals at the old man with the bandy legs who's sprawled in the wet and laughing so hard he might die. How was school today,

134

wee Jimmy? Well, the famous man smelled of medicine and was sick on the pavement . . .

Instead, I will offer dignity.

The car sweeps in the gates of Stevenson's Primary and I step out with a smile, with *bonhomie*, warmly shaking the hand offered by an impossibly young male teacher in plimsolls and over-tight jeans.

At times like these I yearn for my father's charm. The most I can offer is a one-liner followed by awkward silence. Today, there is only silence. The teacher waits a few excruciating moments too long for some kind of engagement before we're rescued by a photographer.

'Everything ok?' whispers Erin.

'Good as it's going to get.'

'Nope.' She puts a hand on my shoulder and rests her head against it, beaming for the camera.

I hold my face in a strained grimace and listen to the rapid series of shutter clicks. 'I'm not following.'

'I mean, Jay . . . ' She waves the photographer away. 'That you need to pull your finger out of your *arse*.'

She smiles again, showing her teeth. She really has immaculate teeth. I wonder if she sharpens them.

The school was a Victorian crumble even in my day. I'm surprised it is still standing. Perhaps it is a Listed Building, protected by councillors who were once pupils, who ignore the strap and other cruelties and believe, with the forgiveness of time, that it is fondness they feel for this place.

It is instantly familiar, the upside-down T of corridors as you enter, classrooms to the left and right and some steps directly ahead. This leads to another corridor, the school office on the right and the canteen and the assembly hall on the left, from where pandemonium is spilling.

'Here we are,' says the teacher. 'The children are so

excited, they've been waiting all day. Are you ready?'

'Is this a Listed Building?' I ask.

He looks confused, poor fellow, as he pushes open the double doors to the hall. I am greeted by an overwhelming cheer. They're lined up in the same rows, Duke, where we sat for assembly, where they would nip me, punch me, give me Chinese burns, and you never stopped them.

I back away . . .

I see myself running along the corridor and around the corner into the toilets, the same fishy toilets, everything still everything in this place, down on my knees in a cubicle, puking my guts up, but no running feet coming closer, no bullies or security or Erin, just a steady dripping from the cistern above my head and a smell of disinfectant at once comforting and repellent.

'Are you ok, mister?'

A little boy in glasses. He looks a bit like Charles Hawtrey. He's wearing grey shorts and a green jumper.

'Are ye no feeling well?'

I nod my head.

'We had custard the day. It wis lumpy an everythin'. Ah didn't feel too good either. Didnae boke tho.'

I get off my knees and sit on the toilet seat.

'You want to see something?' he says.

With great solemnity, he produces a yoyo from the pocket of his shorts. He steps back and flicks it a few times, doing a simple up and down. Then with a quiet *watch this*, he flicks it out in front of him, the yoyo landing on the floor and briefly rolling along before he zips it back in again.

'Walkin' the dug,' he declares.

I remember that I could do that, once.

As I struggle to my feet the boy holds out a warm and sticky hand. Again, he looks suddenly serious.

'Don't mind them, mister. Them back there. Ma

brother's gonna sort them out one day, sure he will.'

He leads me out of the toilet and, holding my hand, guides me back along the corridor to the assembly hall.

I step into the great cheer ...

I make them laugh by pretending to trip over my feet. I clap with genuine delight as a girl in a monkey costume and a boy in a tux do the mirror scene from the *Monkey and the Showgirl*. I offer my best theatrical bow after another recreation, the dream sequence from *A Man's a Man*, a boy reciting *Green Grow the Rashes* while a group of girls dance delightfully behind him.

Afterwards, there are more photographs. The pupils are arranged behind me on the stage, teachers at the sides. I stand on the floor below and in front, arms outstretched in the usual showbiz *ta-daa*. We all smile for the birdy, except Erin, who stands off to the left looking wary and uncomfortable.

The little boy in the shorts and green jumper standing beside me, do you remember him, Duke?

This is my return, see?

I smell the after-fug of a million school dinners and marvel at the tiny chairs. I hear hymns once sung and the tears cried. I remember occasional delight, like the girl in the monkey costume over by the piano, playing happily all by herself, skipping and singing. She too will remember, in time. So be kind to the little boy, Duke. Remember, you were still alive back then, long before the *Shinigami* struck. I wonder what my emailer might have to say about you?

137

Ten

Have you heard the one about the old man, the pervert and the chump? No? C'mon, you must have. Well, when I stop laughing you're in for a treat. And yes, that's chump, not chimp, though there was also a chimp, but not in the joke. A joke can have a maximum of three protagonists.

That's just how it works.

I am dressed in coarse brown trousers, blue cotton shirt with black waistcoat and slip-on black pumps. On my head is a conical straw hat. Leo sits beside me in his civvies and together we watch Charlie, who is standing in the middle of a large, round varnished table, hopping from leg to leg.

It is midnight of some summer day in 1964. In the half-light cast from six hanging lanterns I can only feel as if an ending has been reached.

'This is what it has come to,' I say.

'Indeed,' he answers.

Leo that is, not Charlie, although the chimp stops dancing and looks across at us, as if he too knows the finale has been reached. Then he blows a raspberry and sticks up a middle finger.

This is *Peking Chimp*.

The final film in the Breda Boys contract. A slapstick classic, 'tis said by some. Duke and I are acrobats in a travelling circus in medieval China who get embroiled in a plot to kidnap a princess.

Duke was right.

I wouldn't be directing any more Breda films. Fotheringham was back. In fact, I wouldn't be directing any more films for Rank at all. Earl St. John's loathing for *Wrecking Ball* had ensured that.

With our contract up, the old man was sweet-talking a renewal. I wasn't doing us any favours. Directing had simply underlined my dislike for acting. I started to freeze mid-shot. Duke would stride off the set in frustration. The reason that we were still in Pinewood at midnight was that we'd only just finished filming for the day. Thirty-two takes for a twenty-second scene.

Although it was surprising we were still filming at all. The old man was also working a more troubling schmooze. The fifteen-year-old daughter of the assistant director had visited the set. A big fan of The Duke, she asked for an autograph and got a hand up her skirt. The old man fawned for the executives and managed to persuade Hardwick the AD not to go to the police.

'There's fifteen goin' on twenty and fifteen going on ten,' he told me. 'She's the latter and your brother's got problems.'

Yet Duke got the second contract and I got canned. It was the day we wrapped, a suit I had never met telling me, 'The Breda Boys films will be remembered forever and you played no small part.'

'I know you,' said the taxi driver who picked me up from the studio. 'You're the one with the chimp!'

That taxi took me to Soho's Beak Street, a gloomy basement bar just along from *The Sun and 13 Cantons*. The old man was sitting in a leather seat at a round, zinc table. Twelve of these filled the space between the bar and the low stage, set in an arched brick alcove lit with red and white spots.

'I take it you knew,' I asked. 'About the contract with Duke?'

He waved to the three workmen fitting the granite tops of the half-moon-shaped bar behind him. As they trotted off he rested his hands on the top of his cane and pointed with his chin. 'Like the name?'

I followed his eyes to the neon sign hanging above the stage. The Cannonball Club in scrolling red letters.

'Cannonball Adderley, one—'

'When you were going to tell me?'

'Does it matter?'

'Course it matters!'

'Aye, well.'

'Aye, well?'

'They wanted Duke. They want to put him in romantic comedies. Reckon he's the new Dirk Bogarde. There's no place for you, son. You're the monkey man. When people see you, they see a chimp.'

I tried to muster one last shot but the anger had gone. I sat down and stared at the flickering neon.

'You like it?' he asked.

The half-finished Cannonball was already the old man's new HQ. The place of his dreams, at last. Martinis and jazz, candles in wine bottles, dried wax down the sides – it wasn't naff back then.

'A place of good music,' he said. 'Good booze and . . .' He searched for the elusive word with a hand in the air, rubbing thumb and forefinger together. 'Refinement.' It hung there oddly, both of us aware that the old man and refinement went together like Dom Pérignon and spam.

As I stood up to leave he grabbed my arm. 'It's not a bad thing, you know. *Monkey No See* and all the rest. It's *all* about that monkey.' His other swung arm around the room. 'No monkey, none of this. You were bang on, son. I am nothing if not someone knows when to offer praise.'

★ ★ ★

In truth, I wasn't that angry. I had been liberated, my days my own for the first time in years. I occupied myself with the growing Breda Empire. The property business had taken off, a cash flow for film production. We had a couple of projects and one was my own, *Journey to the End of the Night*, with a possible investment angle brokered through Richmond 'Fatty' Ashcroft.

Fatty was another of the old man's Soho cronies and a partner in The Cannonball. Minor aristocracy with some pile in the West Country, Fatty had access to both cash and an old public-school friend on the MGM-British board. I brought him into the Breda Pictures fold and made an unexpected discovery: Fatty wasn't a movie man but somehow had a gimlet eye for box-office gold.

Our run of hits in the late seventies would be pretty much down to him. Charm with a razor's edge, that was Fatty Ashcroft. You'd be halfway home before you realised you were bleeding.

I'd discover that myself, in time.

Anna phoned me in Kilburn a few times. 'Are you all right? Are you sure you're not too disappointed about . . . '

Being dropped, she wanted to say.

I'd bat back banalities neither of us believed, like *it was an opportunity in disguise*. A loaded silence usually followed, heavy with all kinds of things that I couldn't bring myself to say.

The lightness vanished. I stopped answering the phone. I walked autumn London. I spent a week riding the Bakerloo from Stanmore to Elephant and Castle and was accosted by a kinetic young woman with troubled eyes who had seen me a few times and urged me to keep travelling.

With December rain came a pouring guilt.

I would stand at the kitchen window in the glum

141

dusk, listening to the rattle of trains coming closer, then the flash of brightly lit carriages through the skeleton branches of the trees between the houses and the track. That *rat-at, rat-at* aftersound, it was like memory's pulse, taking me back to my first days in London, when novelty obscured the city's indifference and made it easy to forget a past and place now rushing back towards me like the tide at Esha Bay.

In the hallway the telephone was a regular insistence. *Talk to me, talk to me,* and I knew who was asking.

Eventually, Anna appeared in person. A surge of seasonal enthusiasm had taken me to *O'Shaugnessy's Meats,* instantly evaporating with the butcher's amused stare, as if I was the turkey for expecting there to be any left two days before Christmas. When I returned empty-handed she was sitting on the front step in a green Astrakhan coat, cheerfully waving a bottle of whisky. The light was fading, her smile a secret. It should have started snowing, just then.

'Old Mrs Kelly across the street, she'll be keeking out from the nets.'

'Probably thinks I'm a prostitute. Let's give her something to talk about.' She jumped up and threw her arms around me, lifting her feet off the ground as she did and sending me stumbling backwards.

'Sorry,' she giggled. 'I may have had one or two already. Where have you been anyway?'

'I went to buy a turkey,' I said.

'On December 23rd?'

'Aye, they've all been gobbled up.'

'Boom, *boom!*'

'You wonder why they didn't renew my contract?'

We drank a first and a second. Sitting in the living room at opposite ends of the sofa. Three panels of the gas fire.

We started with Duke.

'He was so drunk they wouldn't let him into the premiere of *Goldfinger*. Did you not see the papers?'

'Can't say I did. I'm not exactly a dedicated follower of the Duke.'

'See. I knew it! You *are* annoyed about that contract. Why can't you just admit it? There's no shame in it.'

And back and fore like that for a while, through another fast glass and then her warm hand on mine.

'I'm worried about you, Jay. No-one's seen you for weeks. What have you been doing with yourself?'

'I dunno. Reading? Walking, been out with the camera. Watching the trains.'

'The trains?'

'The line out the back. In fact,' I checked my watch. 'Quick, I'll show you.'

She hurried after me, through to the kitchen. Full dark now. We stood at the sink with me behind her.

'Trust me?'

'Maybe!'

I put my hands over her eyes and said *listen*. Moments later we heard it. A rising roar moving left to right, rattling the windows and the crockery on the draining board. When it was directly ahead I took my hands from her eyes and let her watch the bright carriages pass in the darkness.

'I've always liked trains,' she said.

'Me too.'

'I can remember the journey down here, when I left. Clear as day but it seems like a lifetime ago.'

'I know. I was so excited, but the funny thing is I don't think I wanted to leave in the first place. It just seemed to happen.'

'I was going to write at the *Courier* and that would be that.'

'Come on, you were too talented to be stuck there. Those Breda Boys features. They were fantastic. Art.'

143

'There's no need to take the mickey, Johnny.'

'I'm not!'

'Really . . . Well, I'm some artist, celebrity tittle-tattle, who's screwing who. Whoops, can't just *say* that.'

'Everybody knows anyway.'

'Exactly. What is it with folk?' She looked at me very carefully. 'Why can't we just say what we mean?'

Three whiskies down, I almost did. She was right. What do we wait for? So of course, I kept waiting.

'You know what puts me off going back?' I said. 'The thought of people thinking I've failed. I remember the leaving do at The Clachan. All those people who envy you but secretly want you to fail.'

'You haven't failed. I'm the one who's failed.'

'Rubbish. You've got a national newspaper column. I'm the monkey man who made a weird film no-one saw.'

'I'm a gossip-monger.'

'I'm a has-been that never was. Over the hill at twenty-five.'

'Enough! Come with me.' She grabbed my hand and led me back to the living room. 'My turn. Do you trust me?'

'Sure.' She stepped behind me and put her hands over my eyes, guiding me forward with her hips.

'Open them!'

When I did I was looking in the mirror above the sideboard. A pale, pinched face frowned back.

'Repeat after me.'

'C'mon, Anna, I—'

'Here and now I do solemnly swear.'

'Here and now I do solemnly swear.'

'To stop moping around like a plum and, em . . . get back in the saddle.'

'The saddle?'

'Say it!'

'To stop moping around like a plum and get back in the saddle.'

'There.' She turned me round to face her. 'Better?'

'Well, I'm smiling.'

'Me too.' She suddenly leaned forward and kissed me on the lips. Briefly, but a beat too long.

'How on earth did we get here?' she added softly.

My rationality scattered, ricocheting off those three whiskies. 'How's that?' It was all I could manage.

'London,' she stated.

'London? Right. Sure . . . '

She sat down on the sofa. 'One for the road?'

'Yes, ma'am.' I saluted for some peculiar reason and sat down beside her, reaching for the bottle.

'I know about Duke and the girl, by the way.'

I stopped mid-pour.

'There's a sanatorium I've heard about, down in Devon. A drying-out place. You can imagine what he said. I asked if he'd prefer Wormwood Scrubs. I should shake your father's hand for heading that off.'

I wondered if she ever got round to that. The old man was dead within a month. January 1965, a Friday afternoon, brain haemorrhage in The Coach and Horses during a drinking game with some American GIs.

My brother and I did what was expected. We drank too much and played endless Duke Ellington records. We talked about the old man, already shaping the myths, joking about who was going to inherit the fedora. We called him a silly old bugger for getting into drinking games at his age and said the usual stupid thing about going the way he would've wanted, as if anyone wanted to go at all.

Looking around that house, where copies of *Playboy* were idly scattered and Patchouli an ever-present scent, where the living room had been newly arranged to bordello chic and the ghost-guests of a thousand parties still offered their air-kisses and casual slanders, where the Moroccan-style white and aquamarine tiles of the bathroom had spellbound many a stoned wanderer, looking around I realised that without our father there would have been none of it.

Later, as I read a statement to the press pack outside, I thought about all the stories we tell about ourselves and others, liquid and shifting as a murmuration of starlings. What if I veered away from this *man of great energy who will be truly missed* and talked instead about how families are dictatorships and we are all the bastard offspring of someone else's failed ambition?

I didn't.

No talent for the ad-lib, I heard the old man say, again so disappointed. *Shoulda let your brother do it*. But beside me Duke was lost in his own failings, immaculately drunk, swaying to a private breeze.

Duke instantly took to the fedora. It didn't take to him. The old man's head was bigger than his and the brim slipped almost to Duke's eyes. I saw a photo in a paper a couple of days afterwards.

The Duke, the Lady and their Grief, the caption said.

Duke was walking along a street; black raincoat, shades and fedora. His face was angled skywards, a picture of contemplation. A few steps behind, Anna was a picture of concern, effortlessly à la mode in white boots and black mini-dress. It was extraordinary to contemplate where she'd come from and where she now was, her appearance like an ongoing farewell.

Yet the photo looked so staged it infuriated me. Leo told me to calm down but I went over anyway.

Ellington was playing, of course, blaring out from the fifties Wurlitzer installed in the living room. My brother was sprawled on the purple velour couch. White shirt open to the waist, sunglasses on.

'You still listening to this?'

'It's called grieving.'

'I saw the photo by the way. The *Mirror*? What's with the hat? You've taken the piss out of that hat for years.'

'I defer to my earlier comment.'

'You defer?'

'That's right.' He sat up suddenly and reached for his glass on the low coffee table. 'I defer to my earlier comment.'

'Where's Anna?'

'Out shopping? I dunno. Why are you so concerned?'

'I'm concerned about you. And her.'

'Course you are. You've always been so concerned about her.'

'I have no idea what that even means.'

'Course you don't.'

I sat down on the seat opposite him. We said nothing for a long time. 'You didn't even like him, Duke.'

He threw back the whisky and pointed at me. 'You. You, little bro, are a cold-hearted bastard and—'

'Can't say I liked him too much myself.'

As Duke leapt to his feet so did I. Before he said anything, I slapped him hard across the face. The sunglasses flew off. Two shocked and bloodshot eyes briefly contemplated me before he sat down again.

I stayed standing. 'Just don't, Duke, *don't*. Wear his fucking hat but don't give me any more of this shit.'

★ ★ ★

It was a private funeral but they came anyway, hundreds of people despite the driving rain of cold February. Men with hats in their hands and women in black lined the steep road up to the church on the heights. We drove

147

slowly past them behind the hearse, up to the old congregational church, stubborn as Calvin himself in the face of the storms that had battered it for a century.

I remembered frozen Sundays. Frightening sermons and tuneless singing made all the more unsettling by the one voice, a wavering soprano, that could hold a note. I would look round for that voice but never find it, the rise and fall like a bird flitting across the dark pews before vanishing.

No bird sang at the old man's funeral. Duke, Leonid and I sat in silence, several cousins murmuring hymns as anonymous as their faces, which I hadn't forgotten but simply never known. Anna whispered the words so quietly that it might have been the Kaddish or Wee Willie Winkie.

Why not? The old man who would cross the street to avoid a minister was having a last laugh, on us.

We chewed our way through *Bread of Heaven* and listened to a eulogy so far off the mark it would need McKeever's lighthouse to guide it home. Then into the rain and ashes to ashes, mud to mud, a slapstick routine begging to happen. Alas, there was no whee-plop as the minister slipped and fell into the grave. It was disappointing. Final proof, I felt, that there is no God.

It was only when I got back to the car that shame at the absence of affection for my father hit me. I guiltily watched the mourners who were still lining the streets down to Inveran, who had stayed out in the rain as the funeral took place and again bowed their heads as we drove past.

I glanced round at Duke, sitting behind me on the back seat. Shades and silence. Was he as grief-stricken as he seemed? Why not? It was clearly a time of absurdities. I looked away from him, to Anna, who offered a smile I could only describe as offbeat. That's the problem with absurdity. Once you notice it you start seeing it everywhere. It's infectious, and far too easy to indulge.

'He spent his whole life waiting for an audience like that,' I said, and tossed another piece of driftwood on the bonfire. The salt-soaked timber began to spit, a counterpoint to the hissing of heavy rain on hot ash.

We were sitting in our Mackintoshes in the same huddled row as when we lit the fire, hours ago. It was full black now, pulsing embers, the sea a presence only in waves I could hear but not see.

I had been the one who wanted to come here after the wake at The Clachan, a need to clear my head of those endless tributes. Yet the memories followed us to the shore, the fire lighting a way back to the ones he once built every midwinter, a wink for his boys and an apologetic shrug for our mother, who disapproved of such pagan practices but always smiled when it was lit.

'He'd have been mortified,' said Anna.

'Mortified? He'd have loved it,' I said. 'He would've made our lives miserable going about it.'

Anna smiled, rested her head on Duke's shoulder, the smile becoming a frown as he shook her off.

Duke lifted the whisky bottle and tipped it back. I took a shot and held it out for Anna, who placed it back in its hole in the sand. We went back to staring at whatever we each saw in the flames.

'Can't believe he put us through that service,' I said. '*Feed me till I want no more.* The old bugger was gorging us all right, stuffing it down our throats. Four hymns, three prayers and two psalms.'

'Five hymns,' said Anna.

'Five? No much wonder the minister looked pleased.'

'Like Easter and Christmas rolled into one.'

'Eastmas.'

'What?'

149

'Eastmas.'

'Give it a rest, you two. Bit of respect, eh?' Duke still stared straight ahead. 'He's not ten hours in the ground. Ten hours. I'm sure he thought it was worth it just to see all those people.'

'C'mon, Duke, it's—'

'Did it never cross your mind that he wanted a funeral like that? Like he maybe, I dunno, came back to it.'

'Came back to it? You're having a laugh, right? *He* was having a laugh. We should have slung him on the bonfire. Proper Viking way to go. He'd have loved that. You sure we found the right will?'

He was suddenly on me, a smack on the side of the head as I tried to get up. He shoved me onto the sand and sat astride my chest, slapping my face again and again. I heard a wailing like the wind rising, which I realised was Anna. She was pulling at Duke's arms, screaming at him. His body suddenly sagged and his arms dropped. He looked at me dumbly as I shoved him away and scrambled up.

She came to me. Touched a finger to my lip. Looked at Duke with such exquisite sadness as he tried to get up and fell back on the sand, tried again and gave up, reaching instead for the bottle.

That way she looked at me.

It could have happened that night, after we put Duke to bed, standing in the doorway like concerned parents, or later on, in the kitchen, when we sat together, drank tea and said so little, her head on my shoulder which I didn't shake off like my brother. Instead, it was the next day, after the walk to the Craigie Falls. 'A beautiful morning,' she said. 'Leave him here to sleep it off.'

We took the path behind the cottage, up towards Ben Chorain, beyond the shieling and east, the Sound below us, a silver shimmering become muted grey as the clouds shifted in front of a vague sun. The uncertainty matched the way I felt, one step after another and my heart beating harder, harder. Only the exertion, I told myself, not expectation, the same heat of effort I felt in Anna's hand as I helped her up the last steep slope before the waterfall, her hand that did not let go as we walked across the smooth flat rocks, into the thunder and the icy spray.

'I love you,' I told her.

Her reply was immediately lost in the waterfall and a long kiss that stripped any further consideration of what they might have been. Only after we shivered back into our clothes and lifted the Mackintoshes that had kept us dry from the wet heather did I again wonder what they were.

To ask her was to misplace a gift, I told myself. And not to ask was never to be disappointed.

Later, we stood at the kitchen window. Duke had gone for a walk. We were watching him in the distance, moving up hillside on the same path towards Ben Chorain. We said we can't let it happen again.

Then let it happen again.

* * *

1965 rolled on and London changed. I made an effort, for a while. I stepped in for the old man and Fatty, and I opened the Cannonball. Ironically, the club became renowned not for my father's beloved jazz, but rock 'n roll.

The Rolling Stones, Pink Floyd and The Yardbirds all played early gigs there, the club becoming synonymous with what no-one at the time called Swinging London. Keith Moon made it his regular for a few months after he was barred from The Ship for letting off a smoke bomb. He had a walkie-talkie installed at his favourite table so he didn't have to fight his way to the bar, through all the Peacock Mods strutting oblivious to the outraged cries of a fedora-wearing ghost.

My generation never fitted me that well either. Take my clothes, the drainpipe trousers too long, runkled at the foot, bringing attention to the winkle pickers that bent up absurdly at the toe, making my legs look like two hockey sticks. Or my manner. I had the air of a policeman in a bad disguise. I tried to let my awkwardness become eccentricity and told myself I was part of the scene when everyone knew I wasn't.

Yet in time the commentariat lumped me in with the counterculture. These labels are usually retrofitted. The Spectacle assimilates. We all want to belong, deep down. We want to be persuaded that this is what we were truly looking at, back then, that we really were trying to change the world.

Sometimes, though, I glimpsed it. A genuine freeing of possibility, a decoupling from what had gone before. But there were a lot of Bobs and few Dylans out there. The Cannonball, all the parties, they were filled with so many others like me, who failed to find the fearlessness to truly let go. Maybe they too looked at clothes that weren't quite right, wondering why they were there at all.

Anna, that was why.

I obsessed about seeing her but avoided Notting Hill. After what had happened, the thought of having to endure the loaded strangeness of her domestic life was beyond agonising. Every time I dragged myself along to a party, pub or band, it was in the hope of bumping into her.

Not that we said much the few times we did meet, our awkwardness so apparent it could be bottled. She avoided my gaze, as if to look at me was to be compelled to talk about *the waterfall*. Then the getaway, the same *good to see you, Johnny* that always seemed like a final farewell.

Then, one time, it was. She vanished from the scene.

Once or twice I nearly telephoned her. One time I even made it to St. Stephen's Garden, walking back and fore until I noticed a policeman was taking an interest and hurried back to the Tube station. This was 5th February 1966, the first anniversary of the Craigie Falls.

It would be my brother rather than Anna who I saw next, months later. First, a telephone call from which I hung up in exasperation. Then a visit, from which I couldn't, a rapping on the door on a Saturday morning.

He stood on the front step, immaculately mod in a double-breasted silver and navy pinstripe boating jacket and matching trousers. Behind him, by his midnight blue Jaguar, stood a representative of a more vintage London style. Slick hair. A three-piece suit under a black Crombie.

'What the hell do you think you're doing?'

'Hello to you too. Who's your friend?' Slick stood very still with his hands clasped. Staring at me.

'One of Dad's.'

'One of Dad's what?'

'One of his . . . I dunno, his men?'

'His men?'

'That's what I said.'

'So you have men now?'

'Yes. I have . . . Look, let's just go inside.' He pushed past me into the house. Straight to the kitchen.

'Make yourself at home,' I said, watching him disappear down the hall to the kitchen. When I caught up, he'd already found the vodka. He poured a stiff one and downed it. Poured himself a quick refill.

'Well?'

'Well what?'

'Don't give me that rubbish.'

I thought Duke meant me and Anna. Instead, he was incensed about Breda Pictures' new film. His latest, *Next Stop Victoria*, had been mired in re-writes, delaying filming. This meant, firstly, that a breathless public had to wait for the masterpiece that was a playboy hiring some crooks to steal a hundred grand, and, second, that *Journey to the End of the Night*, the first production we made for MGM-British at Borehamwood Studios, ended up being released in the same week of October.

'I told you on the phone,' I said. 'We kept to schedule. You're the one who got delayed.'

'So it's my fault.'

'I don't know whose fault it is, but it's not mine. Anyway, it's not as if they're competing with each other.'

'I wouldn't know.'

'You should go and see it.'

'Should I.'

The reviews for *Journey . . .* were better than *Wrecking Ball*. The *Express* applauded Leo's 'chilly visuals', while *The Observer* called it an 'artful, if seedy, tragedy' in which Captain Samson, cuckolded by his wife as he flies around the world, takes revenge not on her and the swinging London scene that rejects him but the passengers on the airliner that he crashes into the Channel.

'Pretty decent dream sequence you might like,' I said.

'All they're talking about is the Breda Boys crap. All over again. I was trying to transcend all that.'

'Transcend?'

'Piss off. Are you really that jealous that you have to undermine me? Is that what it's come to?'

'What it's come to is that you're paranoid. You should cut that out.'

He had poured another, which hovered at his mouth. He held my gaze as he downed it. 'Do me a favour.' He was now pointing. A vague sway. 'Tell me the next time you're working on your hobby.'

'You're dressed like Roger Daltrey and making Dirk Bogarde movies. You should work for me.'

'What, you reckon you're cutting edge now?'

'Sharper than you.'

Duke strode out of the kitchen. I waited hopefully for the slam of the front door which didn't come. I knew how this worked. He wouldn't come and find me. I could leave for an hour or a week or a year and he'd stay right here, waiting for me to go to him to be granted my apology.

I found him in the living room, sprawled on the couch. I thought he was asleep. Then his eyes opened. A gentle gaze, as if he had left from one place and returned from somewhere altogether different. It was remarkable, the pendulum shift of his emotions, that astonishing ability to forget.

'I'm sorry, Johnny.'

'Don't worry about it.'

'Do you remember, all those shitty ferries, up and down the west coast? We'd have pissed ourselves laughing if anyone said we'd end up making films. What the hell am I complaining about?'

'Sure, Duke.'

'I mean it's all just fallen into place. Folk dream about all of this. Couldn't be better.' He was looking at me but somehow through me, with a smile I could have reached out and peeled off. 'I can't do it.'

'What?'

He suddenly jumped up, arms wide. 'I thought I could, but I can't.' His bewilderment seemed absolute.

'What are you talking about?'

'I was getting better, you know. I haven't had a drink for a month.'

'Just tell me what—'

'Can you be there for her? Can you tell her I'll do my best? Do that for me, I'm so sorry.'

With that, I knew Anna was pregnant.

I stood on the steps in the rain, watching the Jaguar purr up the street. Then I was just watching an empty street. I suddenly understood how incredibly easy it was to drift along in a state of stupefied detachment from everything going on around you. While some might find a mindless bliss in this, my less than enlightened reaction when I got back inside was to punch a hole in the kitchen wall.

Eleven

I stand naked in front of mirrors now and then.

Other old men must do this. But how do you bring it up to check, and would they admit it?

It would be more noble to claim it as an existential reflex. To remind myself that I still exist. That I am not yet a ghost. In truth, I'm wallowing, in the comparison of the doddering now to every then.

Somewhere in this pale wattled throat is the spectre of a once-elegant neck. *You have an elegant neck*, someone once told me, whom matters not. It could even have been myself, staring in a mirror at some other time, comparing my body of then to another, even more youthful one, a person now so improbably distant he was likely someone else entirely.

We are so many people in a life, and now a new addition.

The *Shinigami*.

After the last email I read, I asked Akira to track down the rest of them. Maybe there is some kind of threat here. I should be pleased. I have met people so ego-haunted they would feel insulted not to have a maniac come-a-stalking. Why not me? I have inspired feelings of repulsion in direct proportion to the savagery of my asset-stripping and made films so reactionary and so right-on that gun-toting apocalyptas and smoked-out hippies must be equally infuriated.

I should stand my stalker beside me as I look in the mirror, take him through all these reflections on reflections. I will tell him it is only recently I have been defined by these spindly legs and pigeon chest, bones all sticking out as if my skeleton is determined to get a head start on death.

At least there is something authoritative about crumbling, late-period JJ, it being the sum total of my physical evolution. Emotionally, I remain feeble. I was once a voracious reader of my own press, gratified by generosity and overly aggrieved by every hatchet job. These days I assume that everyone I meet is a Nazi – not your fascist-lite Colonel Blimps but full-throttle, wet-lipped Gestapo-types. This way I will always be pleasantly surprised, at least sometimes.

I pad across to the panoramic window. The snow is lightly falling once more, the room, perhaps the whole world, unnervingly silent. I press my body against the surprisingly warm glass and stare beyond the slowly whitening grounds to the cliff-edge, the sluggish sea beyond. Movement draws my eyes to a figure below me. Someone in a bulky red jacket. He strides towards the sea with such purpose I expect him to start running, to leap, legs cycling, over the cliff . . .

I want him to look up, to see the naked old man pressed against the glass like a figure out of Bosch.

It would hardly be fair.

I peel myself from the window and go back to the bathroom to pull on a white dressing gown so all-consuming it might have been designed for a polar bear. Maybe it once *was* a polar bear.

Then a knocking at the main door. Erin. She tries to appear indignant but only succeeds in looking as if she's smelled a particularly bad fart. She's come to escort me to breakfast with her and Frank Stone. Over her shoulder Akira appears around the corner of the corridor. He sees us and immediately stops. He has a black folder in his hand. 'Just give me a minute and I'll come down.'

'I'll wait.'

She pushes quickly past me before I have a chance to answer. I look at Akira who turns and walks away.

'I'm not going to disappear,' I say, as I follow her through to the lounge.

She stops at the big window, hands on hips. 'I'm not saying you will.'

I salute as I turn away.

'You do know I can see your reflection,' she says.

As I dress, I can hear Erin on her mobile phone, staccato sentences like verbal hieroglyphics. She frowns when she sees I am carrying the portfolio bag containing the storyboard. We head down to The Ghillie's Bar. Only once, between calls as the discreet wooden door to the private bar is opened for us, does she address me. A quick compliment on my charcoal-grey Armani suit.

As soon as I step into the bar, Lewis appears. He is becoming more comfortable in my presence, the face salmon-pink as opposed to puce. I ask for coffee and wander across to the window.

The snow still falls. I realise that the figure in the red jacket trudging back and fore across the white wilderness is Frank Stone. He's holding a sheaf of papers in his left hand and seems to be talking to himself, his right hand flailing. Now and then he stops and scribbles something.

'His way of working, apparently.'

I almost drop my coffee. 'Christ's sake, Erin. How long have you been standing there?'

'I read it in an interview. *The flow only comes when I'm moving,* something like that. Seems to work for him.'

'The flow being the script.'

159

'Mm-hm.'

'You told me you were using mine.'

Erin lets her eyes meet mine and keeps them there. 'A few little tweaks, Uncle Jay, you have to expect that.'

As I must expect Stone. He opens the door with a shaking of snow from his all-consuming puffer jacket. If he fell over he'd struggle to get up. Stone knows how to make a better entrance than that.

'Whoo-hoo,' he shouts. 'Cold as a witch's titties but it sure gets the creative juices flowing. Mr Jay!'

Mr Jay.

A greeting to convey both respect and familiarity. He has decided he knows me. Yet his expression conveys genuine delight. That California insistence, I've forgotten how tedious it is. He grins as he rushes over and grins some more as he crouches in front of the fire and warms his hands.

I glance at the bar with forlorn hope. Today, I have promised myself to wait until eleven, maybe ten.

'I have to say—' his expression changes utterly in that pause from aw shucks vacuity to papal seriousness '—that your script is just wonderful.'

'Which bits have you binned?'

He's startled, momentarily. Then breaks out a smile and wags a finger. 'It's that Scottish directness, isn't it?'

'Which bits? You were out there a while with the red pen.'

'I was. Reading. *Admiring*. Just making a coupla . . . snips.'

'The flow only comes when you're moving, eh?'

'Yes.' His face clouds. 'That's right.'

Because whatever you do, don't mess with the mantra. 'My best bits come to me when I'm having a crap.'

Again, he seems momentarily startled then starts laughing. Once more that cartoon yuk-yuk-yuk. 'You're something else, Mr Jay, something else. Isn't he, Erin?'

160

My niece's wariness becomes weariness. 'And just what that something is,' she says, 'who knows?'

'Oh! I just remembered,' says Stone. 'Have you seen this?' He waves his hand in the air and before it's by his side again an immaculate, red-headed PA has materialised with a tablet computer. 'The Hollywood Reporter has voted *A Man's a Man* number sixteen on the greatest films of all time. And your book! Number eight in the UK charts. A star is born all over again!'

'It's like fashion,' says Erin. 'Flares and big collars. Hang around long enough and back round they come.'

I smile at her. Frank smiles at both of us. Then Erin too breaks out a frosty one and now we're all smiling.

'Free publicity for *The Bruce*. I'll take it! And don't *you* have some big days ahead.' Stone's tone has shifted. Maybe this is how he speaks to all his friends. An odd wheedling that emphasises random words, as if speaking to an idiot. 'The *book* signing and the awards *ceremony*. Your *recognition*.'

'Here today, gong tomorrow,' I say.

Stone slaps his thigh, laughs and then looks suddenly wistful. 'You remind me of my father, you know.'

'No, I remind you of old people. Here's something else for you to admire.' He grabs the portfolio bag that I thrust at him. 'My storyboard.'

As I walk away I hear the bag being unzipped then Stone shouting after. 'This is something else, something else, Mr Jay.' Something else to ignore.

There was no need for that breakfast. No need for me to be there at all. Just lip service being paid to my role.

Executive producer. A grand title for an empty role.

My value is to the marketing rather than the creative process. Yet PR must also have a storyline and the essence of mine is nostalgia, the forgotten star making his final film. Get the oldies to the box office, the curious

161

who have sometimes wondered what happened to him? My continued presence in this hotel is proof of my acceptance of the role. As the stylish stencilling of the mirror now hanging on the wall of my suite so eloquently shows, Nostalgia is ever-attractive to me.

Treacherous too, today's jewel tomorrow's landmine. We remember, we remember but do we really?

I open the folder Akira has left and read the ten or so emails to The *Shinigami*. When I finish there is zero chance of making 11am without a drink. I take a bottle from the cabinet and settle back in the low chair by the window. I re-read the emails and the various extracts about *Shinigami* that Akira has also printed out from online dictionaries of religion and mythology.

I discover I am a reaper, essentially, a parasitic being who extends his own life through the deaths of others.

See me hover . . .

There, in the snow beyond the window. Not as many fangs as in that black-and-white illustration. More gummy; a decrepit, soup-sooking *Shinigami*. I search the whiteness for *hinoki* greens, trancing images coming almost too quickly, flooding across me with a deep sense of yearning.

Beyond the glass, I picture Shuzenji, the room called Yamabuki. There is a low, black lacquered table and *tatami* floors, *shōji* screens left and right and sliding doors to the outside deck directly ahead. It is dusk. Anna and I sit side by side, a granite bowl between us filled with floating tea-light candles. I feel such an exquisite sadness. To hold her hand would do nothing to close the distance that has grown little by little each day we have been here, the perfect location, it seems, for her to study what she so rarely speaks of. She is looking across the pond to the Shinto temple on the tiny island where she spends so much time. I will find out why, eventually.

I top up my glass. Again, I wonder about this stranger sending the emails, who knows so much.

* * *

Tonight the book signing, a couple of days from now the civic ceremony. 'Tis the greasy spoon to The Ritz. The Buckfast to the Burgundy. The bacon roll to the . . . You get the message, Duke. A populist slumming of it.

The worthies whose bums will benumb in the Town Hall seats will not queue for me this evening, my Testament in their greedy hands. Too busy at home, half-naked with hanging bellies, searching closets for suits and frocks that they desperately hope still fit, accessories to set it off just so.

You loved all this.

I see your jitteriness as we wait at St Stephen's Garden for the car to take us to Leicester Square. Antsy, an ever-filling glass. Not that you were nervous. Not you, Dukey boy, your edginess simply impatience for the flashbulbs and the shouts as you glided your way up the red carpet, beautiful Anna at your side who you haven't complimented, who you have barely noticed . . .

I knot my tie in the window. I should be able to see Erin in the reflection yet my vision is filled with you, Duke. Her voice is close, almost directly behind, shifting in and out of my awareness. 'A sell-out . . . a hundred and fifty . . . they've cleared a whole floor for you . . .' You were born to all of this, Duke, a facsimile of the old man's ambition. 'It's heart-warming . . . all that affection . . .'

Yet don't be jealous. I will not wink as I raise my glass. It would be crass in the extreme to offer even the tiniest reminder that this could have been your night, your book waiting to be signed by all those people, who will whisper, 'He's looking old . . . I never knew he was so small . . .'

'Jay. Jay!'

I turn from the window, Duke's face instantly replaced by Erin's. And Frank Stone, somehow materialised. Akira is still on the chair beside the bed. He gives a reassuring, near-imperceptible nod.

'Frank's come to say good luck,' says Erin.

Stone, perplexingly, is dressed head to toe in tweed. The Scottish laird as delivered by central casting.

'You're not coming then.'

The laird steps forward. Looks serious. 'This is your night. I don't want to, you know . . . steal your thunder.'

'Very kind.'

'It's *your* night.'

'But you're coming to the civic ceremony, my award.'

'Of course!'

I wait in vain for the explanation as to why thunder is more likely to be stolen at a bookshop than a town hall. Instead, he shakes my hand and then – as if he's decided to go for it – gives me a hug.

'Five minutes. I'll come and get you,' says Erin. 'Go easy on that.' She points at my glass and follows Stone.

I pour another. I sit down at the coffee table and open Akira's folder. I re-read my stalker's email about Simon Warner, the hints of what he revealed before he died. Simon was ages with me, the son of our neighbour, Old Donny. A funny-looking kid, the nickname Simple Simon was inevitable. I can't picture Simon, but remember his cottage a few hundred yards along the road, as neat as ours was scruffy. Simon had a thing for birdwatching. Always out with the binoculars.

I didn't see him that day. Yet he was there, Duke. The email says there was a sea eagle above our cottage and Simple Simon was watching it from the top field. That's when he saw you go into the byre.

Then me.

164

Immediately after. That's what always troubled Simon, apparently. I had no idea that I'd been seen.

'Don't worry, Johnny.' Akira puts a hand on my shoulder. 'He is just a crazy person. He probably doesn't even know himself what he's talking about.'

I reach my hand up and put it on top of Akira's. The other brings the glass to my lips. Then, as I look out the window, beyond the reflections, some words I have read echo with those I have recently heard. I shuffle back through the sheaf of emails until I find what I'm looking for.

I'm making a documentary. Lewis said exactly the same words to me in The Ghillie's Bar.

Now, Duke, I may have been gone from Inveran for a long, long time, but I'm fairly certain the town hasn't become a hotbed of *cinéma vérité* in my absence. Even I can join the dots on this one.

* * *

Unseasonal or otherwise, around here the snow never hangs around for long. It was a source of such disappointment for young JJ, waking expectantly to find that yesterday's fall had all but disappeared. Here on the coast it's never cold enough or hot enough, but perfect for the rain that so swiftly returns white winter or summer blue to the usual dejection of grey. It is one of the reasons I have lived so long in Japan, that land of defined and guaranteed seasons.

Again, I am sitting up front.

Akira taps his finger on the steering wheel and keeps a distance from the security car in front. Gentle Akira, who has always helped me keep my own distance. He is smiling, enjoying the music. Thelonious Monk is the consummate soundtrack to the drive. Dissonance of piano in black.

When I close my eyes I still see the headlights,

sweeping the verge, shrunken snow patches in rain.

'Almost here, Johnny.'

I open my eyes, the windscreen a TV with the channel suddenly switched. Dark countryside has become orange streetlights on wet pavements. We move slowly past a line of people, the multicolour of umbrellas. Only when Akira says, 'They're here for you, Johnny,' do I realise they are queuing for the signing, waiting patiently in the rain for the bookshop doors to open.

'Erin won't be happy.' I smile at a young woman in a red bobble hat, peering and waving enthusiastically as we pass. 'Too many people. Too many threats. Eeeny meeny miney mo, how is JJ going to go?'

Akira shakes his head. Takes a hand from the steering wheel and waves a finger. 'You should not be so faeces.'

'Faeces?'

'That is the word, yes?'

Now I understand. I start to laugh as the car comes to halt outside the shop. 'Facetious, Akira, *facetious.*'

Strangely, when they see me laughing, a few people standing beside the car also start to do so. I have a flash of the old man's funeral. Hundreds lining the streets. They could be the same people; sombre then, laughing now but still gawking, mobile phones bearing modern witness. I get out and shake a few outstretched hands as security hurries me gently but insistently inside.

I wonder with expectation rather than anxiety if Lewis will be in tonight's audience. I didn't see him as we left the hotel and have no idea what I might have said if I had. How would the crowd react, Duke, if they knew what he does? Would their let-down linger, like the sad rain, or would they shrug it off, for although we admire so deeply, we need the certainty of disappointment?

Tonight's MC is Lachlan Anderson; I am supposed to know who he is. He is tall and bald, with a whiff of

166

repressed entitlement. He says, 'Call me Lachie,' pumps my hand as if drawing water and invites me to sit on a low stage behind which is a pyramid display of my biography. I resist the temptation to pull one out from the bottom. Lachie offers me water and I ask for red wine, nodding at the drinks on the other side of the rows of chairs. He nods at an assistant who scurries away.

'I see you have a lackey, Lachie.'

He laughs but the eyes don't. He informs me he is the presenter of an arts programme called *Late Shift*.

'I don't watch TV.'

The nonchalance wavers a little. His gaze shifts to Erin, who has materialised at the table. She gives him his orders while I sip my wine and watch the chairs fill up with smiling strangers.

I have chosen two excerpts. My first recalls when I heard *A Man's a Man* had been nominated for an Oscar; the other is about a Mulholland party, when I found Dennis Hopper asleep beside the pool the next morning, naked, with his feet in the water. Beside him was a bread knife, a hacked-up watermelon and a pile of raw meat. Between readings, I take pre-arranged questions from Lachie about inspiration, how it feels to make a new film, who was my favourite actor to work with . . . Then the floor is opened up to other questions about inspiration, how it feels to make a new film . . .

Everything is everything until a young man in a Che Guevara T-shirt stands up and shouts, 'Bullshit!'

Two security guards move swiftly.

'What about all you've left out of the story?' he asks. I hear strangled words about the Cayman Islands and the minimum wage as security drag him away.

'Well, folks.' The audience eyes turn as one from Che to me, making me think of a thousand Breda Boys performances. 'I guess he won't be wanting a signed copy.'

The laughter is too loud, tension being released. My heartbeat slows to its usual ragged apathy.

Lachie wraps things up. I sign my scrawl on a few dozen books. Old women with a twinkle and young women with none, bashful movie geeks and decrepit creatures like me, determined to reminisce. They remember JJ and Duke, the first Breda Boys shows and the last, wandering off with their wistfulness as other expectant faces take their place; please sign it to Katie . . . to Gregor . . . to my greatest fan . . . to *Shinigami*, my stomach an instant lurch as I look up sharply.

It is not Lewis.

'Sue Shinnie?' repeats a middle-aged woman with an unsettlingly large perm. She's mortified. Thinks she's said something out of turn. Annoyed the big movie star. 'Just Sue, if you prefer, I don't—'

'Of course, no problem. To Sue.'

I sign the last book at nine, just in time, my patter running on fumes. I sense a growing disappointment. Never meet your heroes, that's the rule. Don't they know I have gone years barely speaking to anyone but Akira? He's by my side as I wave my farewells to the still-milling throng.

As we climb the stairs to the ground floor I hear a rising buzz of noise. At the top, across the store, bemused staff stare out the doors and windows. On the street outside, a line of skeletons peer in. They wear black trousers, black tops with stencilled white bones and grinning skull masks. They are chanting something I can't make out, rhythmically drumming on the glass.

'We leave. *Now*,' says Erin.

'A demonstration, Johnny.' Akira sounds so calm, his voice almost dreamy. 'About your business.'

'It hasn't been my business for a long time.'

'You think that matters?' says Erin.

'If I'm the ghoul, why are they dressed like them?'

'You really need to ask?'

'Yes.'

'Oh, for crying out loud.'

Security hustles me between book stacks, *Religion and Self-help*. It makes such perfect sense I have to smile. We hurry through a staff door and down a flight of stairs to a loading bay that smells strongly of oil. Twenty-feet-high doors concertina open and we're in a narrow, dark street.

The three Mercedes have their engines running. There is a brief coldness of rain as I'm pushed into the middle car. Erin gets in beside me and the convoy takes off, coming to an abrupt halt almost immediately. A security guard hurries past with his arm out, shouting *back up, back up*.

'Problem?' says Erin.

We turn to look out the back window as Akira reverses at speed, following the car behind to the other end of the narrow street. Then another abrupt stop. Again, I hear the rhythmic chanting.

It's all a bit exciting.

Erin is repeating the word *intelligence* as the first of the figures dressed as skeletons appears.

It sticks out a tongue and starts to batter its hands on the roof. Others swarm around and join in, peering into the car, waxy deaths heads with dark circles round the eyes, black-and-white teeth painted on either side of the mouth. Here and there are hooded figures in porcelain-white, Guy Fawkes masks. The car starts to rock from side to side, Erin shouting into her mobile as Akira revs the car and we lurch backwards. There's something here, a memory I place in the face of a mask-less young woman standing still in all the movement, staring straight at me.

Instantly, I am in Guadalajara, 1974, the Day of the Dead festival, Mexico; somewhere else Anna and I searched for magic. Booze from dawn until dusk, dancing to Mariachi and further away from each other, the evening fireworks exploding with the same sadness in the young woman's eyes.

I watch her for as long as I can, until the car reaches Stevenson Street, passing under a banner saying *Low Pay, No Way.*

'A debacle. An utter debacle.' Yet there is enjoyment in Erin's eyes. She opens the drinks cabinet, pours two whiskies and says something I don't hear, my head full of firecrackers and the looming faces of moustachioed glitter-drunks in filthy bars, the coldness of Anna's hand and this drink that tastes like Mescal . . .

'Another?'

That I do hear.

'It's quite touching, I suppose,' she adds. 'That people still feel that they can make a difference.'

In the low light of the car her face has taken on a masklike quality of its own. She's grinning as well.

'Are you ok? You seemed—'

'Why were they dressed like that?'

She looks at me carefully. 'There really is no time in your world, is there? It's 31st October. *Halloween.*'

I look out the window. Stare at the half-lit tenements. Out there, up the heights in the full darkness is the cemetery. There you all lie. You've never needed to wait for Halloween to go a-wandering.

'A flash demo. Nothing we could have known in advance.'

'Well, it's something to talk about.'

'Just a pity that Frank Stone wasn't here. Think of the headlines. *Hollywood star caught in provincial riot.*' Her light-heartedness is uncharacteristic. She smiles. Even squeezes my arm.

'Don't underestimate the locals, Erin. I was born here. If they'd caught us they would've eaten us.'

'You spoke very well. They loved you.'

'Local boy done good.'

'Apart from Che Guevara.'

'You can please some of the Trots some of the time...'

'Oh, I picked something up, by the way, before all the excitement.' She produces a book from her inside coat pocket. 'Have you seen this before? It was in the local history section.'

Anna looks at me from the front cover. She's sitting at a typewriter, looking over her shoulder at the photographer, an enigmatic smile on her face. I've never seen this shot before. The book is called *The Breda Girl*, a short biography, published by a local historical society. 'I didn't know about this.'

'Look at the photos.'

There is such delight on Erin's face. Now I understand her mood. She flicks through photos I haven't seen for years and others I never have. Anna is smiling in all of them. She always smiled. I hope this is how Erin too remembers her mother, and feel a tremendous welling of shame. I reach out and touch her cheek, her surprise softening to affection as she grips my hand.

'I miss her,' she says.

'I know. I do too.'

'But you never talk about her.'

I again see her sadness. I understand, I always have, why serious little Erin surrounded herself with one obsession after another, those surrogates for an affection we always made such hard work.

'I was always waiting for you to talk to me about her. After she died I wanted you to keep her with us. But every time I mentioned her you'd change the subject. I don't understand, I never have.'

I sit back in the seat and close my eyes. When I open them again, she is reading the little biography.

Undoubtedly, she will find out more details, fleshing

171

out that life about which I have been such useless source. Yet it is as much as I can do to imagine Anna, the smoothness of her cheek, say, her hand in mine under the volcanoes of Mexico. To speak of her would be to feel her heartbeat, to hear a voice which, even as it whispered so close in my ear, was always so far away.

Erin puts the book down. 'I still don't understand why there was no warning about how sick she was. Dad too. There wasn't much explanation there either. I've never understood any of it.'

I stare at her in silence. Better to say nothing. Better to endure the hurt in her big, serious eyes so like her mother's. I wonder what the book says about us all, Duke? I wonder if Lewis has read it.

Twelve

November 1966, the gloomy block of flats that is Queen Charlotte's Hospital. I was there an hour before visiting time and wandered up and down Goldhawk Road in the rain, preparing all kinds of apologies, from the banal to the ridiculous.

I was the first one in. A nurse whose flinty gaze offered instant and unflattering judgement ushered me into the barracks-like ward, hurrying me between long rows of beds and staring women.

Anna was nursing a baby wrapped in a shawl. She looked up and smiled. There was no surprise in her eyes, even though we hadn't seen each other for over a year. I had a familiar, disquieting feeling that here was another situation that she had somehow foreseen and rehearsed.

'Her name is Erin.'

'Why didn't you tell me?'

Her smile was almost pitying, as if I had just asked the stupidest question in the world. 'Your brother finally decided to pay you a visit then?'

'If I'd have known before, I could have ... I'm so sorry I wasn't here for you.'

'There's no need to apologise, Johnny. I wasn't exactly seeking you out, was I? It was just all so awkward because of what ... ' Her smile. So delicately shy that it brought a lump to my throat.

'It's brilliant, you know. The baby. I'm so happy for

you both.' I even tried to believe it, just for a moment.

'How was he?'

'Not the best.'

'Was he now? Poor wee boy. All too much for Duke. She's three days old and he hasn't been to meet her.'

The smile remained. She didn't seem upset or resigned, this something else she had long seen coming.

* * *

Anna told me a dozen times I didn't need to but in the absence of Duke there was no choice. I'd spent three days trying to track him down. The friends I had phone numbers for either didn't know where he was or weren't saying. She could hardly deal with a newborn baby all by herself.

So I moved back in to St. Stephen's Garden.

The press scrum was waiting when we got out of the taxi with Erin. One question over and over again.

Where's Duke?

It wouldn't take them long to work it out. He was a man of habit. I wasn't going to be surprised by a call from Mustique. So it proved, Duke eventually phoning from a noisy pub that was obviously The Clachan. He was drunk, launching into a long, rambling story about how *my boys ran that Daily Mirror bugger out of town*, as if putting off the question he finally asked.

'Is it a boy or a girl?'

I put the phone down and pulled the cord from the wall. The next call came a few days later. Not my brother but Fat Jack McVeigh, telling me Duke had spent a night in the cells after breaking into The Empire. 'They huckled him onstage. He was going through your old routines, both parts . . . '

Anna, Erin and I took the train north. I left them at her mother's on the heights of Inveran and took a taxi to the

174

cottage. There was no sign of Duke but the sink was piled with unwashed crockery, a weariness of empty bottles on the table. I pictured the farce, my wild-eyed brother staggering from room to room as the wind howled, tipping the drink, babbling his case to empty space.

The image was way off the mark. I found him in The Inveran Empire later that day. He was sitting onstage, eyes closed, nodding to the music filling the theatre, I think it was Ellington's *Far East Suite*. He looked almost serene. The mod look had been replaced by a style more in keeping with a town that the sixties would bypass almost altogether: a tweed suit and brogues. On his head was a familiar, battered fedora, leaning against the chair a silver-topped cane.

'He just sits there for hours.'

Fat Jack and I were standing at the back of the auditorium.

'Every now an then he gets a notion in his heid an scribbles something down on a bitty paper.'

For the first time, I noticed the sheets scattered on the stage around Duke, barely visible in the dim light.

'He paid me. I felt embarrassed but . . . you know.'

'Eh? How much?'

'Two hundred quid.'

'Two hundred!'

Now Fat Jack did look embarrassed. 'I didn't ask for it, he just offered. Would you have said no?'

'Two hundred quid for what?'

'I dunno. Hire? He just sits and plays music. Says he's got something up his sleeve.'

'You're ripping him off. Can you not see he's not well?'

Fat Jack was suddenly angry. A finger in my chest. 'Don't you dare. He can be out of here quick as I let the daftie in. Who do you think smoothed it wi the polis when he bloody well broke in?'

175

I shoved his hand away and hurried down towards the stage.

'You're no in London now, pal,' shouted Jack. 'Didn't take long for you to forget about Jacky, eh, all ah did for you.'

I stopped on the other side of the orchestra pit. I watched Duke nod his head to the music and wondered what was on the sheets of paper. When the music ended he reached between his legs for a bottle of whisky I hadn't seen. He noticed me then, but not a hint of surprise.

'You're gonna love this, little bro.' Glittery eyes that made me uneasy. 'Come up here and have a drink.'

He told me all about it, the mother of all memorial concerts, the old man deserves it, right, a charity gig, see all the names I've got lined up, it'll be like a greatest hits thing, just can't get a running order straight, do you think we could get Basie, imagine that, imagine the old man's face ...

'Are they ok?' he suddenly asked.

'They're here, Duke.'

He swallowed. 'That's great. That's great. Thanks, JJ. Thanks for being there.'

'Her name's Erin.'

His eyes widened. 'I've got a daughter.' He looked away, into the dark of the stage.

'You coming to see them then?'

He looked back. 'Sure.' A smile, quick then gone. 'Maybe tomorrow, eh? Long journey for them.'

The next morning I drove Anna and Erin out to the cottage. As I turned up the drive I saw Duke at the top of the slope, smoking. He quickly tossed the cigarette and hurried away. When we got inside the cottage there was no sign of him. I found him in the byre, sitting quietly on the splitting log.

'You coming in then?'

'Give us a minute. Just doing some kindling ... It's right cold in there, the wean'll need some heat.'

He picked up the hatchet to start the small task that took half an hour to finish, eventually ambling into the kitchen with an armful of kindlers. He turned slowly from the hearth, brushing slivers of wood from his jumper. Only then did he look at Anna, sitting at the table with the baby.

'This is Erin, Duke. Do you want to hold her?'

He looked down at his hands. 'I'm a bit dirty. Maybe best not.'

'You're bloody right. Best not.'

Anna stood up quickly and knocked over the chair. Erin began to cry and Duke took a step forward, saying something lost in the slam of the door. In silence, I drove Anna and Erin back to Inveran.

Duke disintegrated quickly. I thought of a car crash in slow motion, where you think you'll have time to intervene before impact. Somewhere in those immutable red eyes I glimpsed, now and then, hints of someone remembered, ever more distant staging points on the way to a stranger.

I found him hangover-free one morning, full of contrite determination to sort it out, right now, 'I'm gonna be a husband and father!' A flustered Anna called me later to say that Duke had appeared at her mother's and started packing her bags, then tried to drag her out of the house to catch a train. I got another call the same afternoon, from the golf course. I might want to come and get my brother, who had spent two hours hitting dozens of balls from the first tee.

At other times, there was a fragile stillness to him. Sat in the front row of The Empire, scribbling in a notebook that he never let me see. He was still able to work the magic, that smile so charming it could transmit down a telephone line, a wink for me and an angsty *this means so much* as he persuaded the producer of his new film, *The Sandwich Girl*, to put the schedule back.

He tried his best to fill out the bill for *Smile, the Billy Jackson Memorial Concert*. But less luck here for The Duke. Word spread fast in Variety Land, Fat Jack with the telephone whispers. Most of the Scottish acts found other commitments while none of the English ones were willing to make the journey north.

There were whispers too in Inveran. Every day I drove from the cottage to town, up the heights to Anna's house, her mother a frail and absent presence in an easy chair she never left.

We'd take long walks with the pram, up towards the moor and down into town, along the promenade, a stop at Jameson's tea rooms to the coos of the old biddies and the undoubtedly raised eyebrows after we left. Even the seagulls knew about Duke's strange residency at The Empire.

'Poor man's losing his mind and his brother's swanning around playing daddy.'

This I overheard in the Queens Hotel. I'd gone in for lunch and was hidden away in one of the booths when Fat Jack came blustering in, indulging his habit of half a lifetime, *a hauf an a hauf* and the lunchtime special, holding court with the usual collection of bulbous-nosed cronies.

'Think he thinks he's Alfred Hitchcock. Sat there with his grand schemes. Tell ye, it's pretty pathetic.'

'Why'd you let him then?'

'Hey, Jack's no mug. Took him for two hunner!'

'Two hunner!'

'It's rent! What's a man to do? He's no short of a bawbee anyways. Makes a mint in those films.'

'Aye, amazing what they'll pay for a pile of shite.'

'Never mind Duke, you seen the films JJ's been making?'

'What the fuck's all that about?'

'Least there's no a monkey in them.'

'That's no way to talk about JJ!'

'Na, he's moved on from monkeys. He's more the wee dug these days, sniffing around yon Anna.'

'His brother's wife. Man, ahd be beelin. What's Duke got to say?'

'Duke? You could shag his missus in front of him an he widnae notice.'

'Poor man's losing his mind and his brother's swanning around playing daddy.'

'Maybe he *is* daddy.'

I listened for a while longer then stepped out of the booth. Four pairs of eyes turned to me with a shifty mix of embarrassment and amusement. I walked to the bar and slapped down a pound note.

'I reckon it's my round, eh?'

I left the Queens in a fury. It was a time for absolutes, I decided, fuck this ridiculous, neither-nor existence. I hurried to Anna's. We had to get out of this place, start again, just the three of us, somewhere no-one gawked as if we were the matinee down at The Ritz. I was certain she would agree, a confidence that came crashing down like midwinter surf when I turned into Sandford Street. In the distance, she was holding hands with Duke as they pushed Erin's pram.

It was a few days before Christmas 1966. I had been back in Inveran for a matter of weeks that suddenly felt like years.

At The Clachan, sometime later, drunk for only the second time in my life, I made another decision. I left immediately, walking in driving sleet to the promenade.

I was sober, sure I was, just the wind making me bob and weave like the red and green festive lights strung between the lamp-posts, tinkling with every gust, an enchantment leading me to the car, Hansel in the grimmest of fairy tales.

I made it back home, nose to windscreen all along the single-track road, rising waves on the Sound throwing spray across the windscreen. Twice I slammed on the brakes, skidding once on the slick road and just stopping before the ditch, the headlights illuminating a sheep in the rain, staring with such optimism that I leaned on the horn until it clambered to its feet and trotted off.

With the wind, Duke didn't hear the car drive into the yard. I stood at the kitchen window and watched him. He was sitting at the table, on the phone, firelight playing on his smiling face. I pictured Anna in her mother's front room; a whisper and her own smile, tolerant. He put down the phone and blew out his cheeks, the man who knew how close he had come.

As soon as he heard the kitchen door open, he sprung to his feet and rushed over. 'I'm sorry, JJ.'

I just shrugged.

'For everything. No little bro anymore. *I'm* the little bro. You're the big brother. You've been there for her.'

'Sure, Duke.'

He looked sheepish. Then a careful smile. 'I saw them today. I met my daughter. Properly *met her*. Just woke up this morning and knew I had to. The pressure had gone, you know? I'm sorry. I just panicked.'

'You ran away.'

He winced. 'Yeah. Ran away. Not any more. That's gone. All gone. We're heading back to London on Thursday.'

'What?'

'Start again.' He grabbed my shoulders. Ever the glittery eyes. 'The world forgives. I'm proof and I'm gonna say it.' He let go of my shoulders and rushed to the door. 'I'm gonna bloody shout it!'

He did. He stripped to his pants and stood in the yard, half-lit by the spilling kitchen light, the rain exploding in the mud as he shouted his apologies into the storm, over and over again. He looked almost exultant when he came back inside, face flushed and a self-righteous grin.

I told him I had slept with Anna.

'Eh?'

'Up at the waterfall. Right cold, but we didn't notice it.' Then I went up to my bedroom.

He appeared a few moments later. 'The fuck are you talking about? Is that supposed to be some kind of joke?'

'Phone her.'

'You've got problems, tell you.'

'Phone her!'

'Piss off.' He slammed the door.

For a long time, there was only rain, and then sleep. I was wakened by shouting downstairs and the slam of another door. When I woke again a pale, hesitant light was creeping into the room. The previous night seemed so distant and improbable, a story I had once been told.

I couldn't find him. No sign he'd slept in his bed. In the kitchen, last night's bottle was empty. The rain was still falling, squally bursts against the kitchen window. I stood at the sink, sipping a glass of water and looking out, the muddy yard and the hillside only blurred impressions. I must have been staring at the shape on the hill path for a long time before I realised it was moving.

I only recognised it as Duke when he reached the gate at the top of the yard. His Hefner-esque, maroon bathrobe was tied loosely at the waist and flapped in the wind, revealing those ubiquitous pinstripe pyjamas, the designer named Cardin I was supposed to know.

I was sick in the sink then. As I hunched over, spitting and retching, I waited for the back door to open.

When he didn't appear, I went outside. I found him in the byre.

In the dull light, my first thought was confusion, how his pinstriped body could hover in space with no apparent means of suspension. Then I saw the cord from the bathrobe tied around a roof beam. His chin was pressed chin down to the chest, arms hanging limp and his tightly bunched fists an appalling white in the darkness, as if the bones were about to burst through. One foot was bare, the green Wellington boot lying on the ground beside an overturned chair.

Those observations have always troubled me, less their essential horror than the passage of time that my noticing them represented. A second, was it even as much as that, a second's delay between seeing and doing that might have made a difference, one, two beats more to stop looking and start running, grabbing Duke by the thighs and lifting, taking his weight, releasing the pressure on his neck, cursing his ballooning weight and shouting up into the popping eyes peering down at me, Duke, c'mon Duke, over and over and what to do next as I held his thighs and turned, turned, his body like a marionette, looking around and remembering the tool shelves on the wall by the window, shouting an apology as I gently let go of his legs and rushed over, finding an old Stanley knife and apologising again as I stood up the chair and sliced the cord from the roof beam, Duke landing so unnaturally that I knew it was too late.

I removed the cord from his neck with some trouble. I sat on the chair and stared at him. I cursed him before I let myself cry then knelt beside him and stroked his stupid, stupid head. Minutes passed. I think I was waiting to see if he moved. I tried to prise his fingers out of their awful white fists and gave up, looking up at the wooden beam and the cord I had cut. I remembered a morning in another lifetime, a monkey sitting up there, grinning, I was sure it was grinning.

* * *

I called the ambulance some time later. By then I had found a script called *A Man's a Man* in his room. A set of storyboard pictures too, in a portfolio bag stencilled at the clasp with 'DJ' in gold letters. I remembered him sitting in the front row of The Empire, slipping sheets of paper out of sight.

* * *

We walk with our past. Or maybe it walks with us, I don't know. There are times the boundary between now and then seems gossamer-thin, as if the after-trails of the most vivid dream has extended into the waking day. You have the most powerful certainty that all those people are going to come through the door, one by one, gently admonishing you for thinking they had gone at all.

I saw them all, in the days that followed, my father sitting across the table, the catch of firelight on amber as he poured the whisky. My mother, quiet in the rocker with the darning needle and the disapproving glances. My grandparents, as silent as the land they had worked for decades, still coming and going to the rhythm that had perplexed me as a young child and still did.

And Duke. Capering on the shore as the dusk fell. Up in the top pasture, a Spitfire with arms outstretched. Such an achingly innocent presence, unsettling me, who I tried and failed to ignore.

In contrast, Anna wore her grief peacefully.

A dignified thank you for those who came to the cottage in a steady stream. Few stayed long, as if afraid the presence of death might somehow taint them. Soon enough it would be their turn to take the handshakes and offer the whisky, or even sit up with the body, a tradition that seemed less a mark of respect than notice being served that one day it would be you. Anna had passed on that particular trauma and had Duke taken to Fettercairn and Son's in Inveran.

I watched her, the working up to strength with each knock on the door, the slow sink of her shoulders when they left, up and down, like a summer swell on the Sound. I was a near-mute presence by contrast, a cata-tonic con man determined to deceive myself: nothing I could have done . . .

'Are you sure you're ok?' Anna asked, a dozen times a day, troubled on my behalf for the trauma of having found him. Concerned that I had barely talked about it, a hand on my cheek.

My remorse pushed her away. I could barely look at her, a distancing she put down – I saw it in her sympathetic smile – to my grief. In the end I told her, viciously, to leave me alone and stop blaming me for what happened. She'd suggested nothing of the sort but I didn't understand why she wouldn't admit that Duke had told her he knew about us. I thought she was punishing me.

She went back to her mother's. With Anna gone, the mourners stopped coming. I sat alone with the ghosts. Three days later, old Fettercairn knocked on the door to take me to the funeral. A pale, pinched face and ice-blue eyes, a suitably eerie presence for the Reaper's lieu-tenant. There was the coffin in the back of the hearse, 'Duke' spelled out in a corny floral arrangement.

Anna's choice. The sentimentality surprised me, and

it was there again, after the service. The mourners had left for the wake in The Clachan. She was standing alone by the wall that marked the seawards extremity of the cemetery, staring up at dozens of gulls soaring in flawless blue.

'I've always wanted to fly. Imagine I woke up and they had grown overnight, my wings. Where would I fly to?'

She turned with such exquisite puzzlement but didn't seem, somehow, to actually register my presence. It was all she said to me that day, if it was even me she had been talking to. Those birds. I would see so many more, watching her watching them as she waited to soar up, up and away.

Her avoidance of me at the wake was also oddly passive, making it altogether more distancing, amplifying my coldness to the point of absurdity. Days passed and my guilt began to verge on panic. I was terrified to talk to her but phoned once, immediately hanging up. Instead I waited, pathetically, for her to come and offer forgiveness in return for an apology I hadn't offered.

Had she done so, I would have struggled to explain the script and storyboard scattered across the kitchen table and floor. I'm sure she would have recognised Duke's handwriting straightaway.

A Man's a Man.

I was astounded my brother had crafted something so delicately complex and beautiful. His grin of one-upmanship followed me to the bottom of every bottle. He'd written the script out longhand, and when I finally decided what I was going to do, it took me two weeks to type it up and re-draw the storyboard in my own hand. After I had finished I burned the originals.

Then I called Leonid. 'I've written a film. It's based on the life of Robert Burns.'

'You kept that quiet.'

I spent two more days typing up a copy and when Leo eventually got back to me it was by telegram.

Where have you been hiding this stop made some enquiries Warners maybe interested stop what is the problem with your telephone stop.

The problem was it was lying in the yard where I had hurled it, furious with the way it never rang. If still connected there would likely have been warning of the man who had materialised when I came out of the byre one morning, a hatchet in my hand from chopping kindling.

'Mr Jackson. *There* you are.'

His features, somehow squeezed into too small an area of his face, were crinkled in exasperation. I considered hurling the axe at him, Tonto-like, a slow-motion end over end, a comic *dooiing* as it quivered in the centre of his forehead. This was Don Heelpen, though I didn't yet know it, award-winning interviewer for *The Observer*. The article would be called *The Accidental Recluse*.

Not a bad title that.

Johnny Jackson stands in front of his cottage and tells me about the weather. He gestures seawards and says, 'It's out there, under the waves', the ship that gave him and his troubled brother the famous name, The Breda Boys. Behind him is the barn where he found Duke. Three months on, Johnny's taking his time.

Don stayed two days.

There was something compellingly sympathetic about his squashed appearance and odd mix of hipster speak and clipped Oxbridge. My ego too was keen that he stayed. Not only did Don like my films – *I truly do dig them, dear boy* – I was also pleased by how my exile had become a minor *cause célèbre* if only, I wasn't that vain, as a curious epilogue to the tragedy of my brother.

Johnny doesn't go into town. He says he is 'all out of platitudes'. He can spend hours with such distance you wonder if he is there at all. Yet mention film and he'll talk all night. I have been instructed in the art of lighting at 3am, watched a framing masterclass demonstrated by two raised hands, thumbs and forefingers making a square, like a camera lens . . .

When a copy of the interview arrived later I recalled only vague outlines of those scenes. I didn't recognise this Johnny Jackson at all. I'd never been so interesting. The persona Don created followed me around for years, less a memory of the word than the image, I think. Those accompanying black-and-white photos appeared in more and more publications, especially after the success of *A Man's a Man*: a shot from behind as I stare, wild-haired, at Ben Chorain; an expectant look over my shoulder from my chair in the empty living room; a full-face close-up, I'm frowning, a tumbler of whisky at my lips . . . In most I wear an old Aran jumper. Don Heelpen, he made me seem damaged, and people are always attracted to someone else's damage.

He dragged me up the mountain behind his cottage to watch the sun rise. 'A man's a man', he yelled to the breaking light, thrusting a hip flask my way. 'To toast what's gone and all it keeps giving' . . .

The day I read the interview I took a long walk to Esha Bay. I had a bottle I thought I should have rather than wanted. I drank it. I lay back on the wet sand and watched the scud of clouds that each took on the shape of Duke, a whole column of him marching across the sky, oblivious in the crash of the surf to my shouted apologies and my anger, such anger. I thought about Don's image of me and about my brother, the life spent in the skin of someone he'd been told he was. I realised that I had no remaining tethers. I had become the dust of an old byre.

That same afternoon, I retrieved the phone from the yard and plugged it in, calling Leonid to say I'd be back in London in a few days. Then I decided to burn down the byre. I had siphoned a few litres of petrol from the old Morris and was about to start dousing the inside of the barn when I realised that any exorcism would need so much more than a ceremonial torching.

When I got back to the cottage, Anna was sitting at the table, Erin on her lap. I smelled petrol and perfume.

'You're the talk of the town. You know what they call you?'

'I can't say I do.'

'The Hermit.'

'You surprise me.'

'Someone came up to me and said I don't need to worry with a man like that to look out for me.'

I blushed. She's got the strength of the sea. I'll shelter her when she wants me to and let her be when she's had enough. This, at least, needed no embellishment. I remember how Don raised a glass . . .

I sat down opposite her. I watched Erin look at me then back up to her mum.

'How are you doing?' Anna said.

'I'm doing ok. You?'

'I tried to phone you. But I couldn't. I don't know why I pushed you away like that.'

'I get it.'

'I'm sorry.' I waited for more. For her to acknowledge that Duke had told her he knew about us.

'I know. It was such an awful shock. Who knows how anyone is going to react. We lash out, we hurt each other.'

I saw now that she was slightly drunk. A glittering in

188

her eyes. She'd driven over like that, with the little one.

'I feel so guilty, Anna.'

'There's nothing you could have done.'

I slept with Anna. I heard the words and closed my eyes, briefly, but enough to see myself enter the byre. Those short seconds between thought and action.

'There's so much I could have done.'

'You know what, just don't!'

She seemed furious. I said nothing. I had no idea if my silence would antagonise her even more.

'Don't be a bloody *victim*. I'm not having it so why the hell should you? I'm not going to push this pram back and forward in Inveran forever. I don't want men assessing my heartbreak, old biddies and their kindness.'

'They're just being kind.'

'Don't give me that. You don't have a clue. Holed up in the middle of nowhere like some eccentric. Get yourself to town for ten minutes and see if you think the same. See how they look at you.'

The fierceness held for a few moments longer before fading. 'Why are you even here?'

'I live here.'

'Really.'

'You know why.'

'No, no I don't.'

'You. I'm here because of you.'

In the silence that followed I poured us another drink. I watched little Erin, so emptily staring.

'Well, here I am,' she finally said, a tired affection in her eyes. 'Guess we might as well elope.'

She was joking, of course, but I couldn't help the lurch in my stomach. 'What would the old biddies say to that?'

She giggled but her face immediately clouded. 'I'm glad he didn't know about us. I think. What about you?

Part of me wonders if it might have helped. Christ's sake, who knows. I don't know.'

My stomach turned for an altogether different reason. I felt instantly sick. I remembered the evening I told Duke about Anna and I, the shouting from downstairs which I assumed was Duke on the telephone, confronting her with what we had done. Yet he hadn't said a word.

Thirteen

'Mr *Jackson*, you're so . . . *ruthless*.'

'Tis a blue sunny morning after the Night of the Skull People. Frank Stone and I are sitting in the back of the Mercedes. He leans away from me slightly. I think he's going for shocked respect.

'I wish I'd gone now . . . *A Man's a Man*, sure. But not if you're working for him, huh, am I wrong? How much *are* you paying your people? I saw the TV, those were some seriously pissed hombres.'

Stuck in the Mercedes with him, the presence of Stone is almost hypnotising. I drag my eyes away from the vampire fingers clutching the air as he speaks, the odd pouting ventriloquist mouth.

'They're not my people.'

'Me thinks you doth protest too much.'

'It's not a protest.'

'No. Last night. *That* was a protest.'

'It wasn't really much of a protest.'

'There you go, protesting again!'

'I mean, there weren't that many people.'

'Didn't they start banging on the top of the car? Wow! Maybe they wanted to lift it up and carry you away like—'

'Cannibals?' I suggest.

'What?'

'Zombies?'

'*Vikings*. There were Vikings round here, right? They

were gonna carry you off like Vikings. Burn you on the beach.'

'Vikings.'

'Vikings.'

'Dancing round the flames?'

Stone grins. Teeth like neat rows of headstones. 'Yes. That is *exactly* what I imagined.' The smile vanishes and he leans forward, mock-serious. 'Seriously though, what are you paying those people?'

So we return to the start of the loop.

'I'm just messing with you.' I feel a hard squeeze on my arm and open my eyes to an apologetic smile. 'It's a long time you've been incommunicado. I get it. But you need to enjoy yourself. Go with it!'

'Oh, for fuck's sake.'

Stone and I look up at Erin.

I think we've both forgotten she's in the car, sitting up front with Akira. Overnight, any guilty enjoyment about the bookshop demonstration has vanished. She's caught up with the media coverage.

She holds up her mobile to show us another headline. *'Fear and Loathing for Breda Inc.'* Then an exaggerated shrug and grin. 'What do you think, boys, are we fearful or all fucked up?'

'Ha!' Stone slaps his thigh and wags his finger. 'Now that. *That* sounds like someone enjoying herself.'

'Least we've got Renner flying in,' she says.

Brad Renner is the reason we're in this Mercedes at 8am and heading for McIntyre's Cave. The A-lister is in the air. Due at nine to visit crew and set. Then back to the Castle to work the press, pour stardust on last night's debacle. 'We'll retake the narrative,' she says.

Just in time for tomorrow's civic extravaganza, the re-awarding of the Freedom of Inveran to the *Shinigami*. I'm becoming quite fond of my title. Akira showed me the latest email this morning. *I was at the bookshop. I saw*

you through the window of the car but you never saw me . . .
Or some such.

Erin has not mentioned it. She continues to protect me from an anxiety I don't feel. I almost find myself telling her that I know who the emailer is. I still haven't seen Lewis since I found out.

The leading security car barely slows as it veers into the car park for McIntyre's Cave, the security barrier lifted at the last second. Press and TV scatter as Akira sweeps in, the car following coming to a horizontal halt behind us, protecting us from the shouting throng on the other side.

'Let's do it,' says Stone, cheerily.

We get out. Erin and I ignore the shouted questions and head for the steps down to the cave. Stone goes over to the journalists. 'It's good to see so many of you here on . . . ' the rest of his words lost as we descend into the mile-wide, undulating rush of soft-breaking surf on MacIntyre's Bay. I remember these rare days of implausible peace, as if winter is catching its breath.

Stone re-joins us at the cave entrance. As we enter the chamber, I witness a crushing defeat for his sociopathic cheeriness. The set has been trashed. Two of the three lighting rigs hang at odd angles, several stanchions buckled. Only the rig above the entrance still functions, throwing out that strange, mustardy light. Most of the uplighters around the stalagmites have been smashed.

Erin wants to know why she wasn't told.

Frank wants to be alone. He ambles back and forward across the set then picks up his overturned director's chair. I leave him and go back outside to the beach. In the distance, the tide is coming in. I remember the warning when we were kids: *Be careful, it comes in faster than you can run.*

We tested it one day. Do you remember, Duke?

There were a few of us, walking boldly out to meet the onrushing water. We didn't get within thirty metres before someone bolted and then the rest of us.

I walk for some distance across the wet sand before the sharp stab in my left side requests I stop. The waves here can be immense, a violence that seems unbelievable in today's calmness, the surf low and lazy, the mercury water beyond almost flat. It looks so solid, as if I could walk on it, across to the isle of Erbay in the milky distance, Jesus in a long black coat, the onlookers on the beach lined up and staring. As indeed they are when I turn back to land.

They're looking not at me but a figure sitting on the sand. Frank Stone, I realise, as I come closer. I stop when I reach him. His eyes are closed and his hands clasped cross his lap. He is talking to himself in a low voice. *May there be peace in the north and the Great Spirit protect me . . .*

I move on.

I remember reading that Stone sleeps in an oxygen tent. He's likely booked the cryogenic freezer too.

'Another disaster,' Erin explains when I reach the shore. 'Renner's PA just called. He's not coming until his safety can be guaranteed. Asshole. The press will love this. Let's have nothing else, ok? Let's just . . . '

She gestures seawards with such helplessness. Instantly, I'm back at Wendlebury Manor, watching Erin playing by herself at the bottom of the long garden. Beside me on the patio Anna squeezes my arm, acknowledging our shared apprehension that this little girl will be forever alone.

'Let's go and visit her,' I hear myself say.

'What?'

'Your mother.'

'Really? You want to go *now*? For crying out loud.'

'What else is there to do?'

194

'Nice. Very nice. It's not something you do when there's nothing else to do. You go because you want to.'

That remains the problem. I watch her stride away then look back at Stone, who is still sitting on the beach.

* * *

I am bone-cold.

It is these incessant thoughts of graves. I shivered my way back up the steps to the car park. Then I shivered in silence as the motorcade swept back to the Castle and I was finally alone again. Even now, in the steam room that has been cleared for my personal use, I feel a tremor, though now more likely due to the DTs, weakening now as I drain the hip flask I have taken in with me.

When I leave, there are a few peeved-looking guests in the changing room. I almost slip over on the tiles.

'Sorry.' I raise the flask. 'I think I'm steamin'.'

No laughs, not one. Gotta work on the delivery, Duke. I look at my wet footprints on the floor and imagine them carrying on, right out the door. I suppose I should get up and follow . . .

Back in the suite I stand naked at the window, peering at my salmon-pink skin, wiping away the sweat caught in the sagging folds of my belly and breasts. Doubtless a long-range lens is pointing my way, a two-page spread awaiting, me on one side and Frank Stone's beach prayer on the other.

'Do you want to play?' asks Akira.

As I turn, I note with surprise that I am semi-erect. His eyes drop, the two of us now staring at the miracle and wondering about the malfunctioning libido that created it. A wholly different nuance has been given to Akira's innocently asked question about the *Go* board he is carrying.

'Give me a minute,' I say.

195

'You bet,' he says, and can't help breaking into a smile that becomes a laugh both his and my own.

Go is a game I felt I had to learn when I moved to Japan. They have TV programmes showing live matches, an entertainment so compelling in its tedium that I have lost whole days to uncomprehending considerations of false eyes, snapbacks and *atari* combinations. Akira and I are terrible. Our game strategies reflect what our relationship has become, informality within convention.

I watch him study the board in his usual fashion. Leaning forward on his elbows, palms together, fingers tapping his nose. He looks up at me very seriously, as if he is about to impart great knowledge.

'I have a new strategy, Johnny.'

I hold back my smile. 'I'm intrigued.'

He nods very slowly. 'I do this.' He picks up a white stone and holds it between thumb and forefinger. 'And this.' He closes his eyes. 'And now.' He places the stone down randomly on the board. He opens his eyes, looks down and then offers me an excited double thumbs up. 'Success!'

'You think?'

'I do.'

Now I'm smiling widely. 'How so?'

'Because the strategy, dear Johnny, is no worse than any other. I am *improving*.'

'You mean you're not getting any worse.'

He considers this for a moment and then nods, mock-serious once more. 'That too I will take.'

We are on the brink of a ferociously haphazard *ko* battle when there is a knock at the door. Akira shows Erin in and retreats to another room, my niece joining me at the low table in the lounge.

She looks at the board. 'I've never understood this game.'

196

'You're probably a genius without knowing it. It's a game of territory, taking as much as you can.'

'Hostile takeovers?'

'Aren't they the only kind?'

She settles back in the seat and looks out the window. It is snowing again after the bright morning sun.

'I've never known a place that has so much weather,' she says.

'Only one thing you need to know round here.'

'What's that?'

'No waterproof in the world will keep you dry.' I pour myself another large one, courtesy of Mr J&B.

'I want to apologise for earlier,' she says quickly. 'For not wanting go to the cemetery. It was such a ridiculous morning and . . . it seemed like the wrong time. But when's the right time?'

'You should go when you want to, like you said.'

'Then let's go.'

'What? You want to go now?' I realise it is exactly what she said to me back at MacIntyre's Bay.

'You're the one who wanted to.'

'Yes, I did.'

'Well, do you?'

'I do, yes.'

'Then I'll see you downstairs in ten.'

I stare down at the black-and-white stones on the *Go* board. I have seen your headstone, Duke, our father and our mother's too, though not Anna's. Still I have to visit you all. Still I hesitate.

⋆ ⋆ ⋆

When I was young there was no death. It was a time of much narrower confines, the most pressing concerns having enough money to buy *The Dandy*, or how long you could stay out on a school night.

I had seen death, of course, my grandfather and grandmother laid out under white sheets. I had felt the solemnity of others and for those unsettling days before and after the funerals knew I was in the presence of something fundamental. Perhaps it was the suspicion that here was something likely to overwhelm me if I thought about it too much that led me to conclude that death was so bafflingly distant from the immediacy of my world that it wasn't exactly real.

The cemetery, likewise, where I stand now in the razoring scour of a sleet-heavy westerly. As a child, I didn't pay it any attention. Only now and then, my eyes drawn upwards as I cycled home, did I think about the two occasions I watched my grandparents lowered into the ground.

Later, when I was a teenager, I found out the cemetery was built on the site of a Viking graveyard. Frank Stone would be delighted to know this so I won't tell him. I can all too easily imagine the scene he would somehow work into *The Bruce*. Fire against the sky as the ship is set alight, axes and swords and shouts of defiance all so much more appealing to my teenage imagination than these bleak rows of headstones, names gone from memory, lost to moss.

'Jay!'

Can you imagine if we didn't cremate people, Duke? All those headlands from here to Cape Wrath filled with thousands and thousands of stones, we wouldn't be able to move for old bones.

'Can you remember where they are?'

Erin is standing some distance away between two long rows of headstones, hands on her hips as she looks hopelessly around. I realise it is almost thirty years since she has been here.

I remember where you lie, Duke.

I helped with the cord that day as I could not help you

198

with that other. I can still feel its surprising smoothness as we slid you under. I even wondered, appalled, if that was your final thought, the smoothness of the bathrobe cord around your neck as you scrabbled at the noose.

I beckon Erin over. She follows me to the other side of the church, the Viking side. On the western edge, looking across the bay to the islands and the open sea, are the four graves. It is the first time I have seen Anna's. The white marble has such depth. It holds my gaze like an enchantment.

'It's beautiful,' says Erin.

I realise she too has not seen the stone. It was a year or so after the funeral that it was set in place, I think.

'So peaceful up here.'

Her eyes are tender. She seems almost happy, as if she could linger here for the rest of the afternoon. People are drawn to graveyards, even when they have no connection to the dead. I have walked Père Lachaise and Highgate, Kōyasan in the gathering gloom, hundreds of Jizo's little red scarves glowing in the dark. As I look down on Anna's grave, I glimpse a man on a bench away to the right. Does he know the dead or does he just sit? And if he just sits then why?

'Are you going to tell me why you didn't come to Mum's funeral?'

I smile ruefully as I reach forward and wipe dirt off the smooth face of the headstone. No escape here.

'If I had stayed here I'd have turned into an old man who's always talking about who's just died. It's what happens when you stay in one place. But I didn't, so I only find out who's dead long after. There must be so many I don't know about. Maybe I should assume they're all dead except me.'

She's chewing her lip when I turn to her. The vaguest of nods before her gaze moves out to sea.

'I don't know why,' I say. 'I just couldn't. The thought

of flying halfway round the world with her coffin in the hold.'

'And me? I was thirteen. It was ok for me to fly around the world with her body in the hold? I needed you and you weren't there.'

I have wondered many times what Erin must have felt when Mrs Ishihara appeared at Haneda airport in my place to accompany her. Still, self-pity has never suited her. 'When did you ever need me?'

'Then. Maybe now? Can we just leave all this and just think about them? Nothing else, just think about them.'

'I think about them all the time.'

'So do I.'

'And I do need you, you know?'

She clasps my hand and puts her head on my shoulder. No small feat this; Erin is a foot taller and has to bend slightly at the knee to do so. Her body feels tense, my own too, yet when I close my eyes, after a moment, I feel a relaxing in both of us. The spell of the white marble, perhaps.

'So peaceful up here,' she repeats.

When I open my eyes the man on the bench has moved. He's now about ten metres away, leaning against the cemetery wall. He produces a camera and starts taking pictures. Erin has also seen him, but her only reaction is to tuck her hair behind her ear, as if she wants to better show the photographer her profile. I start to move away but she grips me more tightly.

'Let him take a few pictures, what does it matter.'

I see now that the photo-op has been staged. It explains Erin's change of mind about visiting the cemetery. I realise what she wants, something heart-warming to offset the recent media hostility. Uncle and niece together in tragedy.

I suppose I should be outraged. Instead, I just feel a passing annoyance that Erin has wrong-footed me. She

200

has wanted to come and visit her mother and her grief is genuine so what does it matter if she also makes a commodity out of it? It is no less authentic for being cheapened.

We return, arm in arm, to the Mercedes. The quick-fading sunlight briefly swells, the sandstone of the old church deepening to umber, like an acknowledgement of my final farewell.

Why was I so reluctant to visit Anna, Duke?

As if there could be anything left to ambush me after so many years. As if the sight of a white marble headstone could have made any difference whatsoever. My essential feeling remains one of detachment, now tinged by a guilty disappointment that what I have never stopped carrying has been neither added to nor lessened by this visit. It was at least more bearable than it would have been back then, to stand jet-lagged and jittery in the undoubted rain, lowering her into a black pit beside you, Duke, as if, even in death, you had to have the last word.

Akira eases the car across the gravel, picking up speed as we reach the road down to Inveran. Erin reaches across the back seat and takes my hand, her smile a convoluted mix of affection and apology.

The visit to the cemetery, our shared grief and my silent complicity in the photo-op has created a conspiratorial warmth between us. In one moment, I decide to share my final commitment with her. In the next, I change my mind. The warmth fades. As we speed back to the hotel Erin tries to make conversation, giving up, yet leaving her hand on mine for surprisingly long.

She tries again outside my suite, her half-hearted *see you at dinner* a question she can't understand why she's even bothering to ask. When she leaves, I tell Akira we need to organise one more excursion. Just he and I. There can be no security phalanx to deaden the moment.

'Come and get me at eight.'

'Eight it is, Johnny. I'll sort it out.'

I pour a drink and draw the curtains. I am in no mood for reflections. I turn off all the lights except the two reading lamps at either end of the coffee table. Thin, chrome and boomerang-shaped, they lean insistently towards me, super-focused spots leaching very little light into the surrounds. I will try and resist the obvious parallel about only ever seeing what's directly in front of me . . .

How much is momentous in a life? Who justifies, truly, the conceit of an autobiography? I'm embarrassed for all who read my polished little nuggets of nothingness. Like a confused mole, I squint at their meaning, all so neat and so layered, stripped of messiness, the literary equivalent of a Club Sandwich, so much appeal but always so disappointing.

Yet now I actually want a Club Sandwich. What does this tell you, Duke? There is significance here, yes?

Room service answers the phone immediately, as if they have been waiting for my call. I expect an instant pitter-patter of hurrying feet, the rattle of a trolley in the corridor. It takes only slightly longer for the soft rapping on the door. I shout a terse *come in, come through* . . . Only when the waiter is standing opposite me on the other side of the table do I look up.

I do not expect Lewis. My heart gives an inadvertent thump. Even in the near dark I can see the blush on his big forehead. It is hard to imagine anything vindictive of this man. 'Put it down,' I say.

He clatters the bottle and sandwich platter down so hard on the table I expect the glass top to smash.

'Sorry, sorry.'

202

'Didn't know you did room service. Jack of all trades, you. Bit below your rank, eh?'

'I was coming up this way anyway.'

'Grab yourself a glass and sit down.'

'We're not really supposed to.'

'Bollocks to that. It's all about the guests, son. First rule of hospitality.'

He hesitates for a few moments then crosses to the cabinet on the other side of the room, returning with a tumbler. He sits down on the very edge of the sofa directly opposite, as if ready to bolt.

'I've been meaning to talk to you,' I say. He shuffles on the seat and glances towards the door. I pour two whiskies and hand him one. When he takes it, I raise my own in the air. 'To the *Shinigami*.'

I know that he is now definitely blushing.

'Sorry, sorry. Bit egotistical to toast myself. Here's to you. How's that documentary of yours coming along?'

'Is that how—'

'"I'm making a documentary." You told me. In the bar. You wrote the same thing in one of your emails.'

He slams the glass down on the table and stands up. 'I should be going. I don't want to—'

'Sit down, for crying out loud! No-one's going to come bursting in. You think this is a Frank Stone movie?' I top up my drink and watch him sit back down. 'I'm guessing that it's about me.'

He looks down at his glass.

'Helluva dramatic though. The whole *Shinigami* thing.'

'Maybe so.'

In that moment, I know what I'm going to suggest. Yet I'm not sure where it's coming from or if I actually want to. 'Tell you what. I'll give you the big centrepiece scene. It'll make the whole thing hang together. You've spent so much time fretting about me that it's the least I can do.'

'I'm not following you.'

'Let's hope no-one else does. When are you off shift?'

'Nine.'

'Have you got a car?'

'Where are we going?'

'Lewis, son, I'm fenced off. I peer out at the world from a compound. You've done your research, I've been like that for a long time. There was this rainy morning, see, I wandered into a byre.'

He rubs his beard and looks troubled. No psychotic temperament after all, it seems. He's likely wondering about mine, if I'm always this spontaneous. I'm not, I'm a man of tiresome habit, I have to sleep facing north, the open ends of my pillows must face the centre of the bed ...

'Then you can tell me what you want, eh?' I add.

As soon as Lewis leaves I call Akira's room and tell him to take the evening off. I have three hours to change my mind. The Club Sandwich winks. I take one bland bite and leave the rest. Can I really be such a cynic, Duke, if I feel that sandwiches have let me down more than people over the years?

* * *

The gloom is a cindery deepening as Lewis pulls out of the back gates of the hotel. We're in an ancient, rattling Land Rover, as cold as the Arctic air outside. I sit in the passenger seat. Lewis is apologising, fiddling with the fan, trying to clear the condensation from the windscreen. He drives carefully until it clears, revealing the CinemaScope view that I've always been such a sucker for.

So let's indulge the thrill, Duke! When I see a shop on the edge of Inveran, I ask Lewis to stop.

The door gives a merry tinkle as I enter. The teenager behind the till looks startled, as if I am the first customer she's had all day. I feel her eyes on me as I wander the shelves, staring at tins and packets I might never have seen before. I buy a half-bottle of Old Inveran and open it in the car, a caving in to nostalgia that I regret with the first swig. Perhaps it is the screwing up of my face that makes Lewis decline the offer. Do you remember, Duke, this was our first shared bottle? A Friday night in the byre, all day Saturday with my head in the toilet. I will persevere . . .

On the promenade the flags dance in a rising wind, a heavy swell bringing the waves high enough for the crests to be illuminated by the orange streetlights. We follow the lights eastwards and, where the promenade continues round to the marina, take a left, steeply climbing Shore Road.

Once more I pass the entrance to the cemetery. Then we turn into a series of tight corners, headlamps making psychedelic greens of the flashing verge. A few minutes later we reach the top of the hill. The road flattens out as it continues west, across the Moor of the Parting we cannot see, the landscape different from the other side of Inveran, a geological watershed crossed. The Land Rover is buffeted by a wind that meets no resistance, slowly easing as we begin to drop steeply down, the void of the Sound of Skerray soon appearing to our right.

I had forgotten how close the sea is to the single track. I see the glint of shingle and a confusion of waves, now and then an arc of spray lifting gently across the road, the way a tugboat bowser might welcome a big ship back into harbour, as if the Sound has put on *a welcome home, JJ.*

It is full dark now. Lewis slows. He will know, undoubtedly, that the cottage is just ahead. He turns into the side-track and stops, the headlights illuminating a closed gate at the top of the slope.

'Not a bad scene for your movie, eh?'

It is impossible to tell if I am drunk. It is likely, yet not certain. It might only be the wind making me stumble as I step carefully up the slick, rutted track. Yet I manage to follow the headlight beams through the same rusted gate of sixty years ago, the darker shape of the gable end looming closer.

When I reach the yard, I need the torch that Lewis handed me from the glove compartment. Instead, I stand in the dark, letting my vision adjust. My eyes are streaming, Duke, but not tears. Then a troubling thump of my slow-failing heart. As if here I may finally fall and not rise.

You'd like that, yes?

There is no life in the cottage. In the absence of people it has become like every other empty home in the Highlands, a place of abject melancholy, heavy with the presence of ghosts known all too well.

Inevitably, it is now a holiday cottage. Akira found it on a website.

I peer in the kitchen window and switch on the torch, revealing a white table and four different coloured plastic chairs. The kitchen has been knocked through to the front room, the floor now covered in a zigzag patterned carpet. Above the fireplace is a print of *Lunch atop a Skyscraper*.

I feel both a tender longing for something long gone and disbelief that I could ever have been here at all.

I switch off the torch. I force down another mouthful of old Inveran as I stare into the dark cottage, waiting for the illumination of some cobwebbed memory, the fire to flicker on polished flagstones, two boys messing about at the table, one mussing the hair of the other, the parents smiling and indulging but only momentarily, the light-heartedness cut off swiftly by my father's bark, as if it is too embarrassing, too revealing of affection, perhaps, for us all to enjoy ourselves ...

Would I enter the house if my mother smiled? Pull her to me and breathe her scent? Would I shake my father's hand, finally, an acknowledgement and an exorcism? There is no room for such possibilities with you there, Duke. I watch our mum and dad follow your gaze to the window, such disdain in your eyes and such disappointment in theirs. Even my young self can't look at me, rushing over to the box bed to bury his face, as if he suddenly sees what he must become.

Is he not proud of the Blue Plaque of the Breda Boys achievements? When I go back to the gable end and shine the torch up it is not there. I eventually find it at the front of the cottage, lying on top of a picnic table, two stars of a lesser firmament staring up at all the others. I carry the plaque back round to the kitchen and prop it against the window for you all to read.

I sense you behind me now, Duke.

Yet by the time I turn and swing the torch back and fore across the yard you've vanished. I move the torch back to the byre then quickly point it down at the ground, the glittery rain pouring through the beam like tracer fire in an old war movie. I am waiting for my courage.

When it comes, I'll lift the torch back to the byre. I'll let the beam follow its outline, along the sagging roof, down to the door tied shut with blue twine that will take an age for me to untie.

The hairs on the back of my neck stand up as I open the door. It creaks, of course. I hold my breath as I look up, but all I see in the emptiness below the cross-beam is dust drifting through torchlight.

207

I sit down on an old packing crate. I don't know how long I sit there. I point the torch at the ground and click the beam on and off, on and off, watching the same bits of muddy straw appear and vanish. I don't know why I feel so disappointed. When the door opens again I swing the torch up and see Lewis. He stands in the doorway like an invitation, rain tracing in behind him.

'I know. Helluva night for sitting in—'

'Why are you here?'

'Isn't that obvious?'

'Not this barn. Inveran. Why the hell did you come back here?'

His sudden anger is startling. I wait for something to explain it but his face instantly softens.

'I'll take you back.' He turns away quickly and I rush to speak before he steps out into the rain.

'I don't want to go back. Not yet,' I add.

He hesitates for a few moments before again facing me. 'There's always my place. If you fancy it?'

Fourteen

Anna, Erin and I returned to London in June 1967. We didn't talk about what would happen when we got there, though the question seemed to hang in the air for the whole journey. On the concourse outside Euston I finally acknowledged it. I asked Anna if she wanted me to go back with them to Notting Hill.

She did, but would never have asked. I ended up staying several nights. Then I returned to Kilburn but visited every day. Soon, I began to stay over, 'It's too late to go home now, Johnny', eventually moving in full-time a few months later. 'I mean, you're round here so often anyway.' It was a reluctant neediness. She wanted me there; just there, an exact arm's length away.

So we filled a life with domestic intimacies, indistinguishable from husband and wife until that ever-loaded goodnight before we went to our separate rooms. Then that, too, became normal.

Yet all was just shifting shapes.

Her need to have me around was balanced by a melancholy detachment. She existed elsewhere, a place of an emerging Duke fetish; a little shrine in the corner of the living room, framed photographs and a candle lit every morning. And the birds, the birds, pictures found in junk shops and bought from catalogues. She filled the house with them, always one in her eyeline.

These were intense days. Still the door-stopping press, though less as time passed. Even when they slunk off altogether, Anna refused to leave the house. It was me who took Erin on walks and did the shopping, longer and longer trips to delay my return to those epic silences. Yet both times I said I would move out she insisted there was no need with such anxiety in her eyes, apologising for being so distant and 'Give me time, Johnny, give me some space.'

It struck me as the most accidental, even apologetic, of relationships.

I never asked again if I should leave. In time, her answer might have been different. By then I always expected, during one of our frequent, disorientating skirmishes, those seared-in moments of her sad fury and Erin's tears, that she would scream at me to get out. Yet she never did.

That's how it breaks, little bro.

Duke was ever-present. A smile in the photograph as Anna lit her candles, a ghost sprawled between us as we sat at either end of the sofa in the heavy evenings, matching us drink for drink.

I made his film and told no-one.

★ ★ ★

The film industry has a kinked pathology. Profound cynicism meets childlike innocence. I have met people I suspect would strangle their firstborn for the rights to a sure-fire hit. It's so ludicrous to spend millions making stuff up it can't be anything but serious. Everybody's so terrified about someone else killing the box office that they compulsively snap things up. There's a hoarder's relief in knowing that if you're not making it, at least no-one else will be able to.

Seeking the Grail of the killer concept.

It's a near-religious mindset. The more gripping the story *behind* the story the better. It turns that tarnished carpenter's mug into a gem-encrusted goblet. *A Man's a Man* ticked all the boxes.

There was no-one better than Fatty Jones to build the buzz. The co-owner of The Cannonball made Peter Ustinov seem monosyllabic. He built the film like a Coltrane solo, taking only a teaser synopsis to studio meetings, along with copies of Don Heelpen's *The Observer* profile. He talked up my tragedy and how I had retreated into *exile on the edge of the world, where an occult fury of released emotion created this masterpiece*, a hallucinatory re-telling of Robert Burns' life, which turned on how the poet sold his soul to the devil and received Highland Mary as a muse.

Fatty gave Warner Brothers two days to get back to him, three to make an offer on the full-script. When they took four he went straight to MGM – he'd been talking to them on the sly anyway, building that hoarder's anxiety. MGM agreed to finance the same day. One million dollars, with Breda Pictures sub-contracted as producer. The studio's one insistence was an A-lister as lead and Robert Redford signed on, hooked by the sentiment of his Scottish roots. Lucky old Leonid got to indulge a little crush when Jane Asher was cast as Mary Campbell.

We went into production at Borehamwood in May 1968. I sent a second unit to Scotland for landscape shots, insisting all other locations were no more than two hours from London. I'd convinced myself I had to get back to Anna every night but was always relieved to leave in the morning.

The most celebrated scene, where Burns and Mary pledge their love, was actually filmed in Oxford with the River Cherwell standing in for the Water of Fail. Midway through take 33, a disconsolate Jane burst into tears, inadvertently giving us the film's emotional peak.

211

There were other, unidentified grumblings to the press about *God in a combat jacket*. Yet the moment of imminent breakdown often gave the most potent take. Then God would call a wrap and hurry back to Notting Hill and a production where there was only ever one opportunity to get it right.

Fatty persuaded me to do one pre-release interview, choosing *The Daily Mirror*, where Duke had his most indulgent fan base. 'Good PR, Johnny boy, needs the ooze of sentiment,' Fatty declared.

I oozed only weirdness. This piqued an interest all its own, less my cryptic answers than the white gloves I was wearing. I had developed a rash, terrified by the mountain of footage I had to corral into a movie, this the downside of torturing Hollywood stars for hundreds of takes. I didn't explain this, naturally, leaving the interviewer to speculate on *a fear of germs like another oddball film-maker, Howard Hughes*.

Anna would add to the image, an unintended consequence of my coaxing her back into the world. She started taking Erin to the park. Then I persuaded her to take on a nanny to give her some time to herself. I bought her a camera. She wandered west London and took hundreds of photos she never let me see. I was delighted when she told me she was thinking of writing again.

Her return to journalism was straightforward, Duke's death still a sentimental dog-whistle. Her weekly column in the *Express* was called *The Party*. The editor must have expected a re-boot of the showbiz tittle-tattle of *Through the Looking Glass*.

Instead, Anna gave him ruthless satire. The sentimentality that had briefly flared in Inveran had vanished. In its place, a hardness emerged, and a growing disdain for me. Both found their flaring in her new column. *The*

Party was a luvvie cringe-fest, characters like 'Fingers' Hansen, a priapic young starlet chaser, Larry d'Oliphant, a shrill and drunken queen wracked with sexual guilt, and Hailey Halloran O'Halloran, the manipulative host and bitter old silent film star obsessed with 'Death's final cut'.

Then there was The Director. A man of random gnomic utterances which stopped conversation dead. In a later episode, he placed an Oscar on the table, a talking point that nobody talked about.

'He even wears a checked shirt,' I complained.

'Why *have* you started wearing checked shirts?' said Anna. 'And those trousers. You're not the army type.'

'I just mean—'

'What!' She slammed her hand down on the counter. 'What *does* it mean? What does it matter?'

'It matters to me.'

'Look.' The anger had instantly evaporated. 'People think you're strange anyway.'

Such tender cruelties, I thought.

'So who cares? You've got the big hit.' This with a little pat on my cheek, a mother showing affection to a child. She hummed a little tune as she bent to Erin, mussing up the little girl's hair.

A cinematic odyssey ... A new departure in film ... New wave meets old wave and swamps the screen. Don Heelpen gushed about the *spooky meld of the traditional, three-act arc and the avant garde.*

Jump cuts and flashbacks, breaking the 180-degree axis, we pushed it just far enough. We let the film flow and we stopped it dead, a ratatat of dialogue followed by the emptiest of deep-focus compositions: Burns by the sea, only the sound of the wind, the camera held on him for a full minute before moving left to follow an oyster-catcher picking at the shore. Leo framed big landscapes

213

with saturated dream-colours and oppressive, candle-lit close-ups. We stirred schmaltz with disquiet, enough of Redford's beauty to keep the housewives coming, cool enough to bring the hipsters. Here was the sentiment and the harshness of Burns: the dreamer and the player.

Don't take my word for it, read the reviews.

*　*　*

With multiple *A Man's a Man* nominations for the forty-first Academy Awards, off we flew to Los Angeles in April 1969.

It's hard not to be the bumpkin on your first visit to La-La Land. From Iowan, wannabe Monroes to yes ma'am Texan charmers and stunted Celts like me whose eyelids are sweating, the instant reaction is wide-eyed delight. The Californian sun makes it irresistible. Everything is utterly possible.

In some kind of nervous reaction, I retreated into an odd, imperial nostalgia. I ditched the combats and checked shirt and adopted an *Our Man in Havana* style, the Yanks all gee-whizz delight at my living up to the eccentric billing, while I impressed myself with how quickly I was able to ruin a linen suit. The concierge at the Chateau Marmont hid it well but when I glanced back he was smirking.

Anna, Erin and I had a suite. We looked south over Sunset, Los Angeles a sea of white lights. The bumpkin was reminded of Halloween childhoods, an epic field filled with turnip lanterns. Day and night the city hummed as if everyone was talking at the same time, now and then the disorientation of a siren always followed by others. My heart beat more quickly the whole time I was there.

Anna was repelled and fascinated. She was a

214

silhouette on the terrace, staring into the blood and purples of an apocalyptic sunset, white-cotton elegance in a Hollywood Boulevard bar, blue eyes peering over the rims of her sunglasses as she sipped another Daiquiri.

She didn't want to come to the ceremony. Three times she would stare instead at the television to see Fatty, Leo and I make the surreal clamber onstage at the Dorothy Chandler Pavilion. Best Cinematography, Best Film, Best Director. I eulogised about the old man and Duke, milked the rags to riches and babbled something embarrassing about the Scottish Dream, whatever that might be, being just as powerful as the American. The audience lapped it up.

I was still wearing the linen suit. In some pictures I hold an Oscar in the air with sweat stains under my arms. With Fatty in his country-pile tweeds and Leo in an oversized tux we looked almost subversive. The *New York Times* actually called our appearances a *sly, countercultural statement*.

Warners didn't mind.

It was after 2am at the Beverly Hills Hotel. The curious were now drunk, the long-drunk now emotional, some offering a few lines of Burns with their compliments, memorised just in case.

'They're offering a two-movie deal and fifteen per cent,' said Fatty. 'I said we'd think about it.'

The reaction of Leo and I was both instantaneous and similar, a frantically whispered questioning of his sanity.

'*Relax*, dear boys. The game's afoot. Let's see what MGM have to offer, yes?'

He returned later with a fresh Warners offer for three movies, twenty per cent and guarantee of the final cut.

We made it back to the Marmont around five, the first of the dawn streaking the east. We talked about the movies we'd make and the compounds we'd build in the Hollywood Hills, our Malibu beach houses. So much was possible, but you never see the high-water mark until it recedes.

'Quite a night for you, boys.' Anna's words were slurred, eyes raw. Glass in hand, she swayed at the terrace door then walked carefully across to drape her arms around me. 'I was watching you up there and all I could think about was Duke. I could see him, Johnny, right there, beside you. He'd have been so proud.'

Leonid raised a glass. 'To Duke.'

'To Duke.'

And we lifted our hands to a sky become blood-orange, the thrum of the city and the ever-wailing sirens.

'What a god-awful place this is,' said Anna. 'He would have loved it, he would have absolutely loved it.'

Later, after Fatty staggered back to his room I told Leo that *A Man's a Man* was Duke's film, that I had found the script and storyboard. He laughed at me and we never spoke of it again. I sat on the terrace and watched those lurid LA skies. I thought about the film, the psychedelic bridge sequence where Burns sees the devil on the other side and makes the decision to cross.

* * *

It was a major sorrow I didn't enjoy all that followed. Solemn John Calvin, what a gift he made of self-loathing. *Yir nae better than ye should be . . . Nae need for art, God gave you everything you need.* My favourite? *Him, famous? Ah knew his faither.* I decided that my father's greatest achievement was to cut loose from all that folk-guilt. He loved to trot out those bleak aphorisms, always deriding them with a mocking, dissident laugh. I should have screamed them out the window and given the press clustered on the pavement below something to write about.

Sometimes there was only one of them, more often a few, a constant presence for months after we returned from LA. The sense of siege was corrosive. I did a couple of interviews, Sunday profiles, but still the door-stepping, the 'What's next?' questions and the usual gone before.

'What about you and Anna?'

She retreated again, refusing to leave the house. Back flew the birds. Anna drew the outlines and Erin coloured them in. I had dreams that the house was filled with thousands of these pictures, fluttering on the walls, covering the floor as they wafted down from stacks of yellowing paper.

Eventually, I think I went insane. I can even date it.

21st July 1970. Groggy with summer London night sweats, I woke again to the squirrel at 5.30am on the dot.

For days, it had been the same. A scurry on the bay window roof and then an odd whirring, like an old football rattle. I shouted *Shut up!* and the furry little face appeared at the top of the window, upside down as it peered at me. That night, I'd even dreamed about it. 'Meester Jackson,' the squirrel was saying, a creepy, Peter Lorre syrup of a voice. 'They're fakes. *Loook*.' And it gently took my Oscars and bit off their heads, sadly showing me the polystyrene ...

'Spot on!' I shouted. Authenticity would always be just beyond my grasp. At least I'd finally had the sense to ditch the absurd linen suit, returning to my army surplus combat trousers and red- and black-checked shirt. Yet there's Beatnik chic and there's comic lumberjack.

I was always a beat out.

'Always a beat,' I shouted at the squirrel, which shook

its head and vamoosed. I'm sure it shook its head.

A few moments later, I started to hear singing from the room below, *Wee Willie Winkie*. I started to sing along, louder and louder, until silenced by a sudden banging at the door.

'Thanks a lot, *Johnny*. She's terrified!'

A small, shrieking voice was now repeating *the big bad wolf, the big bad wolf* . . .

When I went downstairs they were sitting at the kitchen table. They looked me up and down with almost preternatural calmness, sharing a glance that I fretted about for the rest of the day.

I stepped closer, my heart sinking as I again saw the pictures of birds. I went through to the lounge and tried to ignore the bottle on the sideboard. I slumped down in the red pod chair that Duke and Anna had bought in another lifetime and looked at the Oscars I had placed on each knee.

'Whadaya reckon?' I asked them, and had the sudden certainty that I inhabited a troubled, faraway place.

Soon after, we made the necessary move. Wendlebury Manor was a big old pile in Buckinghamshire. Fatty had mentioned it in passing, some bankrupt cousin having put it up for sale, five hundred acres of woods and parkland. The house sat in the centre of this expanse, the land so flat and the trees so distant that you had a ten minute warning of any trespass on foot. Only one or two for a car but that could be controlled – a gated entrance, two security guards.

The space was instantly relieving. No more the sense of siege. Anna's birds flew off and she took up painting, as if all those sketches she had drawn for Erin to colour in had triggered a deeper interest.

My old *Fisherman's Blues* project became a new

obsession. I let Fatty lead on Breda Pictures. He mixed the mainstream with the art-house and from 1970 to 1975 put together a series of hits: *Down in the Valley, A Winter's Fail* and *Just One More Day*. Yet the kudos mostly came my way.It irritated him, and I offered no demur. Someone called me *the puppet master in his mansion*.

The manor had a ridiculous number of rooms, some of which I must have entered only once. Anna set up a studio in the smallest of the five reception rooms. She bought dozens of prints by Munch, Picasso, Kandinsky, copying them, learning by imitation. Like the photography before, she hid her own efforts from me.

I would sit at the table in the adjoining kitchen and had the connecting door removed so we could see each other as we worked.

I sensed an awkward amusement from our infrequent visitors. Their uncertainty about the exact nature of the relationship between Anna and I wrong-footed them. They awaited a big reveal that I was no more sure about than they.

Later, we had a narrow glass conservatory built along the south wing. Anna would paint at one end, ten metres away from my desk at the other. Again, we faced each other as we worked, a sofa equidistant between us. Our most intimate moments occurred when we sat there side by side, looking out across the vast garden; a neutral space we needed more than we probably realised.

'Imagining just sitting here,' she said. 'For years. Like a time-lapse sequence, the skies all changing.' In the distance, Erin was spinning round and round, arms outstretched. Then she fell over and lay still. 'She'll keep on spinning, growing up, getting older. Never moving from that spot.'

'We'll get old quick enough.'

'Do you remember the big house past Esha Bay, the

whitewashed one where the windows were all dark?'

'The one with the old car parked in the garden, wasn't it a Model T Ford?'

'There was a replica cannon as well, facing the sea. And a set of broken swings. If you walked along the shore you could climb over the rocks into the garden. There was a fence but it'd fallen down.'

'I think it'd been abandoned for years.'

'Don't think so. I saw someone at a window once. He was looking at me. An old man, ancient.'

'You sure about that?'

'I don't think we leave anywhere. Not really. When we're dead and someone moves in we'll still be sitting here. Erin will still be spinning. They'll hear us, now and then. What a racket we made.'

This inspired the final scene of *Fisherman's Blues*. Morag sits outside her cottage, the skies shifting and the garden mouldering, her son's trike becoming rustier. As she stares at the sea, waiting for the long-lost *Makepeace* to appear on the horizon, she is the one thing that doesn't change.

* * *

We began filming in early 1972 and didn't wrap until late 1973. An epic shoot, the Warners brass across from LA three times as the budget spiralled. I had second and third units scouring Scotland for the ideal fishing village. I obsessed about the perfect lighthouse we never found. The single biggest cost was the trawler transported from Hull and installed at Borehamwood, which meant an insanely expensive raising of the Studio One roof. We started to encroach on other productions, aggravating everyone with a stop-start schedule as I re-wrote the script as we went along.

Blues bombed. Rarely has so much expectation been

met with such near-offended opprobrium. In later times, a chattering fax would announce the arrival of the latest review. Nervously, I'd watch it emerge, line by line. Back then, it was a knock on the door of the reception room as the mail was delivered. I remember the day that Roger Ebert's review was handed to me.

We start with something very basic: why is 'Fisherman's Blues' so excruciating to watch? The ludicrous scenes roll endlessly, one after the other like the over-lit waves. So much to create so little. This film is millions of dollars thrown into the air and one of the most indulgent examples of movie-madness I have seen ...

Anna was more devastated than me by the hostility of the reviews. She thought of the film as hers. Early on, she saw herself as Morag, blessing or berating the midnight re-writes which I took back to the studio the next day. She adored the final film. She saw authenticity where others, I think it was *Time* magazine, saw nothing but *disorder, melodrama and inconsistency.*

'Fuck 'em!'

We were in the conservatory, our voices almost drowned out by hammering rain. A few weeks had passed since *Blues* had appeared in the cinemas and sunk like the *Makepeace.* We were drunk.

'No, I can understand it,' Anna said. 'That was my grief. Why should anyone else believe what they didn't feel?'

'Maybe if I had told it better.'

'You told it beautifully. Apart from ... '

'What?'

'Maybe it could have been a bit shorter?'

'You said it was just right! Fatty and Leo said that—'

'Joking, I'm *joking!'* She was smiling as she poured a refill. 'You know what we need to do?'

'What's that?'

221

'Burn the critics.'

I had a folder of reviews. We huddled under an umbrella and walked down to the barbecue pit at the bottom of the garden. Before I was allowed to set fire to the folder I had to stand in the rain.

'Take your clothes off.'

'I'm not taking my clothes off! What if Erin comes back?'

'She's at school. This is a purging, it should be ... what's the word, *multidimensional*.'

This was a reference to what Philip French called the *multidimensional awfulness of Fisherman's Blues*.

'Don't take the piss!'

'Sorry, couldn't resist.' She giggled and sipped. 'Now. Off with them.'

I grabbed the glass from her, downed the rest of the whisky and bumbled out of my clothes. I had to stand with my arms outstretched and repeat what she said. I had a sudden memory of a similar scene from years ago, Anna standing behind me in Kilburn with her hands across my eyes.

'I do here and the by and the very now.'

'I do here and the by and the very now.'

'Set my angst free.'

'Angst?'

'Say it!'

'Set my angst *freeeee*!'

She held a lighter to the folder of reviews and stood staring at the flames.

'*Oi*, what now?'

She turned to me and started laughing. 'Cold, is it?'

I quickly covered my crotch. 'Little bit.'

'You said it ...'

I joined her under the umbrella. I found myself bending down to kiss her. She recoiled instantly, hands on my shoulders. She seemed more than startled, almost frightened. Then, abruptly, she kissed me back.

Soon after, we went up to the manor and made love for the first time in years.

For several weeks afterwards there was a lightness to her I had forgotten existed. I glimpsed the poised woman I had met on the day she appeared at the cottage to interview the Breda Boys. She let me come to her when Erin was asleep, a few times. I would slip out with the first of the dawn. We even went on holiday, two weeks of courtship and caution in Mexico. Sometimes I could almost convince myself her gaze finally rested on me, that it hadn't slipped past to Duke.

Then, in quick succession, came the photographs. The first was in *The Sun*, a shot of Anna and I embracing in the rain while the reviews burned. My nakedness was covered, reader discretion assured, with a large black X. The photographer must have been hiding in the trees. The image was captioned *Fisherman Blue*. I had no idea why they waited so long to publish it.

But it was less this first photograph which Anna reacted to than the episode which led to the second.

Exit the monkey.

Charlie the Chimp died at London Zoo. Before his time, the showbiz life having taken an early toll. I pictured him in his little coffin, the bowler hat they made him wear in the PG Tips advert clasped to his chest.

Anna didn't see the humour. She was genuinely, oddly, upset, and insisted Breda Pictures issue a statement. I could see Fatty's eyebrows rise as I dictated it down the phone. *It is with great sadness that we have learned of the death of our friend and comrade, Charlie the Chimp. A true star of the screen, he leaves us with one last raspberry and a toothy grin . . .*

The BBC took the opportunity to re-run every Breda

Boys film. Anna kept Erin off school so they could watch them together, curled up on the sofa with the curtains drawn. As I listened to Anna tell Erin all about her father I realised that she had been looking for a way back to Duke ever since that day in the rain. Six-year-old Erin started to feel a loss for someone she never knew, her own way back to Duke an insistence that Charlie the Chimp was buried at Wendlebury.

'The garden? Really?' said Leo.

'Really.'

'We have to be pall-bearers?'

So, a couple of weeks later, Leo and I carried Charlie to his final resting place under the big oak at the bottom of the garden, not far from where I had stood naked and recited unto the rain. As then, it was a photo in *The Sun*, looking down from a helicopter as we lowered the white coffin.

That night, Anna turned me away.

'That time's gone, Johnny.' She sounded so gentle. 'Erin. We don't want to confuse her.'

Then something else altogether: 'Just be here for her. For both of us. I want you to just be here. I think we owe it to him. To Duke.'

I was so furious I told her. How Duke knew we had slept together. How that put the noose around his fuckin' neck. I asked what she thought about that, how she felt about hearing that after all these years. I shouted at her to tell me why she was still here and just take her child and fuck off. Then I slammed the door and saw Erin along the corridor in the half-light, a demonic little girl in a horror movie.

I heard and saw all that, in my head, as I turned silently away and closed the door to Anna's room.

I returned to my bed and a dream that would recur, now and then. Duke is dressed as a Pierrot and hangs

224

from the beam of the byre as I try to run towards him. But my legs won't function and I am more and more panicked, shouting *Duke, c'mon, Duke.* Then his head slowly raises from his chest to reveal a grotesque smiling face, the black-and-white make-up mottled and run.

'That's how it breaks, little bro,' he said.

Fifteen

I am on my way to a caravan, Lewis's place. I barely thought about the invitation, I just said, 'Let's go.'

This surely be, Dukey boy, the most interesting evening I've spent in a long time. My delight is inordinate. Yes, pick your jaw from the floor. I'd whistle a little tune if I knew Lewis would take it the right way. Man who mysterious emails sends is of motives dubious, Confucius said that. I should have got Lewis to sign a sanity clause before agreeing to go with him. Yet there is no sanity clause, Groucho Marx said that.

We have driven a few miles from the cottage, up headland and inland, back down to the shore, Esha Bay, a great dark void pulling my gaze as it pulls Lewis's. He catches my eye and I see my own anticipation reflected back; he wants to tell me what he wants as much as I want to know.

Sometime later we turn off the road, down a rutted track, bouncing through deep puddles I expect us to get stuck in at any moment. The track becomes somewhat smoother and the sea appears on our right, so close I could open the window and feel the spray. A few hundred yards further on we veer inland, the track becoming rough once more as we gain a little height.

We turn up a steep slope. At the top, sheltered in the gap between two small hills, a static caravan squats on bricks. In the rain angling through the headlight beams, it is one of the gloomiest things I've ever seen. Mint-green and heavily weathered, a wide front window faces seawards, four smaller windows running along the side towards the back. Curtains are drawn on all.

'That's us,' says Lewis. 'It's a lot cosier than it looks. Once you get inside.'

'I'll take your word for it.'

'You want a drink?'

'You actually live here?'

'I've got a flat in town. Sometimes I stay here.'

The caravan is split into two sections. To the right is a narrow corridor with three closed doors, bedrooms, I presume. Lewis gestures that I should go left, into a small kitchen area with a linoleum floor. Beyond the kitchen, towards the wide front window is a surprisingly large lounge area with a deep red carpet that reminds me of the foyer in the Inveran Empire. In one corner is a brown, L-shaped sofa, a smaller one diagonally opposite with a small table in front of it.

I am invited to sit on the larger sofa and watch as Lewis turns on a portable gas fire. I haven't seen one of these in decades. Leonid and I had one just like it in Kilburn, so much of a hassle to replace the canister that we left it empty for weeks. I remember the slight anxiety if I turned on the gas and it didn't catch, the steady click of the ignition like a countdown to the *boom* . . .

Lewis is about to sit down beside me but changes his mind. He hurries away to the back of the caravan and comes back carrying a wooden chair. He places it a few feet away from me, sits down then stands up, crossing to the kitchen and returning with a bottle and two glasses.

He hands me a stiff whisky, avoiding eye contact. The fluorescent light is unforgiving. I can see the pores on his nose, a sweaty sheen on doughy skin that might retain its shape if pressed.

He looks sick.

227

'Your good health,' he says.

'What now then?'

He shrugs.

'The *Shinigami*'s here, son. He's read all your emails. He's impressed. Is it money you want?'

'No, *no!*' He raises a hand, palm towards me. 'You think I'm interested in your bloody money? I don't ... You really are an easy man to hate.' He stands up quickly. 'First on the left is the loo, second is the spare room. My one's at the far end.' He rushes away and suddenly stops.

'It's a comfy bed,' he adds, softly. The anger has again vanished, in the same way as back at the byre.

Then he's gone. It all happens so quickly. I listen to a door slam and hear myself say a vague *righty-oh*.

For a while, I stare at my glass. I smell the egginess of gas. I listen to the rain start to drum on the roof so loudly that I doubt I could hear myself if I spoke. My reaction is slow, geriatric, first a heat of embarrassment in my cheeks and then the bemused question: what the hell am I doing here?

I no longer feel delight. Yes, we should embrace the new, Duke. To turn our back on spontaneity at our age is to listen to the tailor ask if sir's graveyard suit is to be single- or double-breasted. Yet navel-gazing has its own attractions. And how's about right now, from a nice hot bath, say ...

I walk down the caravan and knock at Lewis's door. There is no reply. I try the handle but it's locked. 'I'm going to call someone, ok?' As I return to the lounge, I remember my mobile is in Japan. I go back to Lewis's door. 'Have you got a phone? If I stay here overnight they're going to start looking for me. You've got no idea what self-importance does to my niece's paranoia.'

The silence again sends me back to the lounge.

I should be angry.

I pour another and prowl around. I open cupboards in the kitchen to the tang of damp and rows of canned food, an alarming number of tins of oxtail soup. I picture Lewis in the half-light, slurping it from the can, dribbles in his ginger beard. He has a strangely conditional presence, as if someone else must be present for him to exist at all. On the wall opposite the big sofa, two photographs are mounted. In one, empty moorland stretches behind a skinny boy standing outside a tent. In the other, a proudly aloof-looking gentleman in a tailored suit stands at the top of the wide, tapering steps outside the Inveran Royal Hotel. I feel an elusive sense of sorrow. I have no idea why he hates me and a more than a little bit of me wants to find out.

Then I go to bed.

I know, Duke, but what would you do?

Second door along, as told. I am instantly asleep, waking with a start at God knows when, so overwhelmed by darkness that I almost cry out. The fluttering in my chest will inevitably become a full arrhythmia, my bladder so insistent that had I not wakened I might have wet the bed.

I peer out of the door like a child sneaking out of his room on Christmas morning. To my right is Lewis. He is sitting on the smaller sofa, wearing headphones. On the little table in front of him is a laptop.

The man on the screen is very old. He wears a mustard-coloured tank top and sits very straight in some kind of medical chair. He looks in pain. As his mouth moves, his eyes widen and narrow in a peculiar rhythm. I edge away, wondering how long it has been since I saw Simple Simon Warner.

* * *

There is no more drama in the night. No other sudden waking and sitting bolt upright. There is no panic of any kind. Just sleep. And even a sense of peace as I wake to an utter silence. The rain and wind has passed, grey light seeping round the curtains. As it swells, I imagine it dissolving the tranquillity I feel, replacing it with something I should be feeling, like confusion, awkwardness.

★ ★ ★

Lewis isn't in the caravan. I stand in the lounge and sip a glass of water, a tremor in my hands. The curtains are open. The Land Rover is spattered with the mud of last night's drive. A grassy slope leads down to a track running left and right along the shore. The tide is in, a lapping on shingle, the grey of the sea merging smoothly with that of the sky, as if the world is curving back on me.

When I come out the toilet, I see a note on the caravan door. *Top of the morning! Popped out for air . . . coffee in the pot* ☺. The cheerfulness is overdone. My tranquillity becomes an instant discomfort. I pour a coffee, adding a shot of Old Pulteney from the half-empty bottle on the counter, and taking another, straight from the neck. My hand stops shaking.

I hear the door open behind me and turn to Lewis's sheepish face. He offers a hesitant, 'Good morning.'

'We need to talk.'

He seems taken aback by my brusqueness. 'Right. Sure. You hungry?'

'No.'

'How about eggy bread?'

'What?'

'No, sorry. You called it French toast, didn't you?'

'I'm not following.'

'Your autobiography. Don't you remember?'

230

I almost expect him to punch me on the arm, like c'mon old friend.

'Your favourite birthday meal. Battenberg cake and eggy bread. You once ate nine slices. I thought you might like it.' His face has brightened, as if everything is now making perfect sense.

The snow begins to fall.

We sit side by side on the smaller, L-shaped sofa with the table. Now and then our arms touch. He has laid out two red fabric place mats, even though I have told him again I don't want anything. His cheeks bulge as he chews, lips tightly closed, as if terrified his mouth might open as he eats.

As he takes another forkful I ask why he hates me. He's surprised. It takes him a while to chew and swallow.

'I don't hate you.'

'Why say it then?'

He shakes his head vaguely, as if he can't believe my ignorance, then shovels in more French toast.

'What about Simon Warner?' I add. Again, I have to wait for him to patiently chew and swallow.

'What about him?'

'I saw you watching him last night. On your laptop. It looked like an interview. Your film, I take it.'

'That's right.'

'He's got a story to tell, has he?'

'He died two years back. Seventy-five, same age you are now. I filmed it in his nursing home.'

'So what's it all about then? Your emails made all these insinuations. What's Simon's little tale?'

'His mind was there, right until the end.'

'I asked what he said.'

Very carefully, Lewis places his knife and fork on the plate. There is a bit of egg in his beard.

'C'mon, tell old *Shinigami* here.'

He slams his hand down on the table, knocking the knife and fork to the floor. 'What the hell difference does it make?' He rushes across to the window, pointing into snow become a wild flurrying.

'When am I going to get to see it then?'

'See the track there? Follow it for a mile then go right. It'll take you to the Inveran road. Fuck *you*!'

Yet I find myself smiling, sitting back and appraising him. I don't believe him.

'Have you got a phone I can use?'

'No.'

'No mobile.'

'Nope.'

'You're the only person in the world who hasn't got a mobile phone.'

'You don't have one either!'

The wind buffets me as soon as I step outside. I almost slip on the steps, the door slamming shut behind me. At the top of the slope I look back. Through the snow, Lewis watches me from the window.

I turn right at the bottom of the slope, retracing the route we drove the night before. The sea is to my left, the tide in. In the distance, waves break across the track where it is closest to the shore. That is precisely where I slip and fall, landing heavily on my side. I lie on the wet track, pain in my ribs and my face at the level of the sea. I watch a wave recede into the jumble of water, the next breaker already forming, swelling up and closer. I taste salt and wonder how big the wave will be by the time it looms over me, crashes down, sucks me back out . . .

It doesn't reach me. Not even an apologetic lapping against the cheek. I move onto my back and close my eyes. I feel pain but no cold. I hear surf and nothing else. For some reason I start to laugh.

When I sit up, Lewis is running towards me. He is carrying a tartan blanket. He helps me to my feet with surprising strength, his eyes full of concern as he throws the blanket across my shoulders.

'I'll take you back. I'll take you back, for Christ's sake.'

We move slowly along the track, my arm around his waist. 'Battenberg,' I say, after a while.

'What?'

'Battenberg.'

He stops with a breathless 'What?'

'You said you had some. I'll have a piece when we get back.'

He looks at me carefully before replying, as if checking I'm not mocking him. 'Sure. If you want.'

It is true. One birthday, along with nine slices of French toast, I ate half a Battenberg. Do you remember, Duke, how you followed me around making puking noises, trying to make me throw up? Today, sitting in front of the gas heater with my tartan rug, I content myself with one slice.

Lewis sits a few feet away from me. A wavering stare. He seems unsure what attitude to assume.

Outside, the wind creeps up the Beaufort, the caravan shuddering to harder and harder gusts. The day has become a dusky gauze, the curtain of a puppet theatre and all those familiar silhouettes. For now, my affection is entirely unencumbered. Once more, ably assisted by the medicinal bottle that Lewis has left at my feet to self-administer, I shall let them dance . . .

'I'm sorry,' he says. 'About earlier. Shouting like that.'

'Don't worry about it.'

'I don't want you to think that's who I am.'

'How long have you worked at The Castle?'

He looks surprised. 'Three, four years, I suppose.'

'You like it?'

233

'It's a five star hotel. It's full of wankers.'

I laugh. 'Of course it is!' I am more drunk than I think I am, or should be. But I'm in shock, Duke, I could be dead, face in the surf with a seagull on my head. 'Why not do something else?'

'What else do you think there is to do round here? Work the ferries? You seen what it's like out there?'

'They don't run when it's this bad.'

'You reckon?'

I look out the window. In fact, there in the distance, a ship is passing. Vague milky lights. A blinking of red. I remember a storm not unlike this one, the vanishing running lights of the *Breda*.

'There's still a romance. The sea. I was going to join the Merchant Navy, once.' I pour myself another. '*Slainte.*'

Lewis repeats the '*Slainte.*'

He's wondering why I seem so amenable. I have to admit to a certain content. Outside, a wild snow. Inside, in the half-light, the tick and heat of an old gas fire. You'd like it, Duke. If you were here with a woman you'd say things like *I don't want to be anywhere else in the world.*

'You're shivering,' says Lewis. 'There's plenty of water for a shower. I'll drive you back when you get out.'

'Tell me what this is all about, son.' My affection surprises me. It is entirely unbidden. I even smile. He stares at me intently then turns away. Again, I seem to be watching him make up his mind.

I spend a long time in the shower. A cubicle barely large enough even for me. The problem, I think, is my bandy legs, at the widest point of the bow both my knees touch the sides. I imagine Lewis having to rescue me again, soaping my knees before dragging me free with a loud pop.

The storm is still rattling when I get out. Lewis has

234

left out some clothes on the bed, over-long jeans that I have to roll up and a garish, baggy green jumper that hangs off me like a punishment.

I'm barely back in the lounge before he thrusts a folder at me. 'Have a look,' he says. 'If you want.'

The folder is a photograph album: stills from my films, publicity shots of The Breda Boys stage shows and movies, a few of JJ and the Duke. Many of them are signed by me and you, Duke, sometimes the old man. Some I haven't seen in years, some I never have. I stare at a photo of you and Anna, must be from around 1965. You're sitting barefooted in a chair in St. Stephen's Garden, wearing a tux with the bow tie undone, leaning forward with your elbows on your knees. Behind you, Anna leans demurely on the chair, face half-hidden by a cascade of blonde hair.

'A rarity, that one. From your brother's fan club.'

I'd forgotten all about that club, although the scrawled signature was most likely written by Anna.

'It's not the rarest though. Look.' He takes the album from me and flicks back a few pages. 'See this?'

The photo is embossed *Inveran, summer 1955*. You, me and the old man are standing at Inveran harbour. Behind us is a steamer, the name white painted on the dark stern: *Claymore, Glasgow*. It's the day we set out on *The Stornoway Way* tour. We're laughing at the camera, surrounded by suitcases. The publicity photos were my idea. We sold signed copies for a shilling.

As I move through the photos I began to hear Ellington. *Such Sweet Thunder*. I look up and see Lewis standing by the CD player in the kitchen. He's uncomfortable, knows he's pushed it too far.

'Any other melodrama you want to roll out, son? How about sticking on a DVD of *A Man's a Man*?'

'Shouldn't I choose one of yours if I'm doing that?'

An instant steeliness. I remember the anger from earlier and recall a line from one of his emails. *All these people, how disappointed they'd all be.* I look back at the photos. 'It's quite the collection.'

'Didn't you say that making a film was all about squatting in someone else's life for a while?'

'Squatting, not stalking.'

He ignores the insult. 'You're right,' he says. 'It's all about the *immersion*. I never really got that until now. I've made loads of films. I started in high school. Little scenes. I ran them together and called it *Inveran 101*. No-one's seen any of them except my dad. He bought me my first camera.' His face is red with embarrassment. 'The documentary's for him, really.'

'So when do I get to see the great masterpiece?' Instantly, his face clouds again. 'What's it called?'

He looks coy.

'Let me guess. *The Shinigami*?'

'Why not? It's the perfect illustration of you.'

'Of my tragedy?'

'Not your tragedy. Everyone else's. All that death you've brought.'

'You're losing me.'

He sniffs. Then comes across and re-fills my glass. 'You're so refined, aren't you? Cause and effect, you're beyond all that. Buy low and sell high. Every one of your accumulations is someone else's loss. Doesn't matter to you. You just see the columns turning red to green.'

'I've no idea what you're talking about.'

'I know you don't.'

'What the hell have I ever done to you?'

'My dad. He'd still be here if it wasn't for you.'

'You're losing me again.'

'The Royal Inveran.'

'The hotel?' I glance across at the picture on the wall. The proud man standing outside the entrance.

236

'You probably don't know what happened when you opened the Inveran Castle.'

'It wasn't my decision to open that hotel.'

'Wrong. You set up Breda Inc. in the first place. That pretty much makes it your decision.'

'C'mon, son, don't be dragging original sin into it. That's the trump card, where's the fun in that?'

'I asked if you knew what happened to the Royal Hotel?'

'It closed down a few years back.'

'Bingo. My dad owned it. Poured his life into it. And overnight the guests disappeared. Pissed off up the coast to your new place. JJ Jackson, Local Legend. He should have cut his losses there and then. Too proud. *I've got a standing*, he said it over and over. *I've got a standing in this town*. He poured more and more into an empty hotel. Then we were bankrupt. Funny that.'

I am now grateful to Ellington, filling the space that has shrunk between us. 'I'm sorry, I truly am.'

'I don't give a shit about the hotel.' He grabs the whisky bottle. 'It was this. He climbed inside *this* and never got out. I'd get calls from pubs, telling me to come and get him. Then one evening it was the police at the door. He'd been hit by a train. They called it accidental death but he meant it, why else was he down the fuckin' *railway*?' He stares at me for a few more moments. Then the anger suddenly dissipates. He sees the bottle in his hand and pours me a top up. 'I worked in the hotel bar. Old Simon Warner used to come in now and then. He came to the funeral too. He had some choice things to say about you. He didn't like you too much either.'

I remember Simon's face on the laptop.

'It seemed crazy, you know, what he told me. But I did some digging. It's amazing what you can find out when you really dislike someone. Enough for a book. Then I thought, why not a film?'

He looks at me with absolute disdain. The affection I felt for this man is almost comically out of place.

'So you think you know all about me.'

His eyes brighten. 'Not everything, I'm sure.' He's expectant. He wants me to ask again if I can see it.

Instead, I close my eyes and listen to Ellington. After a while Lewis suddenly gets up. He returns a few moments later with the laptop, setting it up as *Sonnet to Hank Cinq* reaches its tentative crescendo.

'Just watch it. Please. That's all.'

The last of the late-afternoon light is on the quick-slide to darkness. Lewis hurries into his waterproof and leaves me alone. He has taken a torch. I watch his light bob down the slope and westwards.

On the table the film waits at the menu page. *The Shinigami* fills the top half of the screen. Bold white capitals on black. Below the title is a definition. *Shinigami (death spirit, the Grim Reaper) – supernatural figures or gods from Japanese religion and culture that are related to death.* Below this are the words play film and scene selection, each accompanied by a small representation of a demon's face.

The style is blundering from the off.

I click the *play film* demon and the screen goes black. It remains that way for so long I think it has crashed. Then music fades in, a wistful piece played uncertainly on what sounds like a Bontempi organ.

Suddenly, there is a scream of keys, as if all have been pressed at the same time. *The Shinigami* instantly fills the screen in those same, bold white letters. They slowly fade into a static shot of the Sound of Skerray from our cottage and a voiceover begins, an over-solemn Lewis.

Inveran, Scotland. February 1956. A young man has leapt into the boiling sea to save three drowning sailors from a stricken ship. This is Duke Jackson. At home, his brother

238

Johnny has no idea of the myth they are about to be catapulted into. These will be the Breda Boys, and myth it most certainly is.

Again, the scream of keys. *The Shinigami* flashes onto the screen once more.

Only curiosity stops me switching off. I feel embarrassed for Lewis, but I am also astonished. The feeling grows the longer I watch. Again, I almost switch off. It is increasingly shocking to see my story laid out like this. Lewis knows. He's found out things even I don't know. Yet the incompetence of it and the strident tone, so different from the memories which have scrolled in my head for so long, somehow undermines what is unerringly true.

I pour another drink. The film has returned to the title page. I stare at the words and wonder if a *Shinigami* also has the ability to invite itself to its own death. If so, I offer my summons, my glass in the air, Duke, so ridiculous an idea given my essential cowardice that I begin to laugh.

I find another torch in the cupboard under the kitchen sink and go out into the night, taking the bottle.

* * *

The tide is out. I walk the beach. The torchlight is dim. My shoes and jacket are soaking from my earlier fall. Shingle becomes sand and I have no idea where I'm going. I think I must have reached the beach at Edmonton Bay by now. Emigrant boats once left from here, overseen as I am by the tinsel stream of the Milky Way. I have been all over the world and never seen skies like this.

Lewis is standing a few metres away. I passed him wordlessly some time ago. I didn't have to glance back to know that he had started to follow. He is observing me but pretending he isn't.

239

Yet his gaze too must now be drawn upwards. A vague, milky green has appeared on the eastern horizon. I watch it flare across the sky in a huge and incandescent arc. Then a pastel pink emerges, swelling to mauve and back to pink, languidly following the arc of green and abruptly vanishing, reappearing moments later. Vague white contrails begin to pour vertically through the pulsing rainbow. Behind, against the purple-black background, I can still see the stars.

Lewis comes closer, looking up. There is something unsettling in the careful way he puts one foot directly in front of other, like an animal. The colours deepen and again draw my gaze, the silence magnified by the psychedelic skies. It is so overwhelming that I expect a great fanfare of never before heard music. Only something otherworldly could explain the eerie dancing rhythm.

Lewis is now right beside me. 'The *Mirrie Dancers*', he says. 'What they call the Aurora Borealis.'

'I watched your film,' I tell him.

'What do you think?'

'It's quite the story.'

'Do you think it works?'

He is so anxious. I feel a sudden and growing contempt. 'Is that all you want? Praise. My blessing?'

'No, I just—'

'It's stunning. You've made a masterpiece.'

We stand in silence for a long time. The aurora dances on the beach, the water. I feel him looking at me.

'You think you know me,' I say. 'But it's just a snapshot. All those people we are in a life, all the ones we forget. I don't know half of them any more. I know some of them less than I know you.'

'You think I'm judging you?'

'No. That's the problem. Where's the commitment? *Judge* me for Christ's sake.'

Out of the corner of my eye I see him look away, upwards. 'Why did everything have to happen this way?'

I don't know what he means. I don't even know if the question is for me. He sounds so disconsolate, a little boy on the verge of tears. I almost feel I should apologise for hurting his feelings. It is all too much, Duke. I tip the bottle. I too will withdraw into these beautiful, shifting skies.

Sixteen

I hardened, I know, although I do not see this as my fault alone. I was a man of wilful silences and ballooning weight, midnight pastries and a glass in hand, pondering the desolation of a domestic life I was too dim to understand and too timid to confront. Yet somehow, an inscrutable beacon reassuring me I was still able to do something right, Breda Inc. exploded with success.

Film production I left to Fatty, convinced by the disaster of *Blues* my touch was hapless. Business-wise, I was Mr Midas, spending the rest of the seventies on a resolutely prolific accumulation bender.

Our property investments surged, a windfall used to acquire the Sirocco boutique hotels and the Palisades chain of top-end golf courses. Duke would have enjoyed the golf deal, a latecomer to the game when fame came calling, all plus fours and Harlequin socks, a one-man divot machine at the Inveran links. Jack Nicklaus designed the Palisades courses and they flew him to Palma, Majorca, to dazzle me with so much starlight that I wouldn't notice the jacked-up price. He asked if I played and I told him I'd avoided cults since I stopped attending the Free Presbyterian Church, this confusing the Golden Bear who thought anyone from Scatlan must surely love golf. He stood beside me for the publicity shots with a face to shank a drive into the Med.

Anna had no problem with these trips.

She became the dreamiest of presences, no longer insisting on my nightly return to Wendlebury. Instead, as Erin grew older, she quietly encouraged my absence. I would return to the most distant of smiles and a doubt I couldn't shake that she hadn't actually noticed I'd been away.

Yet after reading the final instalment of *The Party*, I wondered if I'd been wrong. Anna's column in the *Express* ran for a surprisingly long time, and here, at the very last, the strange Director finally spoke at length, a tender monologue about the tragedy in beauty and the sadness in knowing you're not truly of this time. I thanked her for finally making me sympathetic.

She was puzzled. 'Really? That's how you read that?'

Then she patted my hand. That way she patted my hand. Yet every time I came back to Wendlebury Anna and Erin were still there. And although I was relieved they were, I never quite grasped why. We were the most reluctant of families, every holiday a Mexican stand-off.

Erin grew into a subdued little girl, dominated by her mother. Only rarely did friends from her primary school visit. Instead, it was mother and daughter who played games, painted and watched movies.

Her eventual interests were solitary or obsessive. For a while, she made lists, the longest rivers, the highest mountains, accompanied with intricately drawn maps. When she was ten she discovered short-wave radio via a Soviet-built, Vega 206 advertised in a newspaper. Both hobbies seemed wilful statements of her need for space.

Anna was hurt. She'd stand at her daughter's bedroom door, Erin with her headphones on, turning the dial with epic patience, writing mysterious signal transmission codes in a leather-bound logbook: 34333 ... 24212.

In a heroic effort to engage, I built a radio shack for her at the bottom of the garden. I worked on the plans

243

for days, honing the design that took me a month to actually build. I only needed assistance in the last stages to raise and secure the walls, and brought in an electrical engineer to fix up a dipole antenna so Erin could scour the bands for even more remote stations.

Some evenings, I would stand outside the conservatory, looking down across the garden, the shack in the distance, a dim yellow glow in the window. I wondered about other families and the idiosyncrasies of intimacy and distance, and how many others had sombre ten-year-olds proudly present them with their latest postcards from Ecuador, Russia, Australia . . .

These were 'QSLs', I learned, sent in return for reception quality reports, sometimes with stickers, calendars or other little gifts, once a proselytising letter from a religious broadcaster in Nigeria telling Erin that *only Yahweh forgives*. From the God-free zone behind the Iron Curtain she received such frequent letters from Radio Moscow that I expected a visit from MI5. She mounted the cards very carefully in a folder and took them to school with her every day, occasionally updating us on her favourites. Once it was a series of postcards of *Soviet Architectural Achievements*, sent by the grooming commissars of Radio Moscow's English bureau. Each was embossed in gold lettering with MOCKBA: blocky buildings on Gorky Street; the egg-yolk yellow presidium of the Academy of Sciences; the brutalist skyscraper of the Ukraina Hotel.

'Which do you prefer?' she asked.

I chose the gunmetal grey Krymsky Bridge, empty of people and traffic apart from three presumed Ladas.

'Mum?'

'That one.' These were the cathedrals of the Moscow Kremlin, bathed in apocalyptic, reddish light.

'Hmm. Smithy likes this one best.' It was a mid-shot of an impossibly cute girl holding a red flower in the yellow-flowered gardens of the Bolshoi Theatre, a composition straight out of Socialist Realism 101.

'Who's Smithy?' asked Anna.

It turned out Peter Smith was a twenty-six-year-old with learning difficulties who worked as a decorator. He too was a collector, of stamps, and saw Erin showing her cards at Wendlebury Primary when he was painting the gym. He had driven her home several times, stopping before the gatehouse to let her out. Erin said Smithy hadn't touched her inappropriately and no action was taken.

Anna was beside herself. She withdrew Erin from school and harassed the police to bring charges they couldn't justify. Then she insisted I bring in the Breda lawyers who, likewise, found no way to sue the school for negligence. The reception room became a classroom, mother becoming teacher, happy in the midst of trauma at finding a way back to her daughter.

I shouldn't have mentioned *Bad Jack* to Anna.

Leo called it fascist nonsense, Fatty saw box-office gold. Anna read the script in an afternoon and insisted on punishment by proxy for Peter Smith. *Bad Jack*, a revenge tale about a farmer who kills a group of Manson-esque hippies who rape his teenage daughter. My opinion swung it and I produced. *Bad Jack* was a controversial smash, prompting for and against demonstrations outside cinemas by the National Front, who saw in Jack a hero of post-sixties reaction, and the Women's Liberation Movement, outraged by the deliberately ambiguous rape scene.

A week after the film was released Peter Smith was beaten into a coma by an anonymous gang which broke into his house. It took him over a year to recover. 'The system's broken,' Anna said to the policeman who told us. 'Sometimes there's no problem with a bullet in the head.'

It was 1978 and the Moral Panic was upon us. As

with *A Clockwork Orange* before and *Video Nasties* and *Natural Born Killers* later, *Bad Jack* took the tabloid rap for film violence causing all manner of social ills. The manor was picketed for weeks, Breda Productions London office as well. I had dreams where I was looking out from the top floor of the house, watching a vast crowd of people swelling in the distance like in a David Lean epic, flooding towards me ...

Febrile.

I didn't know what it meant when Leo said it. He'd come over one weekend, to 'break the siege'. We drank vodka and sat outside, on the vast lawn which seemed to symbolise the astonishing distance between Kilburn and the present day, what our relationship once was and what it had become. We skirted around all that I wanted to talk about; my unhappiness and Anna's quiet anger, Erin's monosyllables that detonated like tiny cluster bombs of despondency.

'You live in a febrile atmosphere,' he said at the gate-house as he was leaving.

I looked it up. Leo was bang on. I was overtaken by the most urgent need to get away, all of us.

When I suggested a long trip, Anna's one insistence was that we leave it three weeks until the school holidays. The itinerary appeared as an end-of-year project, presented to me in an A4 folder (each of us had an identical copy), a list of ten locations from Scotland to Auckland that Erin and Anna had decided we would visit over the next three months, complete with hand-drawn maps and stats about GDP, key export sectors, cultural practices, top attractions ...

* * *

The trip began in Inveran. An epic drive north in a brand-new Mercedes 240-D that ended in the gloomiest of visits to Anna's mother. She was sixty-seven but looked twenty years older, the outriders of dementia in her watery grey eyes and already an unsettling, repetitive pulling at her bottom lip.

We sat in silence for too long and finally escaped to MacIntyre's Bay, Anna and I arm in arm what felt like solidarity more than affection, watching Erin playing with a red kite that dipped and flitted like old memories. It had been so long since I had spent any extended time with them.

It was Japan where we truly reconnected. Something in the quietude of the people, perhaps, that stillness even among Tokyo's seethe, where I felt an incongruous sense of space and distance. Here was a place of reflection, somewhere to rest the gaze, awhile, on each other.

We all felt it. Australia and New Zealand were jettisoned. We went first to Shibu, days of rain on steep, wet streets, the yellow lamps of elegant *ryokans* behind cypress, calling to each other from our respective sections of the public *onsen*. Then on to the sake shops of Takayama's dark timbered streets, *yakitori* from a booth that Erin insisted we visit again and again, returning to Kyoto and a step back in time to Gion by night, ghost-geishas in soft lantern light, spilling laughter from the little restaurants lining the Shirakawa canal, where Anna and I stood on an arched bridge and she fell in love, though not with me. 'Here,' she said, 'is where I want to live.'

Yet I wondered what here was. Japan looked in all directions at the same time and never seemed sure where to let the gaze rest. We dazzled ourselves in 360 neon, ate hamburgers in the disorientating pseudo-authenticity of a fifties-styled American diner called *Speakeasy*, strolled afterwards by the river, along the Philosopher's Walk in the dusk shadows of a different, deeper Japan, old men and drooping trees, a trace of incense and then a Zen temple emerging from the gloom. I glimpsed Sakyamuni on the altar and asked if I could live here, the gentle eyes posing both question and answer, no more strangeness here than elsewhere, Johnny-san. You can spend a lifetime in a place you were born and never feel part of it, or a minute in somewhere you've never been and know that it has been waiting for you your whole life.

I told the board I was taking a year's leave. Fatty became interim CEO of Breda Inc. Leo took on Breda Pictures. I don't think they believed I would come back. When I did, the world had changed.

The bespoke tour specialist we had been using to navigate the confusion of Japan found us a full-time interpreter.

Akira Minamoto was twenty-two, fresh from a linguistics degree at Stanford. I immediately took to this gentle young man with the bum-fluff moustache, who was happy to act as chaperone for Erin, grateful, I think, for delaying his entry into the anonymous life-grind of the salary-man.

Akira liaised with the real estate companies and Anna drew up her shortlist. We spent a week contemplating a forest bungalow in Nagano, the duplex opulence of an apartment in Azabu, Tokyo, and a stunning old, wood-built *kyōmachiya* town house near Daitokuji temple in Kyoto. Yet in the end it was a seventeenth-century *ryokan* in Shuzenji, two hours south-west of Tokyo.

It was raining as we were shown around.

The *ryokan* sat in a halo of dense forest, separated from the house on three sides by a long, tapering pond. Anna's eyes lit up. She instantly adored the bright spaces of the *tatami*-floored rooms with their sliding *shōji* screens. She insisted we be taken in the rowing boat to the small island that housed a little Shinto shrine. It was the elegant combination of openness and enclosure which, I am sure, gave her such a reassuring sense of comfort at Shuzenji.

We enrolled Erin at the American School in Chofu, Tokyo. Akira was retained as a driver and he took her back and forth every day until, exhausted by the epic commute, Erin demanded we move to the capital.

I felt this was more a reaction to Anna's shifting attention. The overly cosseting mother that Erin professed to hate but secretly adored was rediscovering herself in the quiet of the *ryokan*. She was writing again, stranger in a strange land pieces that would eventually be taken on by *The Japan Times*, and painting too, an ink-wash class at the local college. I think Erin expected Anna to drop it all but she didn't, arranging instead for Erin to stay in Tokyo during the week.

Anna had settled. Into that quietude I would be admitted, now and then, to share cautious intimacies.

'If I told you this was the happiest I have ever been, would you believe me?'

Things like that.

It was December. We were sitting at a table on the decking separating the house from the pond, holding back the cold with a bottle of Suntory ten-year-old. A fabric canopy angling down from the first-floor balcony sheltered us from thickly falling snow. I stared at the lanterns running along the house, votive light becoming softer. I could believe anything on a night like this.

'Of course.'

'It's not that I've *never* been happy. I may even have been happier, a few times.' She reached a hand out from under the parasol and let the snow land on her palm. 'But it was always a bit like this, see, it always melted away ... Profound or what, eh?' She rubbed her wet hand on my face.

I wiped my face, poured us a refill from the emptying bottle and raised a glass. 'I'll take it!' I announced.

'What?'

'Your fierce affection.'

She giggled and raised her glass. 'To fierce affection.' Then, after a moment, 'Do you think my daughter hates me?'

'I think your daughter is thirteen.'

'She probably won't like the painting.'

'Of course she will.'

'No, I don't think I'll bother.'

I looked again at the inkbrush painting on the table, intended as a Christmas present. A winter landscape, two rolling hills to the right and a smaller one to the left, a winding river between. Two dark figures on the extreme left held hands. It took skill to create something so simple. She'd spent all day on it, sitting under the eaves of the little Shinto pagoda on the island in the pond, wrapped in her red duffel coat. She went there daily now, snow or rain, rowing across.

'I don't think she wants to be here.'

'She'll be fine. When I was her age I wanted to be a cowboy. Helluva way from Inveran to Dodge City.'

'The Bandy-Legged Kid!'

'You betcha, perfect for riding a horse.'

'Anyway, what I mean—'

'I know what you mean. I'm just saying we could give her all she wanted and she'd find a way to complain.'

'You think we're doing ok? Are we good parents?'

She registered my surprise. I never allowed myself to think of myself as Erin's parent. 'Far as I can see.'

'But you're blind as a bat!'

'So what's your excuse?'

Such was the pattern of our intimacy. Deflecting in humour what we might have discovered, had she the patience to wait as I searched for the right word and if I believed I could ever find it.

'There's still plenty you see, though,' she added, cryptically, reaching across and squeezing my hand.

I had a sudden, disorienting feeling that Duke was close. I knew as I looked at Anna that she was thinking about him as well. Then, just as quickly, he was gone.

When we first moved to Japan we talked about Duke a lot, what he would have thought about living here, would he have enjoyed it, trying to establish his presence in a place with absolutely no connection to him.

'You know what we should do,' I said, 'when Erin breaks up for the holidays?'

'What's that?'

'Go skiing. She loved that trip they went on. Fancy it? I'll get Akira on the case.'

'You've never skied in your life.'

'Rather that than have her moping around.'

'How long do you want to go for?'

'Weeks. *Months*. I want a log cabin and a big fire and I want to drink whisky and read you haikus.'

Her smile flickered, faded. I watched her gaze move to the island, the outline of the low pagoda just visible on the edge of the light from the *ryokan*. I thought I knew what she was concerned about.

'Don't worry. You can paint there, same as here. A new perspective.'

Niseko was a cluster of villages at the bottom of Mount Yotei on the island of Hokkaido. We bumped north to Sapporo on a tin-can turbo-prop, white-knuckle air pocket drops over the Tsugaru Strait. The journey was almost as nerve-jangling as the high-speed zip to Niseko in a Toyota LiteAce van, a custard yellow lozenge skittering between high walls of snow on both sides of the road.

251

Erin softened. Perhaps it was the terror of the journey, like some kind of shock-therapy, or simply being somewhere new. She transformed into a little girl again, for a while, delighting in her mother's presence and mine, laughing at my stiff-limbed snowplough as she carved elegantly past.

We spent the evenings in our cabin, afternoons too after Anna twisted her back and skiing was too painful, despite the codeine. Board games by the fire or just reading, watching strange game shows. When Erin slept we talked about where we were going and where we had come from, going to meet it again, Inveran, out there beyond the glistening snow on the edge of the light.

'Do you think we're running away?' she asked.

'Staying in the same place can be much the same.'

'I used to think that I'd always end up back there, one day. I'm not so sure now. Maybe it's too much like admitting your time is up. I had a cat that did that once, took itself off to die. Imagine knowing that.'

'Maybe it's just a reconnecting.'

'But reconnecting means that you've lost something, misplaced it. I've never felt that. I feel closer to home than I ever have. You think about it more, when you're not there. It becomes more present, somehow.'

'I wonder what Erin thinks about when she thinks of home.'

'That's what we're building at Shuzenji. A home for her.'

She leaned towards me on the sofa. Rested her head on my shoulder so I could not see her eyes.

'Me and you,' she repeated.

She lifted her head and offered her lips, her eyes still closed. *Me and you*, I thought as I kissed her.

We spent another two weeks in the cabin, then returned to Shuzenji. Erin's hostility continued to slip away; perhaps she was simply getting older and more mature, or even starting to value the home that Anna said we were trying to build for her, *me and you*. Day on day, Anna would row out to her island to paint. I even started to take an interest in Breda again, made a few phone calls, before the morning I realised the 'you' I had not seen in Anna's eyes was not me at all.

It was a Saturday, a steady wind in the cypress. Anna had gone to town with Erin. I was at my desk.

I had a new idea for a film, *The Bruce*, a hallucinatory alternative take on the life of the famous Scottish king, a swirl of images that excited me with possibilities but hadn't settled into coherence. This was my own doing. I'd sit down to work but as soon as an idea began to form I would quickly let it go, as if unwilling to disappoint myself with the gap between ideal and representation.

So, as usual, I was prowling, tumbler of Suntory to hand. First my bedroom, facing the bed that Anna and I shared most nights now, a source of satisfaction but apprehension as I waited for her mood to shift, as it inevitably would, and she returned to her own room. Then into the kitchen, looking out the long window, where a flurry of blossom-like pink snow suddenly blew past, so fleeting and gone it might never have happened. Onto my favourite room of all in which to kill time, the one we called *Kan'ami*, after the famous *Noh* actor. I stood in front of the masks we had started to collect, three mounted rows on the wall of empty-eyed, staring faces. I went through them one by one, trying to mimic their expressions, gurning and grinning as the wind gusted and the timbers of the old *ryokan* groaned like disappointed punters.

I took the hint and went outside, onto the wooden deck. As I looked across the pond to the little island with the shrine I realised I hadn't been there since we first looked round the *ryokan*, almost a year ago. I thought of it as Anna's island, a private place she returned from with ever more impressive paintings. If she had been here I would not have gone.

It only took two pulls on the oars to reach the little wooden jetty. I tied the boat to the mooring pole. She'd cleared the weeds from between the cobbles, and weeded on both sides of the narrow stone path. Fresh-planted geraniums and pansies lit a multicoloured way to the shrine.

I passed two slender stone pillars, about head-height. Unknown *kanji* carvings, scoured clean, scrolled vertically on both. Then the shrine, a heavily weathered wooden structure built about two feet off the ground, the walkway running around all four sides reached by three stone steps. A traditional sloping pagoda feathered out over the internal walls, plain solid wood at the base and anonymous, bleached carvings at the top, a lattice strip in-between.

I peered inside and saw Duke, grinning.

The framed photograph stood in the middle of the small, square altar, a little jar full of incense leavings directly in front. On each side of the photo two stubby white candles had been lit. At the back of the altar were two identical, mottled ceramic statues of a white fox with a big, bushy tail. *Kitsune* were mostly benevolent spirits. But they could sometimes be tricksters.

I could only laugh. I turned my back to Duke and sat down on the wooden platform. 'Fair enough, big bro.'

Hours later, mother and daughter now returned from their trip, I still felt that odd light-heartedness.

I gave Anna a long hug. 'I've been to the island,' I whispered.

I felt her instant tension. One long, stretched moment later she stepped back and looked at me. 'I knew you

254

would.' She looked at me with such affection that I felt a lump in my throat.

'I thought I'd be angry.'

'Are you?'

'No.'

'There's nothing that I'll ever be able to do about it, you know. He'll always be there.'

'Closer than I thought.'

'See! You are angry.'

'No. I'm not.'

'What do you want me to do, Johnny, pretend he didn't exist?'

'No. I'm not saying that. I'm not saying anything. I just found my brother's shrine, that's all. I thought you were past all that.'

'All *that*?'

'Yeah, all that.'

'And?'

'And nothing.' The thing is I wasn't angry, I wasn't angry in the slightest, I was even smiling. 'I feel like he's still watching us, like he knows everything that's going on, like he always did.'

Anna was looking at me strangely. 'What's that supposed to mean?'

'What?'

'You said "he knows everything that's going on, like he always did".'

'I mean how he knew about me and you. The waterfall.'

'You told him that.' The colour had drained from her face. 'When?'

'Well . . . I dunno. A long time ago.'

'I know it's a long time ago, I mean *when*?'

I saw Duke's photograph and smelled incense. I held her gaze. 'The night before he killed himself.'

She put a hand to her mouth. As if she was going to

255

be sick. She looked horrified. I watched her hurry out of the kitchen but said nothing. I poured myself another and turned to the window, waiting for pink blossom to tumble again on the wind and this time I would know I had truly seen it.

She hadn't come to bed by the time I'd fallen asleep. When I woke up the next morning I assumed she'd slept in her room, but when I peered round the door she wasn't there and the bed didn't seem slept in. It was only when I went outside and saw the rowing boat tied up across at the little island did I realise where she must be. Yet when I shouted she didn't appear.

In the end, I had to wade over, watched by an anxious Erin, my feet making wet prints on the neat cobbles, birds and insects fussing as I hurried up the path to the shrine, calling out for Anna.

I found her lying on the wooden platform. Peaceful, as if she were asleep: that would be the cliché. She didn't look that way at all.

Inside, on the altar, the candles were burning and Duke was smiling.

★ ★ ★

I used to wake with a sense of foreboding. Remnants of troubling dreams I couldn't actually remember.

In the absence of recollection, I crafted my own images. Wild seas and empty, scoured landscapes, looking out from our old cottage, watching a rowing boat pitch and sink on the Sound of Skerray, standing in a storm atop the Esha Cliffs, certain I'd just missed someone stepping off.

Yet all those struggling in the waves and plummeting into darkness had no faces. Just blank spaces. I knew who they were and had no need to see their eyes looking at me as I lay in bed, staring up at the checkerboard pattern of the wooden ceiling beams, creating my unremembered dreams and slowly coming back to myself, disorientated, the only clue to how much time had passed in the cold cup of coffee on my bedside table which I had not seen Akira bring.

It was Akira who offered to move into Shuzenji. He would look after the place. Look after me. He picked up Erin from Tokyo every weekend, bringing her back to a home now become a mausoleum.

She was thirteen. I told her that her mother had died of a sudden heart attack, an undiagnosed condition. She forgave me for not turning up at the airport to fly back to Scotland with the body. I had a teacher chaperone her instead, and asked a furious Leo to collect her at Glasgow and accompany her to the funeral in Inveran.

Erin tried so hard to get close yet gave up in the end, driven away by a coldness I hated myself for. She followed a friend to boarding school in Lausanne, returning every holiday, to begin with, then occasionally, and eventually not at all.

Others came, to begin with. Leo, once, to berate me. Fatty to insist I extend my sabbatical, take all the time I needed. Breda Inc. was a big beast now, a Godzilla of Corporations they inevitably called us. Don't worry, Johnny, it's in safe hands: Fatty Ashcroft's safe, pudgy hands.

I pretended an interest for a surprisingly long time. I'd drop ambiguous hints about returning as CEO. I insisted that my opinion was sought for every Breda Pictures productions then rarely offered it. I demanded that board papers I didn't read were Fed-Exed to me, sometimes phoning into conferences where I never spoke. My final involvement could only have been my last. I flew to London and insisted on chairing the most excruciating of board meetings, where they stared at me as if I was Alexander Selkirk, suddenly re-appeared for Sunday lunch.

I veered off agenda. I had a magnificent idea for a new film. I was so impatient to tell them. *The Bruce.* Months and months of ten-hour shifts on a little Shinto island where my dead brother Duke grinned from his altar with such encouragement, with *thumbs up*, as if yes, Johnny, *yes*, here's the film to better *A Man's a Man.* All of them, they'd get it too, when I explained.

So I did. At length.

Afterwards, into the great and perplexed silence, strode deadpan Fatty Ashcroft. 'Well, it's quite the story, Johnny, quite the tale. No-one can accuse you of losing the plot, dear boy.'

★ ★ ★

It was the most beautiful of May days, I remember, when Fatty telephoned Shuzenji to tell me that the board had unanimously voted to replace me as CEO. I asked Akira to bring a bottle and two glasses.

'I have been retired,' I told him.

'No. You have been given the gift of time.'

I looked across to the little island with the hidden shrine. I was forty-nine and Akira was right, there was nothing but time, all the sweet and sour tomorrows and tomorrows that I would turn my back on as I faced, instead, all those yesterdays. Time passed was still time, but a gift?

I raised a glass. Akira followed suit.

Seventeen

The Mirrie Dancers are leaving the stage, creeping black from east and west. I offer the bottle to Lewis. He's no drinker, I see how his face puckers. I wonder if he's humouring me. As the last of the lights fade we walk back across the beach. He giggles a little when he stumbles on the sand.

The rain is heavy by the time we get back to the caravan. We huddle in a loaded silence by the gas heater. I know he wants to ask me more about his film. He breaks the tension by announcing he's hungry.

He makes instant noodles and babbles as he slurps. Camping trips with his dad. They'd play rummy, stuck in the tent while it rained. Once there was a thunderstorm, his dad terrifying him by warning him not to touch the poles in case they were struck by lightning. Their best trip was to Loch Monar. They camped out for three days. He wrote a story about it that was published in the school magazine, with a horsefly called Bigfoot and two men in a rowing boat.

'My dad wrote then. Poems. He never told anyone, I mean, you just didn't ... The film, I made it for him.'

'So you said.' My tone is sharp. I refuse the comparison I am being forced to make between this heroic father-figure and the fedora-wearing ghost sitting in the corner looking shifty.

'Those memories. Do you trust them?'

He looks surprised. 'Yes.'

'I never have. Like I said, all those people we are in a life, they all look back in different ways. How do you decide which one's doing the remembering? What makes you think their memory is the right one?'

'Instinct.'

'Or maybe you just decide this is what I am going to think and stick with it.'

'What's wrong with that?'

'There's no truth in it.'

'Maybe, but there's peace. I don't want to think about what my dad became. I want him as he was. I want him to watch *The Shinigami* and tell me "that's great, Lewis, I'm proud of you".'

I think of those endless JJ and the Duke or Breda Boys rehearsals, the old man's hair-trigger temper. I cannot feel Lewis's deep content as he wakes in a tent to a smiling father and a cup of tea.

'Just fuckin' get it right this time.'

'What?'

'That's all I got from my dad.'

'I still need him, you know. After all these years.'

I can't imagine this. It is extraordinary to the point of idiocy. A pitying affection for Lewis sweeps through me once more. It is still there as I help him to bed, much later. He is asleep in seconds.

I watch him for a while then sit down. 'Well, son, your film really is one of the worst things I've ever seen. That's why it's perfect, it fits the story. I always was a bit hand-held, know what I mean? Never had that Steadicam view.' I take off Lewis's shoes and pull the duvet across him. I pat his hand. 'I'm proud of you.' And I go back through to the lounge to watch the film again.

★ ★ ★

Are you impressed, dear Duke? Not with the aesthetic, forget all of that. What I mean is what Lewis knows. It is extraordinary to see them all laid out, all these scenes we have watched and re-watched.

Everything memorable comes in threes. Like those jokes about the Englishman, the Irishman and the Scotsman. Just enough detail to be satisfying. Can you imagine the Four Little Pigs or the Four Billy Goats Gruff? It would get tedious. It's why no-one likes singing Ten Green Bottles.

Lewis is also working to the law of three, although I suspect this is more by accident than design.

The first involves a ramshackle reconstruction. It is the day you died, Duke. The scene starts with old Simon monologuing in his chair. We cut to the actor playing young Simon, a pock-marked kid who can't stop blinking, panicked Morse Code repeating *what am I doing, what am I doing?*

What he is doing is birdwatching, striding across a hillside under summer-blue skies. This is intercut, incongruously, with stock footage of an eagle wheeling over a snowy moor. Next is a long shot from Ben Chorain, down towards our cottage. Simon lifts his binoculars to a close-up of a man in a dressing gown going into the byre. Another man hurries after him and we cut to an extreme close-up of Simon's face, an exaggerated frown. Then back to old Simon, decrepit but animated: 'There's no way he could have died before JJ got in there, no bloody way.'

So what really happened inside the barn? asks the voiceover. The answer offered is a silent, lingering shot of the Sound of Skerray, time and space to come to the inevitable conclusion that Johnny Jackson, somehow, details sketchy, had something to do with his brother's death. What can you say, Duke? The evidence of old, half-daft Simon Warner is incontrovertible . . .

The second disclosure is just as dramatic. This I knew nothing about. Lewis truly has done his research.

We begin with a close-up of the cover of the Inveran High School magazine, 1966. Two hands appear in shot, turning the pages and holding the magazine open at *The Local Hero at Home*. There's a photo of you, Duke, not one of your best. You're sitting in the front row of an empty Inveran Empire, a scatter of papers at your feet. The pupil, Mhairi Archibald, must have interviewed you while you were organising the Billy Jackson memorial concert that never was.

Below the photo is a transcript of the Q&A. We hear two voices reading an extract. Bizarrely, the voice reading Mhairi's questions is male. I suspect the reappearance of the pock-marked kid . . . The other is Lewis's, channelling his inner Duke. Undoubtedly, his dad also told him he was good at impressions. I have a mental image of Charlie the Chimp slapping a hand over his eyes.

'What's next for Duke Jackson? Any scoop you can give me?'

'You've got a future ahead of you, doll. I can just imagine you door-stepping me.'

'Not even a little hint?'

'Well, seeing as you asked so nicely, I've just finished a script. It's called "A Man's a Man" and it's about Robert Burns.'

Cue the screaming organ keys.

Think how different my life would have been had this interview been uncovered before? It's amazing it wasn't, given the media typhoon that followed your death. Take solace, Duke, that your last interview was with one of the Inveran schoolgirls through which you once cut such a swathe.

Yet it is the shock of Lewis's final disclosure which

makes the whole so much more powerful than the sum of the three parts. I know, Duke, you're as sick of it as I am. All these effects and their causes, who knows where they actually lead back to. But let's load the old film one more time, the rasp of your boot on a toppling chair, a frantic coupling beside the Craigie Falls, three Chinese sailors tumbling in the Sound of Skerray. Who knows, who cares; spin the bottle . . .

It is near the end of the film.

We are told that Anna and I have moved to Shuzenji, Japan. There follows an interminable montage of clichés; snow monkeys in hot pools, plum blossom, doe-eyed girls giving the peace sign . . . Then, accompanied by Lewis's solemn voiceover, we see the photo which flashed round the world, briefly, after Anna died. A journalist with a telephoto lens has caught me sitting on the little island where I found her. I am wearing a black *yukata* with my head in my hands.

A sudden heart attack, the story went.

We cut to a beach now quite familiar to me, Edmonton Bay, the sand stretching in that long, elegant half-circle. The camera tracks in on a sheet of paper held down by pebbles. It is printed in *kanji*.

Yet the death certificate tells us something different. 'Multiple drug toxicity – alcohol and codeine. Event of unde-termined intent.'

Should it shock me, to hear this stated so bluntly after so long? I feel only hollow. On-screen, the death certificate breaks free in the wind and tumbles into a glooming sky, fading from sight. It is a near-perfect image. It is how I have always thought of Anna. Perhaps Lewis is a genius after all.

I realise I am crying. I find myself stumbling through to Lewis's bedroom, shaking him roughly until he wakes, disorientation becoming alarm as he quickly sits up. 'I watched him,' I am saying. 'I watched him. It was

263

less than a second.' I start repeating it. 'It was less than a second.'

* * *

I wake just after seven. Somehow, I have managed to get from my last remembered location, the sofa, to my bed. My trousers are down at my knees and I have one shoe on and one off, as if I couldn't be bothered any more, or had simply passed out. I have a vague memory of shouting at Lewis.

Like a guilty tolling, my heart gives a hard thump. Another warning. I see my blood cells as old men on Zimmers, shuffling round my calcified arteries. One by one they do not waken. It's easy to age. Just let it happen – although first you must accept there's no choice. It is much more difficult to be young. Yet the sense of compulsion fades, the pressing need to do something.

I watch the vaguest of light swelling round the edges of the curtain. A similar lightness grows within myself. I decide I will make porridge, stand in the little kitchenette as my reflection in the window fades, the darkness lifting, stirring the pot as my mother did every morning forever . . .

I find no oats. Instead, I borrow Lewis's jacket from the rack beside the door and go outside. A cold but gentle wind is blowing in from the north-east, the waves a soft running and the tide in.

I find a flattish black rock by the shore and sit for a long time. The only sign of my hangover is a press of melancholy. I glance back at the caravan. The light is on in the lounge and I have the most insistent vision. I am living there all by myself. I am sitting on the sofa looking out at the sea, the light, the way it shifts from washed-out translucence to the most incredible depth.

Perhaps this is where I have always belonged. For a

moment, the *ryokan* at Shuzenji is so utterly irreconcilable I am almost embarrassed. To live in Japan seems like a rejection of myself. I have wasted years staring into bamboo and hinoki green when all I've ever needed is leaden grey.

As grey as Lewis's face.

He is walking along the track towards me, wearing a waterproof so incredibly yellow it can only be making his hangover worse. He sits down beside me and wraps his arms around his knees.

'I'm not a drinker.'

'You surprise me. You know what I want to do?'

He takes a moment, as if making sure he won't throw up when he opens his mouth. 'What's that?'

'Go fishing.'

He's surprised. 'I thought you wanted to go home?'

'Have you got a boat?'

'In the shed.'

'Then let's go.'

The thought tips him over the edge. Quickly, he scrambles to his feet but only gets a few feet before he is noisily sick. When he turns back to me he looks sheepish, but brighter. 'I think I'm feeling a bit—'

Again, he doubles-over, retching.

It is an hour before Lewis feels up to it. We cross to the shed opposite the caravan. It is rotting, collapsing, despite being built against the slope on the western side in a hopeful attempt to avoid the elements.

With some difficulty, we open the warped door. Inside, on a trailer, is a white painted, wooden rowing boat. An outboard motor is mounted at the stern but this is a day for the oars, the grey now cleared to a blue so resonant it almost rings, so cold the world seems frozen in place. We wheel the trailer to the shore, careful on the slope. The Land Rover will be needed to pull it back up.

'I've not been out in the boat since my dad died. We bought it at the same time as the caravan. I had this idea that it would give him something to do. We went out once, I think. Didn't catch a thing.'

'Did he enjoy it?'

'He didn't enjoy anything much by the end, Johnny.'

It is the first time he's used my first name. I sit in the boat as he pushes it further into the shallows before jumping in. In his yellow waterproof, knitted hat and wellies, he is completely at home, pulling the oars with ease. I look round and realise I have no idea what the parts of a boat are called. Again, I feel that desire to stay, to have Lewis tell me all he knows about boats.

I tell him he looks the part.

He smiles. 'Maybe it's a genetic memory.' He points with his chin. 'I could tie those in my sleep.'

On the bottom of the boat, the line of hooks is hidden among brightly coloured feathers. You were useless at tying a line, Duke, a bumble of thumbs. I had to do it half the time, yet you were the one taken fishing by the old man. *Bit rough for wee boys, son.* When I was finally deemed big enough I refused; to accept was somehow to forgive all those humiliations. There is no warmth in my memories of boats, I have no desire to tarnish Lewis's by telling of mine.

After a while, he looks around, as if checking his bearings, then pulls in the oars. He sits down beside me, hands me the fishing rod and throws the darrow line over the side. He returns to his seat and starts to row again, more gently. I hold the rod horizontal, feeling the slight drag of the line in the green-black water, the tip of the rod quivering slightly with each pull on the oars.

'I'm sorry about last night,' I say.

'You were drunk.'

I stare at him until he looks away. 'I watched the film again.'

He sniffs. He's not going to ask what I think. He's trying to convince me he isn't bothered any more.

'Do you really think I had something to do with Duke's death?'

'I told you, I'm not interested in judgement.'

'But you're right.'

He pulls hard on the oars as he stares at me.

'You need a re-edit. I gave you the central scene, JJ returning to where his brother died. Re-enact it. Get that daftie of an actor back. I'll do an interview. Know what I'll tell you? That some seconds are longer than others. That I walked in there, saw Duke hanging like a fuckin' puppet and I hesitated, I *hesitated*. Simon's right, there's no way he could have died unless I did something. But he's wrong at the same time. Because I didn't do anything, just for that moment. And that's the moment he died. That second could have been a day. That's when he died.'

'You can't know that.'

'Sometimes you just do. What can I say,' and I tap the back of my shoulder. 'Call it a hunch.'

'No.' He's adamant, shaking his head. 'I'm not having that.'

I have no idea why this should matter to him. 'What are you going to do with it anyway?'

'How do you mean?'

'The film. You could make a fortune.'

He stops rowing and leans forward on his knees, the oars lifting into the air, dripping. The boat glides. I have the strongest feeling that when it comes to a halt we will simply sink like a stone.

'You don't get it, do you? You think this is all about getting back at you.'

'Isn't it?'

'Wouldn't it be easier just to shove you over the side?'

'What then?'

267

'Nothing.'

'Nothing?'

'See, when I started making that film, I had all these ideas. I was going to send it everywhere, TV, newspapers. It'd be a sensation. I might even get an Oscar. Like you, think of the irony. Best Documentary.'

I look away.

'I know, it's pathetic. I'm just a ghost, people look right through me.' He drops the oars back into the water. 'You, though. I wanted you to know me like I know you. I wanted you to see me.'

'I see you, son. I see you.'

He rows further west. There is very little between us and Canada but sea. The space is unnerving. I almost cry out when I feel a tug on the rod. The brief vibration is instantly familiar, even though I have not been fishing since I was a boy, the rocks off the Albannach Road. Now a stronger vibration.

'We've hit them,' says Lewis. 'Get them in and cast out again.'

I do as I'm told, reeling in the line in the way so easily remembered, a few turns with the rod almost horizontal then lifting it steadily to near-vertical, a beating in my chest that is nothing to do with my failing heart but only excitement. I pull gasping mackerel from the hooks and lay them glistening in the plastic box Lewis has given me. Otherwise, he doesn't help, just watches with an assessing look. When the last fish has been unhooked I throw the line back over the side.

Over the next twenty minutes I haul in three more catches. At least fifteen fish are dying in the box.

'Best gut them,' he says.

'*Gut them, Bucket Boy.*'

'What's that?'

'What my dad said to me when he brought the boat

268

in. That was my job. Duke caught them and I gutted them.'

He hands me a wooden priest and I pick up a writhing fish. I smack it on top of the head and have a quick image of Akira, how he bows to any creature he kills, the trodden spider or the fish taken home from the market. I feel a pang of guilt that he has no idea what has happened to me.

'Here.'

I take the knife from Lewis and start to gut the fish. I am sweating but my hands are red and cold.

'We should have these for our tea,' I say. 'Few fried tatties and a glass or two.'

Instantly, I realise this familiarity is absurdly inappropriate. I feel a heat in my cheeks. We are not friends.

He seems troubled once more and shoves the oars into the water. 'We should get going. I'll take you back.'

'Look, Lewis, I'm—'

'No. Don't say it.' He's rowing furiously, throwing water, trying to spark his anger. 'I'm not having that.'

'I'm sorry.'

He lifts the oars and lets the boat glide. 'Just *don't*.' He leans towards me. 'Don't you dare feel sorry for me.'

I realise I have a dead fish in my hand, its little face agog with a perplexity I can fully understand.

We head in. The boat slips across the water, a glossy black dappled by white bubbles left behind by the oars. There is no more wind and the temperature drops. I feel two subtly different kinds of cold, one rising from the sea and one falling from the sky, chilling me from feet up, head down.

To the west is the long, sweeping beach at Edmonton Bay, directly in front of me a shorter, rocky shore, about a hundred metres away. Set back from this shore is the caravan, snug between two small hills. East, at the

269

highest point of a low promontory, I can make out the vehicle track.

Over that crest, a little later, flashing blue lights appear. Three police 4x4s. One of them turns up the slope to the caravan, the other two stopping at the bottom. Yellow bibs quickly emerge.

Lewis sees me staring and glances over his shoulder. He keeps rowing for a few moments then stops, letting the oars skim the water. I think I hear someone shouting.

He gives me a rueful smile. 'I'm surprised it took them so long.'

There is another sound in the distance, a low-pitched droning which I look round to place, but cannot.

Lewis rummages in the cargo box under his seat. He takes out a pair of binoculars and spends a long time looking at the shore. When he hands the glasses to me his face is red. He looks startled.

'Quite a turnout.'

I watch a policeman emerge from the caravan, then another. At the foot of the slope five others stand in a group. One talks into a walkie-talkie clipped to his shoulder and all of them are looking towards us, one with a pair of binoculars. Along the shore is another figure. Erin. She strides back and forth, the ubiquitous phone clamped to her ear, gesticulating wildly from sea to shore.

I move the glasses to the second of the three 4x4s. Someone else has a pair of binoculars trained on me. Akira, I realise. I wave at him and a moment later he does the same. We are both smiling.

Then, round the promontory to the east, the drone reveals itself, a police or coastguard boat. The drone rises in pitch as it throttles down, cutting a V of spray and heading straight for us.

'You're a director, aren't you?' I say.

'Eh?'

'Frank Stone, he's probably the one standing in the bow of that boat with the bull-horn. What scene would he have, right now? What's the best scene in an action movie? The one we all want?'

Lewis is a confusion of blinks.

'Chase sequence, there's always a chase sequence. Does the motor work?' I pat the outboard behind me.

Bullit, it is not. It is not even OJ Simpson in his Ford Bronco, the LAPD in lazy pursuit. This is more zimmer versus Lamborghini, Lewis hunched forward at the tiller, as if coaxing the boat forward.

The cutter makes up our head start almost instantly, slowing to match our speed. The *MV Hunter* has two vertical stripes at the bow, one red and one blue. A jaunty line of multicoloured triangular flags stretches from the bow up to the radar mast and back down to the stern. A man with a yellow life vest and a bigger beard than Lewis is leaning on the railings at the bow, shouting something into a loudhailer. We have barely reached the edge of Edmonton Bay.

I lift the binoculars and look at the shore. The convoy of police vehicles is following us along the shore track, the blue lights still flashing. If Lewis turned suddenly would they do the same thing? Back eastwards we would go until Lewis turned again. Back and forth along the coast, all day long.

I wave at the man in the cutter with the loudhailer. After a moment, he waves back.

Abruptly, Lewis cuts the engine.

We drift.

Alongside us, the drone becomes a lazy putter.

Lewis seems distressed, a man who has suddenly grasped the ridiculousness of what he's doing.

The bearded man again raises his loudhailer and tells Lewis to stop. He waves a vague acknowledgement. I

271

feel a surge of fondness which instantly deepens as he opens the tiller box and tosses me a half-bottle. I drink and the sun swells, making Lewis an inscrutable presence. I hand the bottle back. The non-drinker takes a hit as he glances at the *Hunter*, edging closer.

'There's nothing to worry about. It's not as if you kidnapped me.'

'That's what it looks like! Why'd you ask me to take off like that?'

'I'll sort it, son, don't worry.'

He laughs harshly, waving the bottle at a second man in a yellow life-jacket who is leaning from the stern of the *Hunter* and tying a line to our mooring ring. 'What do you reckon, do you believe him?'

Lewis is right. I am treacherous, to be avoided like the skerries I can just make out to the west, there and gone in ocean glitter, swelling sun. Can you even be sure they are there at all?

'Are you ok, Mr Jackson?'

I am helped onto the cutter. Lewis remains in the rowing boat. A police officer clambers down and puts a hand on his shoulder, as if he expects him to try and swim for it. But Lewis is immobile, looking at me. He's waiting for me to tell the police that they've got it all wrong.

'You missed one thing,' I shout above the engine.

The policeman looks round as well.

'The voiceover at the start. You say it was Duke who rescued the sailors from the *Breda*. It wasn't.'

Lewis stares.

'It was me.'

He tries to smile and seem unconvinced. But he knows, and then he looks so disappointed.

As I say, I am a treacherous man.

* * *

272

After the chaos, I return to the Castle Hotel. That is, I am returned. First by a convoy of three Mercedes and two police cars, then by six security men, three behind and three in front through hurried corridors. The danger that was no danger now passed, they are pulling out all the stops.

Fade-out

I lie in scalding bath water. I place a little white face-towel on top of my head in the traditional Japanese fashion. I am convinced, but have no way of proving it, that this offers respectful acknowledgement to the snow-crowned monkeys in their hot pools who showed humans the way of the *onsen*.

Afterwards, I stand naked once more at the panoramic window. My skin has taken on the colour of boiled salmon and the steam rising from my body clouds the glass somewhat, although I can still see a few boats on the sea below me. Soon, the light of this perfect, ice-blue day will fade. All will become silhouettes and the projections easier. There I will sit in a rowing boat in the distant east, killing the last of the mackerel, watched by Lewis, who is pleased with me, who rows us with strong, easy strokes back to shore . . .

We can travel a long way for peace. There is a sacred place in Japan, Mount Kōya; the heart of Shingon Buddhism and a place of many monasteries. For a few years after Anna died I went there. I was a spiritual dilettante, of course, seeking the quick fix, indulged by monks happy for my contributions to the upkeep of Henjoko-in, happy in turn to be bamboozled by their dawn rituals.

All I needed was a caravan . . .

I feel bad for what I said to Lewis as I left. It's compulsive, for sure, that need to have the last word.

Yet there is only so much he can know, and what he does will never be enough. His is a doleful presence. He will be ever-suspect for being so pathetic, whatever I might have said to the police. And just like you and Anna, Duke, he won't let me be. I'm the *Shinigami*, cue the Bontempi!

That's what causes these never-ending meditations, yes, meditations, stop sniggering. And so many more to come. It's why I'll live to an unseemly, *biblical* age. What does it matter, in comparison, if millions one day crowd the Odeons of the world to sit, appalled, through Lewis's film?

I hear a sudden, impatient rapping at the door. Instantly, my sagging ball-sack retracts. I have been flash-chilled. The steam no longer rises. My niece Erin is another who will forever keep coming.

I make her wait in the corridor. I have to dress. Her concern will undoubtedly be over-played and I have no desire to sit here in a dressing gown, the confused old man she would like to be presented with. I choose grey slacks and a black silk shirt, and a pair of what I think might be deck shoes.

As soon as I open the door she is upon me. Arms around my neck for a few long moments. Then she stands back, holding me by the shoulders, concerned eyes flicking across my face.

'I don't like deck shoes,' I say.

'That's ok. I know you don't.'

She puts a hand on my cheek, a look of genuine concern in her eyes.

'Would you prefer me to be a gibbering mess on the sofa?'

'What?'

'I'm ok, Erin. My shoes.' We both look down at my feet. 'I was just telling you about my shoes.'

275

'Of course you were. Well, thanks. Thanks for telling me about your shoes. Can you not let me feel relieved?'

'There's nothing to feel concerned about. He was harmless. He invited me and I went with him.'

'But I didn't know that, did I? I just wanted to give you a hug and ask if you're ok.'

'And I am.'

'So I see.' She crosses to the big window and stands looking out at the darkening day. Hands on her hips.

'Good publicity for *The Bruce*, eh? You can't buy that kind of coverage. Stone must be happy as a pig in shit.'

Her head dips. The vaguest of shakes. She remains there for a few more seconds then quickly wipes her eyes, turning and striding to the door. 'I've never understood why you think I don't care.'

'Look, Erin, I don't know—'

'Just *stop*. I was going to ask if you wanted to postpone the event tonight. No need for that, is there? You're here and you're A-OK. I mean, the disappearance and reappearance of the famous Johnny Jackson? What a story. They'll be eating out of your hand. Deck shoes or no bloody deck shoes!'

With a feeling of great weariness, I remember the Freedom of Inveran.

'Can I just suggest . . . '

She gives me what looks like a mint. You're handed something similar after landing at Singapore, that most paranoid of places. Just a sweet, innocently offered, likely some kind of homing device.

Then she leaves.

A few moments later, there is another, softer knock at the door.

Akira.

'I saw Erin in the corridor. She was . . . '

'I know. She's concerned. It's her way of showing it.'

'Do you want a drink?'

He is already heading to the drinks cabinet. My refusal prompts a quick, searching look but no more.

'I missed you,' I tell him.

* * *

They come at six. I am quick-hustled along corridors. Smell of mahogany and heavy light. Doors open, peering faces shoved back inside. A stuffed stag is told to *freeze*, a gun at its head, Highland aristos in the haughty portraits lining the walls ordered to *look away, look away*, the busts of some incarnation of the Duke and Duchess of Argyll whisked off their marble plinths on each side of the main door, an explanation in the distant explosions I see as the Mercedes zips down the drive: *possible IEDs in the cranium, Mr Jackson, we couldn't take any chances . . .*

Instead, it is a quiet descent in the lift with Akira and Erin, the only sound a sentimental lounge-jazz version of *Loch Lomond*. My niece wants to know why I am smiling but won't ask. Only in the car, as the entourage sweeps out the back gate, does she say anything. 'So, you're ready?'

I nod dumbly.

I have no idea why I am sober. I am entirely under-equipped to deal with the press of dignitaries I am introduced to as we enter the Town Hall. They're horrified at what happened. They do not believe my disappearance was innocent and feel somehow responsible. They're hugely impressed I've come at all. 'The show must go on,' I say, and a woman with gold chains around her neck who would be more at home carrying sacks of tatties than the burden of office clasps my hand with tears in her eyes and says, 'Yes, yes, indeed, you truly are the best of this place . . . '

277

Did you hear that, Duke?

I show my gratitude with my best approximation of your Dean Martin dazzler, which is actually a sickly, gummy troubling. The crowd is instantly uneasy, stepping back, clearing a path through the ghost-fog of outdated, over-applied Chanel, tired suits all shiny at the elbows and best shoes that were never that good. Now and then I glimpse a troubled-looking younger man or woman, who have the instantaneous realisation as our eyes meet that they have reached a crucial crossroads and must either immediately leave this place or accept the same sag and swell.

When I reach the stage they all clap so enthusiastically, a standing ovation as my eyes scan the rictus, painted smiles, as if one by one they might fall forward and clatter down, each a cardboard cut-out.

I try to look overcome. I move my hands up and down. The applause fades into the still vigorous, lone clapping of the mayor, grinning at me like another stalker-to-be, a suspicion heightened by a fawning eulogy that ends with a bear hug and an almost coy presentation of the inevitable quaich.

'The Freedom of Inveran!' I declare. 'I am again honoured. But I wonder. What did you leave out last time?'

This received with an explosion of laughter.

'So, tomorrow my cows will graze on the bowling green. It's the only way to get my game down pat.'

More laughter.

And so on.

Palm of yer hand, I hear the old man whisper. He seems pleased, at last, as another ovation begins . . .

Erin is chipper. 'A triumph,' she whispers. Control of the Spectacle has been reasserted. Tonight's success will be followed by Brad Renner's long-delayed arrival on set tomorrow, before we leave for more book signings; Glasgow, Edinburgh then London, a BBC interview and a guaranteed Ten O' Clock News slot. My nausea feels inversely proportionate to her satisfaction.

She's still at my side when we enter the drinks reception in the council chamber, taking questions from journalists rushed north when the news broke of my disappearance. She lets me answer two or three before ending things by suddenly grasping both my hands and saying that she feared the worst when I vanished, that the anti-Breda protestors had shown their true colours . . .

I stare at her as the doors to the chamber open. She winks. 'I know. But we've got to play the game, eh?'

As the well-wishers surge towards me I have the queasiest of suspicions that the whole *Shinigami* episode with Lewis was a set-up arranged by my niece, that he is not now sitting in his caravan thinking about long-gone camping trips with his dad but smoking a cigarette in the back room of Inveran Snooker Club as a man in a black suit counts hundred pound notes into his hand.

Then the mayor. Back again. A rattle of chains as she thrusts a glass of champagne into my hand. 'Did I tell you I know him?' She is leaning towards me, conspiratorial, but her flickering eyes include the others clustering around.

I say nothing. I want to hear her say his name.

'Lewis Chapman. My daughter went to school with him. A funny little boy.'

'Wasn't he just.'

This from a mono-browed, bulbous-headed man with a bright yellow tie I suspect he thinks is wacky.

'Yes, he *was*, wasn't he?'

'You can just imagine this, somehow.'

'Funny how it slips into place, with hindsight.'

'Not that it makes it any less troubling.'

I say nothing. They will see what they want regardless of any protest that they've got it all wrong. And if they ever see *The Shinigami* they will say the same about me, the entourage nodding seriously as it shuffles and murmurs and turns to Lewis with its most sympathetic of collective frowns.

I escape to the toilet, accompanied by two security men who hover by the sinks as I sit in a cubicle with my head in my hands. Sometime later, there is a tap on the door. I open it to Akira.

'We're done here.'

'For tonight?'

'Not just tonight.'

'Ok, Johnny.'

The most genuine thing about my return is the way it must end. With the quiet turning of my back.

Did you expect drama, Duke? Perhaps Akira should upturn the buffet and create a distraction as I slip out. It is what Stone would do, I see him as we return to the chamber, flailing to a rapt and clustering audience.

Instead, we make a selfie-interrupted way through the crowd then slip out a door at the back of the chamber into a dark corridor. We hurry along, following the light of Akira's mobile phone and look, Duke, there's the entrance to the Museum of Inveran, a decent set-up that, come on, where's the joke about the *relic*, my photo in a display case, my old school tie on a plinth . . .

I slip on the stairs down to the emergency exit and Akira steadies me. No alarm goes off as he pushes it open, just a dark alley and cold, stabbing rain, like a crow pecking my bare head. With a tweet of outstretched keys and a blink of orange hazard lights, Akira unlocks the Mercedes.

As we head out of Inveran, I feel a tentative letting go. We're not free yet, I know that, these things are never quite so easy. Any second now I expect the descent of the security detail.

Bring them on, Duke. Bring on you and Anna, anyone else who happens to be near, those teenagers on the street corner, the fuzzy shapes in the steamed-up windows of the chip shop, staring at the flash Merc as they spill out the door trailing orgasmic aromas of black pudding and pickled eggs. The *Shinigami* insists that you all line up, he orders each of you in turn to tell him what he should be thinking, you've all got such opinions. Everyone is so fuckin' verbal, from the whispers in the cypress that told me to come to the white rush of Arctic surf telling me to leave.

I close my eyes. It's about right. I am ever-emerging from deep sleep, that hand on my face waking me again, hot and sticky as only a grubby wee boy's hand can be. Shorts and specs and more answers then than I have managed since.

He had to start asking questions, the poor bugger.

What now, mister? Where to?

I have no idea. It's disappointing, Duke, I know. I guess they just don't make gods like they used to.

www.sandstonepress.com

 facebook.com/SandstonePress/

 @SandstonePress